A Tiger in Suburbia

Anna Woiwood

Copyright © 2023 by Anna Woiwood

All rights reserved.

No part of this book may be reproduced in any form or by any electronic or mechanical means, including information storage and retrieval systems, without written permission from the author, except for the use of brief quotations in a book review.

This novel's story and characters are fictitious. Some mention of real life persons, products, novels, and places are used to create a realistic world for these imaginary characters to live in. Any resemblance of the main characters to actual persons, living or dead, or actual events is purely coincidental.

 Created with Vellum

For Regan,
who inspired the novel's title,
and for the women who suffered.

Content Warning

This novel depicts some events that may not be suitable for all readers. Please note that there are references to alcoholism, domestic abuse, instances of self-harm by cutting, time period homophobia, and pregnancy complications.

Chapter One

Vera remembered the quiet stillness of it.

The hum of the air conditioner, the far-off cries of the neighborhood children in the thick of summer, the birds chattering amongst themselves in the trees, the occasional passing of a car – infrequent on the suburban street.

These were the only muted sounds she could make out in the silence of the home's interior.

Her hand stilled on the newspaper wrapped plate in the cardboard box, stopping to listen. Searching, searching for any sign of life.

There was the cry of the children outside again, and she flinched. Would they come barging into the house again? Begging for refreshments from the afternoon heat, disrupting her in the unpacking of the home yet again? Would Henry break another godawful teacup from the China set Roger's parents had gifted them as a wedding present?

Vera knew Eileen Wilson invariably would count the teacups and know one was missing. And she would hold it against her daughter-in-law. How she could be so careless to misplace such a thoughtful and expensive gift.

Another black mark against her.

Well, there was hardly anything she could do with the thing busted to pieces at the bottom of the waste basket.

The children's voices rose outside and then swiftly drifted away.

Her shoulders released their tension.

She unwrapped the plate in her hand, submerging it in the sink of soapy water.

She looked at the kitchen around her, at the boxes piled high.

It seemed that since arriving two days prior to this wonderful, spacious suburban home the boxes had only multiplied instead of reducing in number despite her best efforts at unpacking them.

"It's like you don't do anything all day." Roger had accused her over his egg - which she had cooked for him - and newspaper - she had retrieved and laid out for him - that morning.

The silence was getting to her.

She left her post at the sink, leaving the plates to soak, the box of dishware still half-full.

She flipped on the radio. The latest hit 'Sh-Boom' played from the speaker as she picked up her pack of Chesterfields and the ashtray from the countertop. She moved through the home that still smelled of fresh paint and new carpet.

There was the comfortable armchair in the sitting room, next to the picture window at the front of the home. Roger had begun sitting there in the evenings, watching the newly purchased RCA color-television set.

There was a mini-bar that had been pieced together upon their first night in the new home. It occupied the corner of the room.

She thought of how Roger had poured her a bourbon in

celebration of their first night in the new house. His hard-won getaway from the city had come to fruition, and they were now a part of upward mobility. They had escaped the small, cramped two-bedroom apartment on the Upper East Side. They now had four bedrooms, three bathrooms, a sitting room, a den, a basement, a room with a washer and dryer – wasn't Vera thrilled?

Then he'd gotten a little handsy with her and they'd ended up on the living room floor with her underwear around her ankles and his warm fluids between her legs.

She stepped over the spot on the carpet she had scrubbed clean that first evening after Roger had gone to bed. She sat, without decorum, atop the chair, slouching down, legs spread wide, atop its comfortable surface.

She lighted a cigarette and surveyed the way the light filtered in through the window panes. The way her cigarette smoke caught in it, shimmering, darkening the fresh, clean white of the walls and ceilings. Staining it with her cigarette smoke. Making her mark on the house Roger had purchased.

Rosemary Clooney came through on the radio.

Vera eyed the minibar, the way the light shone beautifully through the amber liquid of the bourbon sitting atop it.

She smoked lazily.

She got up and poured herself a nip.

She sipped it, relishing the burn in her mouth, the smooth aftertaste.

She closed her eyes and listened to a Perry Como song that had started. His voice made her dizzy and warm.

Vera smoked as she poured herself another drop of bourbon.

She turned to eye the boxes that remained unopened on the opposite side of the room. It seemed they were bottomless, that they may may continue to multiply, that she might be unpacking for the rest of her life.

She sipped the bourbon and stubbed out the cigarette in the ashtray that sat precariously atop the arm of the chair. Taking the tumbler of bourbon, she sat cross-legged on the living room floor.

She pulled items from the boxes, categorizing them in her mind. This should go in Henry's room, this would look nice in the den; this was Emma's favorite toy, she should put it in her room.

The alcohol made her feel loose and lethargic.

She found herself staring idly out across the front lawn. Green, green grass and green leaves, greenery everywhere. Nothing was dirty, no trash strewn about, no homeless people huddled on the street corner. Only green. Peaceful, serene. And deathly quiet.

"Mommy, Mommy, Mommy!" The quiet disrupted.

Vera startled, struggling upright as the girl came racing into the home through the back door, voice growing louder and louder as she tried to locate her mother.

Vera did not respond but knew it would only be a matter of seconds before she was found.

"Mommy?" Emma's tall, lanky form appeared before Vera.

Vera squinted against the slowly descending sun of the day to look up at the girl. "What is it?"

She hoped to God nothing was wrong with Henry. Another black mark on her if Roger were to find she'd been drinking instead of paying attention to the kids. It would be all her fault, wouldn't it?

"Are you okay, Mommy?" Emma was looking down at Vera as if she were the concerned parent.

"I'm fine. What's the matter?" Vera demanded, irritated the child had caught her out drinking in the mid-afternoon. Well, what did it matter anyway?

Emma would soon be eight and seemed to have a sharp

mind. Always observing, always taking note of every little thing Vera did, always judging her every move.

"Mommy, Henry found something in the woods."

"Found what?"

"Come! Come and see!" Emma cried excitedly, already racing away.

It took Vera a moment to pull herself up. She was unbalanced on her feet, needing a moment to recover before she could race after her daughter. The girl was rushing ahead, nearly out the back door. Vera knocked her moccasined foot against a kitchen chair and cursed.

But Emma was already outside, and Vera was close behind, feeling the heat of the sun on her skin. No longer in the protection of the air conditioning, the elements of the world accosted her, making sweat form on her brow, between her breasts, her capri-clad legs. It was so warm; she was so warm.

Emma disappeared into the woods that lay beyond the edge of their new lawn. The brush was thick and high, and Vera did not want to go further, but Emma was calling out to her. She could hear Henry's excited voice even further. She could not turn back now.

She stepped into the unruly woods, thickets and shrubs scratching and clawing at her bare ankles, leaves and twigs brushing against her cheeks, catching at her hair.

She saw Emma up ahead and Henry a bit further. He was leaning over something, peering down into the earth.

She was out of breath by the time she reached the clearing in the woods.

"Look Mommy! It's so deep!" Henry cried.

She saw immediately what was before her. "Be careful! Henry, you get away from there." She cautioned as she moved closer, reaching out to pull him back.

She looked at the opening in the earth before her.

Perfectly stacked stones formed a neat circle. As she neared the edge of it, the forest around her cooled and a damp, musky smell rose to greet her. She peered down, down, following the perfectly laid stones around the edges until they disappeared into darkness.

She stared, transfixed, into the deep, deep darkness.

"What is it, Mommy?" Henry was asking.

"I told you, dummy. It's a well." Emma hissed.

Vera could not turn away. As if the darkness were beckoning to her. As if she could simply slip down, deep down inside the well and disappear from the surface of the earth. As if it might just swallow her up.

The idea took hold of her, making her tingle with unexpected excitement.

"It's so deep! Watch!" Henry exclaimed and threw a rock down inside.

The action startled Vera, breaking her from her trance.

"Henry!" She grasped at the boy. "Don't you play near there; do you hear me? Don't either of you go anywhere near this well." She eyed her son and daughter.

"But we won't..."

"Don't come near it again." Vera spoke firmly.

They knew she meant it.

They pouted but agreed reluctantly before racing away from Vera, as if they couldn't get away fast enough.

She turned again – as if unable to leave, as if it were calling out to her, a hand grasping her ankles, holding her to that very spot. She stared down into the well again. Worried by the strange consolation she felt in its presence.

The cool wind stirred the branches overhead, chilling her.

The rustle of the leaves frightened her.

She backed away, the trance broken.

She made her way swiftly through the forest, back toward the sun-drenched lawn of the new home.

She felt as if she were entering into another a time, another place entirely. The cool, dampness of the well so far away from the bright light of day.

But the feeling it had aroused lingered. She couldn't shake it no matter what she did. Another drop of bourbon, another cigarette.

But it wouldn't release her.

It was only an old well, wasn't it? She tried to console herself as she dozed off vacantly atop the living room armchair.

Chapter Two

She startled awake. Drenched in sweat, breathing heavily.

She'd kicked the sheets away, searching, searching. The girl. Down the well.

"Jesus, Vera." Roger rolled over in the bed, reaching for her flailing body.

She stilled in his embrace, eyes wide open. Remembering, reassuring.

It had only been a dream. Hadn't it?

Emma would be asleep in her room.

Her breathing calmed, she wiped at her forehead, feeling the coolness of the air-conditioned night make the sweat all over her body freeze and cool against her skin. She sat up in bed.

"What was that all about?" Roger demanded, awake and annoyed with her for disturbing his sleep.

"It was only a dream." She exhaled, bracing her face in her hands.

"It was one hell of a dream. I think you scratched me." He

was looking at his arm in the dim light that filtered in through the window from the moon and streetlights about them.

"I'm sorry." She rolled her eyes to the ceiling.

"Jesus, there's blood."

She looked at his arm and saw the gash she'd gotten into him with her neatly manicured nails. She stood from the bed and went to the bathroom, flipping on the overhead light so it flooded into the bedroom. She rummaged around for rubbing alcohol and bandages. She returned to the bed, and held his arm gently as she wiped away the blood and then covered it neatly with a Band-aid. It was as if she were bandaging up Henry or Emma when they slipped and fell.

Roger grabbed her before she could return the supplies to the bathroom. "You'd better be careful."

She slid from his embrace to return the items to the cabinets. She relieved herself and then washed her hands, feeling wide awake.

She padded back into the room and sat at the edge of the bed, reaching for her pack of cigarettes.

"Well," Roger said impatiently, neither seeming capable of sleep again.

"Henry." Vera placed a cigarette between her teeth. "He found a well in the woods the other day."

"A well?"

Vera nodded as she exhaled a cloud of smoke. "It's old. Pretty deep." It would come back to her at odd moments, in lucid, hyper-realistic dreams. The depth of it. The coldness. The perfectly arranged stones. The darkness. She'd dreamed of it since the day they'd found it.

But that evening Emma had been there beside her. Looking down into the well's depths and then, as if something had reached out and grabbed hold of her, she had disappeared inside the hole.

She'd reached for her, trying to grasp at her, but the darkness had consumed her.

"It's just an open well out in the woods?" Roger was looking at her incredulously.

She nodded as she inhaled her cigarette, tapping off ashes into the ashtray on her bedside table.

"That's not safe, Vera."

"I told them not to play near it." She assured him.

"You'll show me. I'll have it covered. I wouldn't want to be liable for a neighborhood kid playing out in the woods and falling inside." He huffed.

He wanted to cover it. And that would solve everything, wouldn't it?

The thought sent a horrible sensation shooting through her body.

She inhaled again. Roger was watching her.

She put out the cigarette and climbed into the bed beside him.

They laid in silence together. Neither seemed to sleep the rest of the night.

She drove him to the station in the morning – an arrangement they had worked out since they only had one car. He kissed her goodbye on the cheek, and then she rolled down the window to light a cigarette – Roger hated the smell of it in the morning – and drove back through the sleepy town.

She supposed it was quaint. There was a small strip of downtown. The barbers, beauticians, post office, a small dress shop, the local library sat a bit up the road, a town hall, the school up a hill. There was a stream that separated the downtown from the rest of the town.

She drove over the bridge and turned into the grocery store, an excuse to stay away from home. There were not many items she needed. Perhaps some more milk, eggs, bread, Emma had wanted jam, a carton of cigarettes for herself. It was excuse enough to stop.

She walked the brightly-lit aisles, looking with tired eyes at all the packages. She laughed to herself, that this should be considered the highlight of her day.

After gathering the essentials, she found herself in front of the wine selection. She chose a bottle of something not too extravagant, but not too cheap and then went to check out.

The woman at the register tried to chat kindly with her. "You're new around here, aren't you?"

"Hmm?" Vera hummed and looked at her boredly. "Yes, I suppose so."

"I haven't seen you before." Her name tag read 'Mary'. She looked tired and old.

Vera wondered just how long she had been trapped in this grocery store.

"Well, I'm sure you'll be seeing more of me." Vera turned her lips upward in what she hoped was a kindly smile, unaccustomed to such small talk with the clerks in the city who hardly had the time of day for anyone. They wouldn't even acknowledge you, let alone notice if you were new or not.

There was a young, pretty boy who was bagging her groceries. She could feel his eyes upon her, furtively looking her over, apprising her from beneath luscious eyelashes. He had a youthful innocence about him. Not a day over nineteen she guessed.

"That will be $11.86." Mary informed Vera, looking from her to the young bag boy.

Vera pulled open her wallet and busied herself with finding the right change. She handed the money over and clipped the wallet shut.

"D-do you need help, ma'am? With the bags?" The young man stuttered.

Vera took stock of the bags she had accumulated. In the

city she would have brushed off the help and snatched it all up. But there was something charming about him, something she did not want Mary to see, so she nodded her assent to him.

She could feel Mary watching her, something protective and wary in her gaze.

Vera walked ahead of the boy.

His name tag had read 'Billy'.

She led him to her car, opened the trunk and stood aside to light a cigarette as he – with exaggerated care – lifted the items inside.

He closed the trunk carefully and looked at her more assuredly than he had beneath Mary's watchful eye.

She took a quarter from her purse and handed it to him. Their fingers brushed. She smiled. "Thank you, Billy."

"You have a good day, Mrs...uh..." he paused, realizing he did not know her name.

"Vera." She said.

"Oh," he looked surprised by her informality. "Vera then."

She smiled easily in return before getting into her car.

She did not look to see if he was still standing there, because she knew he was.

The children were drowsy and confused as to where she had been. Henry was near tears, wrapping his arms through Vera's legs despite his six years of age. He was still a baby. She ran her fingers through his sandy blonde hair and thought of him falling down the well.

She fed the children and sent them out to play in the yard. "And don't go near that well." She cautioned.

She set to work cleaning up after the mess that mornings brought. She washed the dishes and placed them in the dishwasher - marveling that the machine was meant to make things faster and yet she still had to scrub at each dish as she had done before in their apartment in the city. She collected up the dirty clothes, stripping the beds bare, and started a load of laundry. The washing machine in the basement was convenient, but she thought it would be more convenient if it could also fold and sort the laundry too. As she waited for the wash cycle to complete, she vacuumed the house and dusted the shelves, surprised by how much had accumulated in the short while they had lived there. The washing machine chimed and she moved the wet articles to the drying machine and started it, then went to work cleaning the kitchen floor.

She ended up leaving it half done, pouring herself a glass of wine and lighting a cigarette instead.

She was sitting at the kitchen table, watching the floor dry, when she heard the ring of the doorbell.

Vera put out her cigarette and walked down the stairs to the front door. She could see the outline of a woman on the other side. She smoothed a hand over her hair, down the front of her house dress. Her hand shook as she reached for the doorknob, turning it to reveal a beautifully pieced together woman standing on the other side, holding a casserole dish in her perfectly manicured hands. Her dress clung splendidly to her curvy frame, her dark red hair swept atop her head in a tidy hairdo.

"Well hello! You must be Vera Wilson. I'm Kitty Daniels. I live two houses down. Right over there." She nodded with her head.

"So nice to meet you." Vera smiled anxiously. "Please, come in." She took the casserole from Kitty and pushed the door open for her.

She led her into the kitchen. She could feel Kitty looking over the dirtied ashtray and half-drunk glass of wine, the abandoned floor mop.

Vera placed the casserole dish on the stovetop and turned to watch Kitty. This suburban creature, so sure of her place in this town. Vera the new interloper. Had Kitty been sent to test the waters with the new neighbor? Would she go running back to the others and tell them how Vera smoked too much or drank too much?

"You have a lovely home." Kitty was looking at her.

Astonished, Vera found her smile was sincere, perhaps even shy.

She felt perhaps she could like Kitty.

Something about Kitty, some little crack in her facade, made her seem less like a stranger.

"Would you care for a drink?" Vera asked.

"Oh," Kitty clasped at the necklaces about her neck. A gold chain and a pearl necklace. "No. No thank you. I have to pick Junior up from a friend's house across town. I only just came to say hello and introduce myself. You know, it would be so nice if you and that dashing husband of yours would join us for our weekly parties. Tomorrow evening it will be at Sharon's. She and Bill live just up the road."

There was no way out of it, was there, Vera surmised. She was to be a part of this suburban life.

In the city she had not felt like the other young mothers she passed on the street, sat near at the playgrounds. The women who walked and talked in pairs about their babies. Cooing over them, elated and happy in their roles as mothers as if it were some great prize. Didn't they also have to deal with the discomfort of a baby sucking at their nipples, the diaper changes, the spit-up, the sleepless nights, the anger from their spouses when the baby needed their attention?

Yet, they spoke happily, confidently to one another as if all of that didn't matter...

Those other mothers were not her confidants. The people she knew and felt known by were Mrs. Kalman in apartment 2B, who Vera sat with in the afternoons after dropping off some extra bread or milk because she knew it was hard for her to get out. Or Mr. Pasternak in apartment 3C, who would speak to her of the old country and supply her with vodka. These people she had understood.

This perfectly put together woman before her she did not. She did not feel a part of this world and yet she would have to assimilate. She would have to try. For Roger. Roger was so happy there, wasn't he?

"We would love to." Vera forced a smile. "Shall I bring anything?"

"Oh no, no. It will be your first party. We couldn't possibly impose."

Vera nodded.

She had never understood the fraternity of women. In college she had spent most of her time away from crowds, lost in her own world. Always watching from the outside, never a part of it. She had been focused on her studies. Working harder, harder than anyone else.

And where had that gotten her?

Kitty shifted, looking as if she might say something more.

Vera looked at her and found desperation in Kitty's eyes. A need for her to include Vera in this neighborhood ritual, as if her participation were vitally necessary. As if they were kindred spirits in this suburban world.

"I should...I should go. It was so lovely to meet you." Kitty was smiling.

"Likewise. I look forward to the party on Friday." Vera followed Kitty to the door.

"By the way," Kitty turned before she stepping out the open door. "Your children have already met my Eleanor and Junior. Please let them know they're welcome over any time they'd like."

"Thank you. I will." Vera said.

Kitty smiled warmly and then with a quick nod, she turned to leave.

The dryer was buzzing.. The laundry would be ready.

Vera closed the door and wished Kitty had stayed. The home felt empty in her absence.

Chapter Three

Cigarette smoke hung like a cloud about the room. Bill Haley & His Comets played on a record player in the corner.

Vera's eyes flashed over the crowd, vision blurry from one too many highballs. She could make out Roger in the corner talking to a woman who had introduced herself to them as Louise. She was young, prettily made up, blonde hair sat carefully about her face. Some other wives she'd been introduced to, Judy and Sharon, were not too far away, as if they all couldn't wait to sink their teeth into her husband.

Roger entertained them merrily, his cheeks warm with drink, eyes sparkling in a curious way she had forgotten.

She extracted a cigarette from her pack and it was Dale, Louise's husband, who held up a lighter to the end of it.

"You're really beautiful." He said to her, the drink loosening the mood.

It had begun tediously. The introductions – Sharon and Bill, Kitty and John, Louise and Dale, Judy and Philip, Darlene and James, pregnant Margaret and Ken. The men had gone off to smoke and drink in the kitchen at first, the women left to speak to themselves. They looked Vera over as they spoke amiably to her. Asking her about herself, but nothing too serious. How long had she been married? What were her children's names? Did she plan to have more? The things of womanhood. The things they all shared.

They had to prove she was one of them.

It had been terribly formal until the men slowly filtered back into the room. The records were put on, people began dancing as the drinks were served more freely, Bill happily mixing concoctions in a corner.

His highballs packed a punch.

"Would you care to dance with me?" Ken had spun out of nowhere and was extending a hand to her.

"Oh, but I just lit a cigarette." Vera tried to protest, but Ken had grabbed her up and pressed her close to him.

He smelled of aftershave and detergent. His chest was not as broad as Roger's, but he had a kindly, boyish face.

Though, through the haze of the room all the men rather blurred together in her eyes. Who was one from the other?

His hand slid to the small of her back, holding her close. She could feel the heat radiating off his body.

He danced her over to where Bill was eyeing her from behind the bar. She politely dislodged herself from Ken, letting him kiss her on the lips, and then leaned up against the wall, puffing at her cigarette to catch her breath while motioning to Bill for another drink.

She caught Roger looking at her curiously from the corner of the room.

She lifted the freshened drink in a salute to him and pressed its cool surface against her warm forehead.

She was suddenly overcome with exhaustion, wishing to be far away from the hot, crowded room.

She did not like the women, she decided. Nor did she like the men, the way they pushed and pulled at her.

She was not one of them, and it felt as if they expected her to be.

Roger appeared at her side.

"I want to go home," she whispered to him.

They walked side-by-side down the quiet suburban street, the sounds of the party fading into the quiet of evening. It felt as if they might be the only two people alive in the world, it was so deafeningly quiet suddenly.

Her heel caught in a crack and she stumbled.

Roger caught her arm, held her upright as they walked on in the silence of the evening.

The hum of cicadas, the call of a distant owl, the chatter of the nighttime animals started up an evening symphony. It was a far cry from the noise of the city. The shouts of drunken people, the sirens that wailed up and down the streets, the hum of motors.

She missed the noise of humanity in the deafening quiet calm of the suburban night.

Roger helped her up the stairs. She kicked off her heels in the front foyer, knowing her feet were blistered and aching, but the alcohol coursing through her masked the pain. She would have to face it in the morning.

She went to the kitchen to pour herself a glass of water while Roger, appearing far more sober than she, went on up the stairs to check on the children.

She took the water glass and collapsed on the chair in the corner of the living room. She lit a cigarette and stared absently at the streetlights that bled onto the darkened wall across from her.

She heard only the ticking of a clock in the silence of the night.

A door clicked shut. There were Roger's footsteps as he came down the stairs and into the living, unbuttoning his shirt as he did so.

His eyes were upon her, watching her as she sat smoking in the dark.

He moved past her and went to the minibar to pour himself a bourbon. He did not offer her any.

He sat on the couch near to her, holding the glass in his hands.

"You could try to like it." His voice was dark.

"Come off it," She answered hoarsely.

He drank back the bourbon and stood. "I'm going to bed."

She didn't respond. Instead she put out her cigarette and lit another.

When she began to drift off atop the couch, drowsy from the evening, she made herself get up and put herself together for bed. She slid beneath the sheets beside Roger and let her eyes close.

But sleep suddenly felt far away.

She turned on her side, staring at the drawn shade over the window.

"It's a good time..." Roger's voice came to her in the dark. He was not asleep. "Now that we're here and not in that apartment."

She felt her chest tighten, her body stiffen. She feigned sleep; she did not respond.

"Maybe you'd be happier if you were knocked up."

As if he had forgotten the first two times.

And then he rolled over and she could hear his breathing even out.

She did not sleep. Not until the early morning.

The kids were screaming and tearing through the house when she awoke in a pool of sweat, head pounding, light pouring in through the slits in the blinds. Roger was absent.

She stumbled from the bed and made it just in time to vomit into the toilet.

She washed out her mouth and turned on the shower. Slipping from her nightgown, she stepped beneath the stream of water and let it wash away the stench of the night.

With the steam of the shower still circulating through the room, she wrapped herself in a towel and lit a cigarette, inhaling as if it were a lifeline.

She listened to the racing footsteps of her children and thought about what it was that Roger wanted. What he had wanted for years since Henry was born. But she'd put him off the best she could. The apartment was too small, they couldn't afford it...

But now Roger was advancing at his firm and they had this four-bedroom home. Roger had made sure it was four bedrooms.

She stubbed out the cigarette in anger and lit another, wishing she could stay hidden away in the bedroom all day.

But she could hear the commotion the children were making, could hear Henry was now in tears after the sound of a thud.

She finished buttoning the front of her dress, put out her half-smoked cigarette, and went out of the room to find what had happened.

Henry was at the bottom of the stairs, rolling about and crying.

"He thinks I pushed him, but I didn't!" Emma was in tears, afraid she might be in trouble.

Vera ignored her daughter and went to Henry. "What happened?"

"She pushed me down the last few stairs!" He whined.

"Are you hurt?" She carefully rolled him over to look him over. There were no apparent bruises.

"He's fine! He's just being a little baby." Emma taunted.

"Emma! Go to your room." Vera scolded her.

"I didn't do anything!" Emma shouted back.

Vera fixed her with a deadly gaze. The girl's face sobered. "Go." And she went.

Henry sniffled and she scooped him up into her arms and took him to lay on the couch. "She didn't push you, did she?" She asked, smoothing her hand through his sandy blonde locks.

He looked at her through his long, watery eyelashes. And then slowly he shook his head.

The both of them were a headache. Far too much for her to deal with feeling the way she did.

She left Henry to whimper on the couch and went to the kitchen. Where was Roger?

There was the sound of a lawn mower nearby. She glanced out the window and saw him pushing the machine up and down their lawn, sweat dampening the white of his T-shirt. He was a boy playing with his new toy.

When she glanced up, she noticed her daughter was peering at her from around the corner, her eyes moist with tears.

"Come here." Vera held out her hand to the girl.

Emma slunk guiltily toward her. And then wrapped her arms tightly about Vera, pressing her face into her stomach. "I'm so sorry, mommy."

She stroked her brown hair, pitying her.

The dream returned to her at that moment. Emma slipping down, down the well. Away from her.

The sound of the lawnmower died down. The back door opened and Roger stepped in smelling of freshly cut grass.

He looked from Vera to his teary-eyed daughter. "What the hell's the matter with her?"

Vera shook her head. "Only a little quarrel. It's all right."

Emma looked up at her father. Vera could see that nothing registered on her face as she beheld him, as if he were a stranger to her. She backed away and raced out of the room again.

Roger took down a glass and filled it with water. "You're only now getting up? Where's breakfast? They're probably starving."

Vera reached for her cigarettes. "Why don't you go shower and I'll have it ready when you're done."

He looked at her disapprovingly.

She tried to ignore him and moved about the kitchen with learned domestication.

He left her to shower.

Chapter Four

She awoke with a start and stumbled, hands coming to rest on cool stones laid out before her as her legs collapsed on the soft forest ground.

A bird was circling overhead, crying.

Dirt and twigs clung to her feet. Something ached on her cheek, and when she lifted a hand to touch it, her fingers came away bloodied.

Her breathing sped up.

She looked around frantically as the early light of day filtered through the thick forest about her.

She'd had a glass of wine or two the day before, a bourbon with Roger, and then the evening blurred in her mind.

She looked down and saw she was dressed in her nightgown, dirtied from the woods.

The cool, damp smell of the well she was draped over floated up to accost her.

Roger had covered the well with wooden boards until the professionals could come to seal it shut.

The thought relieved and frightened Vera all at once.

She longed to languish near the well in the quiet morning

yet was spooked by the urge, still not understanding what it was that had drawn her to its precipice in the first place.

She stood on unsteady legs and backed away from the strange comfort of the cool, damp spot in the woods.

Heat rose the further she moved away, the forest ground uncomfortable on her bare, scratched feet. The freshly cut grass was a welcome relief as she rushed through the yard and into the looming home. Her heart was beating rapidly, listening to see if anyone else was awake.

But it was as silent as the forest had been.

The clicking of the clock.

Nearly six-thirty.

She fumbled for a cigarette to relieve her frayed nerves, sinking down on the kitchen floor with a wet cloth as she went to work cleaning up her feet. She would need to shower and hope to hell her cheek wouldn't be too badly cut.

As she was wiping down her left foot, Roger appeared in the kitchen doorway. He was looking at her with a strange expression. She could see his eyes taking in her ripped and dirtied nightgown, the cuts on her feet, her arms, her cheek...

"What the hell happened?" He moved no closer to her.

She exhaled a cloud of smoke and shook her head. "I don't know." And she didn't.

"Go clean yourself up. Don't let the kids see you like this." He spoke roughly.

She cleaned up the mess she had made of the kitchen floor while he watched her, then slid past him and up the stairs to their bedroom. She showered and covered as much of the damage as she could. The cut on her cheek had hurt like hell, but she managed to get it to stop bleeding and then had covered it with make-up so that it hardly showed.

The children were awake and running about when she emerged from the bedroom, dressed and pieced together.

Roger was sitting in the living room with the newspaper.

Henry raced by, pausing to put his arms about her and then went on and Emma sidled up to her mother sleepily for a hug.

She looked up and her eyes fixed upon the cut on Vera's cheek. "Are you okay, Mommy?"

"I'm just fine, baby. Just fine." Vera reassured her, holding her close, turning her face away.

"We'll be late if you don't get them fed and changed soon." Roger spoke from the corner without looking up from the paper.

Vera stared pointedly at Roger's inattentive face, rubbing her daughter's back. "Emma, baby, will you help your brother dress for church while I make us pancakes."

Emma's face lit up at the prospect of pancakes and reached for Henry, practically dragging him up the stairs.

Roger was looking Vera over when she happened to glance in his direction. "You look nice." He said, turning back to his paper.

She turned from him and went to the kitchen, putting an apron over her dress so she wouldn't get a thing on it, and looked down at the counter.

A splatter of blood.

The only remnant of the strange morning.

She wiped the blood away and then, feeling queasy, pulled out the ingredients for the pancakes.

She couldn't eat a thing, could only sit smoking while she watched Roger and the children eat their breakfast. She had the strangest urge to cry, feeling her eyes water as she washed the dishes and scrubbed down the countertops, the kitchen table.

They piled into the car and Vera examined her cheek in the rearview mirror, relieved that the scratch was hardly noticeable.

Roger drove them into town, to the Baptist Church off the

main street. Kitty and John and Judy and Phil attended the church as well and had invited them to see if they might like it too since Roger had been raised Baptist. They had sporadically attended an Episcopalian church in the city, but now Roger felt they should be more faithful since they were to become a part of a community.

Vera felt dread in the pit of her stomach, thoughts of the church she'd grown up in flooding her as they walked towards the entrance. Sundays spent being told how horrible humanity was, how wretched and sinful. The way the pastor had gazed at her and how she had avoided him as if she knew what his longing looks meant.

Emma's hand slid into her mother's. Vera squeezed the tiny hand.

The minister stood waiting at the front door to greet his constituents. The Reverend George Johns welcomed them with a kindly, welcoming smile on his wizened, red face. His hand lingered in Vera's grasp, his eyes looking her over in a way that made her stomach turn. "What a beautiful family." He spoke to her before turning to address Roger. "You're new here in town, are you?"

"Yes, sir. We arrived last week and have heard great things about your church here."

"I am happy to hear we receive such high marks. We'd certainly be glad to welcome you as part of our congregation. I do hope we see more of you." His eyes darted back to Vera.

Roger did not seem to notice. His arm slid about her waist as he guided them into the stately chapel. So much larger and grander than the small church in the city.

He chose a pew toward the middle. Henry wanted to sit by Roger and Emma pressed herself against Vera, as if shy in the new surroundings.

Vera looked about and saw Judy and Phil, who waved from where they sat. Vera turned then to see Kitty and her husband.

The red-headed woman left her husband's side to come greet them. "It was wonderful to see you at the party Friday. We hope you'll come to Margaret's next Friday." She looked deep into Vera's eyes. Hopeful.

The organist began playing, and the congregation settled.

And it was in the settling that Vera became acutely aware of a woman who sat exactly three rows ahead.

It was the prim, straightness of her back, the perfect bun of slick, black hair that rested at the nape of her slender neck. Two broad shoulders adorned in a smart, black collared jacket. The only thing out of place was one errant wisp of hair.

The world was lost to Vera, entranced as she was. She longed to know what the woman looked like. She wanted her to turn and notice her in return.

The service had begun, but the morning greeting was lost to Vera. Someone tried to speak with her, but she could only nod politely.

The woman ahead turned to greet someone. Vera watched the stain glass filtered light catch on the gold of an earring, and then the sharp, striking profile of the woman's face came into view.

Vera committed the curve of it to memory, as though she might never see her again. The deep-set eyes, the wrinkles that creased when she smiled at the person sitting near to her, the way her red lips moved as she spoke.

Roger nudged Vera. They were to stand to sing the opening hymn.

The woman was no longer looking to the side but had returned her attention to the front of the church. She rose with everyone else and Vera had a perfect view of her figure. She was tall and stately, a gentle curve to her hips encased in a black skirt that perfectly matched the black of her jacket.

The organ blasted out the first hymn and Vera felt hot. Emma was clinging to her and Roger was standing too close.

She felt as if she might jump out of her skin, restricted as she was. She wanted to leave, she wanted to approach the woman and have her speak to her as she had spoken to the person next to her.

What was it about the woman, Vera wondered, as they were seated again.

An elegantly aged hand was lifted to the slender neck. Perfectly manicured, red fingernails grasped at the errant strand of hair, twirling it as the Reverend took the pulpit to speak.

Vera felt beads of sweat collecting on the back of her own neck, warm between her legs.

The woman was alone.

The man beside her was with a woman beside him.

No one sat on the other side of the woman.

Vera felt relieved by this. Ridiculously happy for some inexplicable reason.

Who was she? Vera needed to know.

The service went by in a blur.

The final hymn came all too soon, and then the congregation began to disperse.

Vera's eyes remained on the woman, wanting...oh, what was there to want?

The woman had turned to speak to someone who had come to her on the other side.

Roger was pushing Vera out to the aisle in the opposite direction so she could no longer see the woman. Vera tried to keep an eye on her, but another family appeared before them, the wife trying to speak to Vera, but Vera's eyes were lost to the crowd dispersing, scanning, searching, searching frantically.

"It's so lovely to see new faces at service. What's your name, dear?" The wife before her was asking. "These are my children, Dan and Steven. Say hello, you bashful boys."

The boys were looking sheepishly at Vera.

Vera could feel another pair of eyes upon her.

She looked up and her heart clamored in her chest.

The woman, who was speaking to a young couple at the back of the sanctuary, was looking directly at her.

Her face was more beautiful from the front. Her dark eyes were wide open, the signs of age making her more beautiful than if she had been a young woman, as if she had grown into her beauty over the years.

Those eyes held Vera's for what felt an eternity.

Roger was nudging her.

The woman looked away.

"Vera, where's your head?" He was irritated with her but trying not to show it in front of the people now standing before them.

The boys were looking at her hungrily, and the slightly pudgy woman who had introduced herself as Elaine was waiting patiently for Vera to say something. They were so ugly to her and right over there...

Vera looked, but the woman had disappeared.

Vera glanced frantically about but did not see her anywhere.

She had disappeared. Vanished into thin air as if she might not have existed at all.

Bereft, Vera circulated with Roger until they finally made it out into the light of the summer day.

Vera lit a cigarette, warm and bothered in the sunlight, as the children raced about and Roger said his goodbyes and thanks to the Reverend.

Chapter Five

Though Roger was sore with her, he rolled over that night and climbed on top of her. Bothered as she was, she wanted him inside of her. It felt like a relief as he pressed into her. But it was too short, too little. He fell asleep afterward. Once his breathing had evened out, she let her fingers finish what he never seemed capable of.

She lay breathless in bed. Wide awake.

The image of the woman danced through her mind. Haunting her into a fever.

She slid from the bed and went down to the living room to pour herself a nightcap, to sit in Roger's chair and smoke and listen to the quiet stillness all around her.

What would the woman be doing now? Asleep? Would she be all alone somewhere or with someone? She hoped it was alone.

It sounded like heaven to be alone. To do what one wanted.

She fantasized until she put out her cigarette and had to touch herself again.

Vera tripped her way back to bed. She realized she had forgotten her diaphragm with Roger.

She did not linger on the thought, the drink bringing sleep as soon as she laid down beside him atop the cool sheets, her body so warm. So very warm.

Roger shook her awake the following morning. "I'll miss the train. Get up." He was doing up his tie.

She stumbled from the bed and managed to slip into her house dress and pin up her hair. She made him coffee, scrambled him an egg, and then drove him to the station.

He did not kiss her goodbye.

She caught sight of her face in the rearview mirror and found the gash in her cheek visible in the oncoming light of day. She touched it, feeling unsightly. She slid her sunglasses on and lit a cigarette.

She watched Roger's retreating form climb up the train station staircase and scanned the people walking toward the tracks as she smoked. Searching...

But why would *she* be getting on a train for the city?

It was a preposterous thought, Vera realized, and eased the car back onto the main road through town.

But as she drove, she continued to search. She peered down each side street as she passed, carefully looking at the few people out and about at that early morning hour. A woman's figure appeared out of the post office. Vera nearly hit her brakes at the sight of her, wishing, hoping...

But when the woman turned to cross the street, Vera realized it was just another woman.

It was not *her*.

Vera returned home and found Emma curled on the couch with her teddy bear. She sat up tiredly and reached for Vera.

Vera took the girl in her arms and Emma buried her face in Vera's chest.

Vera longed to regress, to be a little girl again, to have her mother hold her when the world no longer made sense to her.

Her own mother, however, had never been affectionate with her, preferring to hold her at an arm's length.

They made breakfast together, Henry asking if he could help when he appeared in the kitchen bedraggled and tired-eyed. Vera let him get the toast from the toaster and showed him how to butter it. He seemed to like the chore.

The children ate at the table while Vera watched, smoke swirling about her head.

She cleaned up after them and then pieced herself together meticulously. She hid the cut on her cheek, did up her eyes, and lips, and slid into a nice day dress. Then she took the children to Kitty's.

"I'm going into town; would you mind watching them?" She felt guilty for dropping the children with her, but Kitty had offered at the party Friday. If Vera ever needed, she should not hesitate to ask.

And Kitty looked pleased to watch them. "Would you mind getting me a gallon of milk? We ran out this morning." Kitty pressed some money into Vera's hand.

"Of course." Vera put it into her pocketbook and got into the car.

Needing....well, what did she need?

She drove into town.

There had been no aim, only a want to get away.

She thought of all the places the woman might frequent if she were to also be in town. Vera passed by the library and immediately thought to look there. She parked on the street and made her way into the stately looking building. Searching...

But there was only an older, gray-haired woman seated behind the counter. She introduced herself as Marjorie.

"What brings you to the library, dear?" She asked, eyeing Vera curiously.

Vera fidgeted. "I would like a card. I just...just moved to town."

Marjorie helped her with the paperwork and handed her the metal card with a number prominently embossed on it.

Vera thanked her and left the stuffy, dark library, lighting a cigarette as soon as she stepped outside.

She walked down the street smoking, staring into store windows. Searching...

People looked at her oddly. She began to feel self-conscious without a purpose in the town.

And the woman was nowhere to be seen.

She was being foolish. Foolish and self-indulgent.

She should have gone home to fetch her children from Kitty's, relieving her of the duty.

But there was the milk to get.

Vera returned to her car and drove to the grocery store.

She wandered aimlessly down the aisles, realizing that for her story of errands to be true she would need to return with something more than Kitty's milk.

She purchased food for dinner, another pound of meat, a loaf of bread, some canned vegetables, another bottle of wine.

Mary sat at the register. Her tired eyes looked Vera over warily.

Billy was at the end of the counter. His eyes shone brightly at Vera's presence.

"$7.56." Mary announced with little preamble.

So they would not be friends, Vera decided.

She paid.

"I'll help you with these, Ma'am." Billy did not ask this time.

She followed him out of the grocery store. He seemed to remember which car was hers. He did not work quickly to place the items in her trunk, but rather took his time. "I saw you at the party Friday," he said.

She startled in the lighting of her cigarette. She did not remember seeing him there.

"I live there. When I'm on break from school." He spoke as he shut the trunk.

"They're your parents, you mean. Sharon and Bill." She realized.

He bowed his head. "Yes, ma'am."

She pressed a dime into his hand. "You should have said hello."

His smile returned as he accepted the payment. "Thank you, Vera." He made a point of saying her name.

"You're welcome, Billy."

She returned to her children, to Kitty who was grateful for the gallon of milk and made sure to let Vera know that the children were no problem at all and that they were welcome any time. But Vera knew she could not abuse this privilege.

There would likely be few afternoons of leisure until the children went to school.

Only a few weeks away.

She daydreamed of the freedom it would give her in the afternoons. So she could close the bedroom door and curl herself in bed and smoke and drink away the afternoon without anyone to care for.

She longed to do it now, but Henry banged his knee and Emma had a terrible tantrum over a missing doll and her head began to ache by the time she had to drive to the station to pick up Roger, who seemed even more sour than he had that morning.

He poured himself a glass of bourbon and sat on his chair the moment they walked in the door. The children avoided him.

Everyone remained silent when their father did not speak as they sat around the dinner table that evening.

"I'm afraid I won't be home tomorrow evening. I have a late dinner with a client. I'll stay in the city." He told her before he went up to bed that night.

She stayed in the kitchen, washing the dishes and putting them humming away in the dishwasher, cleaning out the sink with Borax, wiping off the counters, the kitchen table, then sweeping the floor before taking out the trash.

She sank onto Roger's chair and smoked and drank back a bourbon and it was only after everything else in the house went quiet, and she was a little lightheaded and high and exhausted, that she made her way – falling against a wall as a she did – to the bedroom, into the bathroom where she closed the door and turned on the light and undressed enough so she could wipe herself clean with a washcloth - beneath her arms, about her neck, and then to wash off her face, to place cream onto her skin, to roll curlers into her hair, to slip into a night-gown and brush her teeth, her eyes fighting to stay open so that when she finally slid into the bed beside Roger she was out like a light.

There was a calmness in the home the following evening because of Roger's absence.

The children helped her with the dishes and she allowed them to watch the television, since Roger was not at home. Vera sat idly on the couch, smoking and reading a novel she'd taken out of the library. She had not had a moment to read since the move, but without Roger to bark orders at her or look disapprovingly upon a less than perfectly cleaned home, she was left with the luxury of time.

The children fell asleep, and she had to carry Henry up to his bedroom. She tucked them in. First Henry and then Emma. Emma whose eyes came open when Vera sat on her bed.

The girl was looking at her curiously. "Mommy, are you happy?"

Vera felt tears prick her eyes. "Oh, Emma." She whispered and crumbled, wrapping her arms about the girl, pressing her face against her soft cheek, inhaling her scent. The smell of innocence and girlhood.

She loved her and hated her all the same. She wished she could make things different for her, but she didn't know how.

She dozed off, wrapped about the girl.

Sometime in the middle of the night she awoke with a crick in her neck. She slid silently from the bed, pulling the blanket up and around Emma, kissing her cheek, before slipping from the bedroom.

She went to the living room to pour herself another drink and light a fresh cigarette.

She curled herself on the couch and stared out the window.

The house was silent, and for the first time since arriving she adored the silence.

The woman's face came to her as she sat in the stillness of the night.

If she closed her eyes she could see it so clearly. So vivid and alive. As if she might have been standing right there before Vera. An apparition in the night.

Vera longed for it to be true.

It set off a reaction in her body, an ache between her legs.

She climbed the stairs to her bedroom and rubbed herself to satisfaction. And then again. And then laid spread out across the otherwise empty bed and blew smoke rings to the ceiling.

She slept in until after ten the following morning. It was not until Henry came barging in, throwing himself atop her half-naked body, that she roused. "Henry!" She pulled the sheets up and around herself. But Henry didn't care. He wrapped his arms about her and pressed their bodies together.

She spent the afternoon putting the house back into order so when she picked Roger up from the station that evening, it was as if he had not been gone at all.

Chapter Six

The Friday evening gathering was hosted by Margaret and Ken.

Roger hated dancing, but he let the buxom Darlene press up against him during a slow number that played on the record player.

Vera watched as the attractive woman swayed in his arms, her red claws sunk into him like talons. She imagined what it would look like for Darlene to lift her head, and Roger tilt his down so he could look into Darlene's smoky eyes. Roger would hold her closer and she would part her slightly smeared red lips, and he would bow his head to meet her in a kiss.

How easy it might be.

How strange that the thought of it neither repulsed nor aroused Vera.

She blew a stream of smoke from her post leaning against the doorway, watching.

She sipped her whiskey sour.

"Hey there, darlin'. Won't you dance with me?" A body pressed up against her from behind, an arm wrapping about her waist, holding her close.

She laughed, uncomfortable, too many drinks inhibiting a proper response. "I told you, Ken, I'm not much of a dancer."

"But you went at it with James and Bill." Ken's hand had wandered upward, clumsy fingers caressing beneath her breasts.

Vera placed the cigarette between her lips and stared across the smoky room to where Kitty sat talking to Ken's very pregnant wife, Margaret. She was attractive, even in her engorged state. It seemed to suit her to be pregnant as she was. They had five children already. Vera had overheard Margaret worrying about where the money would come for the new baby, but in the moment Margaret looked carefree and happy as Kitty said something that made her laugh.

And here was Margaret's husband with his arm wrapped about Vera. Something pressing hard against her lower back.

"I have to go to the powder room." Vera attempted to maneuver away.

"Dance with me." He held her tighter.

"Let go of me." She spoke firmly and resolutely and far more soberly than she felt.

And Ken relaxed his grip.

She got out, got away. Saw Roger talking to Darlene and Bill and Sharon. Heart pounding rapidly in her ears. She saw a side door that led to the outside world, to the darkness of night.

She escaped the noise and heat of too many bodies, too much noise.

The air was fresh, smelling as if it had just rained. The wetness of newly paved roads and dampened greenery accosted her.

She still held the tumbler of whiskey in her hand, her cigarette burnt down to the near end. Another puff and she stubbed it beneath her heel while balancing against the side of the house.

A car door opened somewhere off in the distance, and a laugh rang out.

Vera pressed herself against the house, peering out to where she could hazily make out the street.

Two figures emerged from a car parked down the road from Bill and Sharon's home. Two tall, lanky young men from what she could tell.

In the dim streetlight she could make out the familiar features of the driver. He was saying something the other boy was laughing at. The other boy put out a cigarette beneath his sneaker and they slapped hands, bumped shoulders in parting.

Vera had ventured to the edge of the house so when the unfamiliar boy ambled down the road and the other turned ever so, he saw her.

His face softened, easing into a smile. He held up his hand in a wave.

She lifted her hand and waved back.

He looked both ways before crossing the street, heading straight toward her.

Her stomach knotted.

She sipped her cocktail and stood helplessly watching him as he approached.

"Vera." He spoke cordially.

She looked him over, taller than him in that moment because she stood on higher ground than he. He was long and lean and handsome. He smelled of cigarettes and strong aftershave.

"Billy." She nodded.

"Another party?"

She held up the drink. "What else is there to do around here?"

He looked at her uncertainly until the corner of her lip quirked upward and then he smiled at her.

"Got a cigarette?" She asked, having forgotten her pack inside, not wishing to go after it just then.

He nodded and reached into his jacket to pull out a pack.

They sat under a patioed back porch on a double glider patio chair. It swung ever so. He lit her cigarette – his were Marlboro's and felt heavier and richer when she inhaled. Drunk as she was, she did not mind the difference.

He was watching her as she smoked. She found she liked his eyes upon her, drinking her in.

"I hope you don't mind my saying so but you're very beautiful." He spoke bashfully.

She felt her lips curving upward. She laughed. "Beautiful."

"You're not...you're not like...well you're different." She had flustered him.

"I'm beautiful, do you think so?" She turned to look at him. He could not meet her gaze. "Beautiful." She laughed again. "I'm practically old enough to be your mother."

"Oh, no. That can't be." He protested. "I mean it." He spoke resolutely, firmly.

She smiled and puffed at his cigarette. "I believe you."

They sat in silence, gazing out toward the forest that lined the back of the property. She thought of the well that lay hidden now. Deep and cool and covered.

The sound of the party filtered out through a cracked window. She wondered if Roger would be looking for her. She wondered if anyone would notice her absence.

Perhaps Ken with his roaming hands and wanton need for her. Did Margaret deny him for nine months so once one child popped out he was quick to reproduce another? How many others did he fondle in the interim?

The seedy feeling depressed her.

Billy was looking at her shyly from beneath his beautiful lashes.

She knew he would not paw at her carelessly.

His crush on her was total, smitten in her presence, afraid to lose whatever it was that had come between them by doing something so stupid.

She wondered what it would be like to kiss him.

It would be so easy to do. No one would see, no one would know except him.

"How old are you?" She finally asked, downing the last of her whiskey sour.

"Nineteen. Next month."

A child.

No, she would not kiss him.

She could see his lap in the darkness. A bulge had formed.

A door opened somewhere in the distance.

"Vera?" A voice was calling for her. Kitty.

Vera stood up, smoothing out her dress. Billy did not move. "I should be getting back." She stubbed out the cigarette beneath her heel and moved away from Billy, leaving him out in the darkness on the patio chair.

"There you are!" Kitty exclaimed when Vera came into view. "Roger thought you'd gone on home, but I told him you'd just gone outside to get some fresh air." She spoke as she pulled her back inside to the insufferable noise and warmth of the house.

Roger was looking at her from across the room, something curious in his expression.

After another drink, he appeared at her side. "Let's go."

She let him have his way with her that night.

She woke up sick on Saturday, vomiting twice before she could put herself together enough to make breakfast for Roger and the children. The day was a blur of feeling nauseous and cleaning. The only redeeming moment was when Roger suggested they go to the restaurant downtown for dinner. Vera would not have to cook, would not have to clean up after another meal.

And while she sat in the restaurant, curiously peering about at the other clientele, hoping...a warmth overcame her at the idea that they should return to church the following day. The possibility of another glimpse drove her mad.

Henry upset a glass, milk spilling out across the restaurant table and Roger scooped the boy up, angry, and took him outside. "Roger!" Vera quietly tried to protest. He was only a boy, after all. But she knew that Roger would not hurt him. He would scold him, perhaps pop him on the behind, but he would not hurt him. He was not violent.

She helped the waitress clean up the mess, apologetic. The waitress smiled at her kindly, assuring her it was all right.

And Emma sat beside her, nearly in tears.

"It's all right, baby." Vera assured her, pulling her close into her side.

Henry came back sober faced and wide-eyed at Roger's side like an obedient dog.

"Perhaps we can't take the children to nice places." Roger said later that evening as he lay in bed, Vera sitting at the side rubbing lotion on her hands.

"They're still young."

"They're old enough to be able to control themselves."

"It was an accident."

"They need more attention, more structure. You let them run around here like they own the place." Roger accused.

Vera took a deep breath. "You're right." It was all her fault, wasn't it? For having gotten pregnant with the children in the first place. As if she had wanted it...

But wasn't she supposed to want it?

She got up, grabbing her cigarettes.

"Where are you going?" Roger barked at her.

"To smoke in the living room."

He let her go.

The morning came all too soon. She had a headache from downing a glass or two of bourbon and then stumbling to bed far too late in the early morning.

But there was an excitement as she dressed meticulously for church. Piecing herself together so no blemish could be seen on her face – the fading scar on her cheek perfectly covered – and her dress neat and pulled perfectly into place about her lithe frame.

Beautiful.

Billy had told her she was beautiful.

As she brushed out golden curls about her face, she supposed that she was beautiful.

Older than before, but there were remnants of what she had once been. Weren't there?

"We'll be late." Roger was calling from the bedroom.

They arrived on time.

Vera searched the throng of people but came up short. Not a single one was the woman from the week before.

She worked her way distractedly through the usual greetings and pleasantries as they made their way to the pew they had sat in the week before.

Vera watched, waiting.

It was at the first hymn, as they rose, that she spotted the woman again. Late, moving carefully about people as she took her seat three rows ahead of Vera.

Her face was kind as she smiled at those she passed. Some words were spoken between her and the man who sat beside her. Her lips were painted an attractive shade of soft red.

Roger had to pull Vera down when it came time to sit, as lost as she was.

The whole of the service flew by in a blur. Too fast and yet not fast enough. Reverend Johns spoke slowly and deliberately. His voice rising into a fury to make a condemning point. "And the righteous man shall live without sin!"

The closing hymn sounded. The congregation roused to life again and in the midst of it Vera lost sight of the woman.

Judy and Phil appeared, blocking Vera's line of sight. They spoke of the party Friday and of how wonderful Reverend Johns' sermon had been that day. Vera could hardly speak.

The woman appeared and then disappeared in the sea of people.

Until Vera no longer saw her and decided she had gone.

She excused herself from Roger's side and went to the ladies' room. She closed herself in a stall and felt a wave of grief and sadness overcome her.

But what had she expected? To speak to this woman whom she did not even know, had no connection with, no reason to know at all?

She relieved herself then pulled her pantyhose back up her legs and smoothed out her dress before exiting the stall to wash her hands at the sink.

There was the intense aroma of freshly picked flowers and something that could only be found deep in the woods that came to Vera as she stood at the sink.

There was the flush of a toilet in the stall next to the one she had just emerged from.

She had not been alone.

And as she looked up into the mirror, her eyes caught with those of the very woman who had haunted her thoughts for a week.

The woman froze, as if struck by something, before a small smile flickered on her lips and she continued forward to the sink.

Vera's chest tightened exquisitely.

"You're new around here, aren't you?" The woman's voice was low and warm. She spoke as she reached for a paper towel to dry her finely aged hands, adorned with a simple gold band about her right-hand ring finger and a simple diamond on the left middle. The tips of her fingers matched her lips.

"Yes." Vera managed in her presence.

The woman eyed her as she pulled a tube of lipstick from her purse and applied a light layer to her lips. Vera watched with intense fascination.

The woman clicked shut her lipstick and straightened to her full height. Her dark hair pulled tightly into a bun at the nape of her neck, her simple black suit tailored to her tall, slender physique. Her dark features. She was severe and beautiful.

Truly beautiful.

Vera watched as the woman dropped the lipstick into her purse and then she extended her strong, tanned hand toward Vera. "I'm Joan."

Chapter Seven

In the city Vera had delighted in getting lost in the anonymous monotony of streets. When the children had been small enough to cram into the stroller she'd pushed them aimlessly down the street, delighting in being another nameless, faceless passerby that no one paid any mind to.

Now the streets were replaced with winding asphalt and sprawling lawns and a forest of trees encroaching upon the manmade settlement.

Her only escape was the woods.

Having washed the kitchen to a shine and started a load of never ending laundry, she walked into the summer heat through the shade of the woods. She could hear the children's voices rising and falling off in the distance, screaming with the delights of summer.

Only too soon would those hot summer days come to an end. School was a mere week away, the children's freedom truncated by desks and structure and learning - her freedom regained.

She walked through patches of shade and light.

A branch caught at her leg and she nearly stumbled forward but caught herself on the trunk of a tree.

The well was before her.

Covered over and closed up. Safe.

The world around her cooled as she approached.

The top was a solid block of cement.

A cloud covered the sun. A sadness gripped her.

She sat on the edge of the well and pulled her pack of cigarettes from her shirt pocket.

She smoked and listened to the rustle of wind as it brushed through the branches above.

The sound of children had died away.

She could perceive nothing more beyond the circle of the well.

She pulled her legs up beneath herself, sitting cross-legged.

Smoke slid from her lips.

Her eyes scanned the horizon of the forest, seeking where its depths led.

She had not thought of Joan since awaking that morning, but the image of her hands came to her. Vivid and present. The curve of her rosy red lips as she had smiled at Vera. The way the light coming from an overhead window had illuminated her dark features so attractively.

What was it about Joan?

She wondered and French inhaled for the hell of it.

Her eyes caught at the line of something manmade far off in the distance. A roof line.

She climbed to her feet, moved with piqued curiosity through the forest.

A path uncovered itself. Faded and grown over.

As she walked further a house revealed itself.

Old and stately. Surrounded by forest but well kept. The shingles a deep green that complemented the wood of the trim about the windows. A picture window with old window panes peered out from beneath the cover of a wraparound front porch.

She came to a halt in the forest, afraid to go too near.

She stood smoking the last of her cigarette, feeling a sense of warmth emitting forth from this house in the woods. It felt as if it belonged amongst its idyllic setting whereas the homes along her street did not.

She wanted to be near it, inside its welcoming walls.

A bird cried out, startling her.

She wondered if she could be seen, feeling as if she were intruding upon something she should not be, so she put out her cigarette and retreated back through the woods, back to the manicured lawn that led to the back porch of her home.

The sun had begun its descent from the sky, and she wondered how long she had been in the woods. It had felt like no time at all and yet when she stepped inside to look at the clock she realized that she was due at the station in ten minutes to retrieve Roger from the train.

Roger was unhappy with her when she showed up late to meet him and unhappier still when dinner took longer than he wanted.

The week went on like this.

On Thursday they were to enroll at the school.

Henry threw a tantrum, wanting to play with his new friend down the block. But Vera had bribed him with the promise of ice cream afterward so he would change into his nice shirt and put on his shoes.

Emma looked nervous, her nearly eight years bordering on the verge of self-consciousness.

They drove to the school. She parked before its tall structure and watched as other mothers and children made their way into the double doors at the front. A man she presumed to be the principal stood at the entrance, greeting those who passed by.

The three of them stared at the scene before them while Vera killed the ignition. "Well, let's get this over with." She got out of the car and stubbed out her cigarette beneath her heel.

She took Henry by the hand and put an arm about Emma.

They walked up the steps and were greeted by Principal Nelson. He had a friendly smile, but Vera did not like the way he looked at her, from head to toe. She felt her cheeks color, and she held Emma closer at her side.

"We're very glad to have you here, Mrs. Wilson." His smile left a grimy feeling as they slid past him and went into the main hall.

It smelled of an institution of learning. Old and worn but filled with youth.

Some children ran by, nearly knocking into Vera.

Doors ahead of them led into a crowded gymnasium. The noise coming from within the doors was overwhelming as mothers and children alike maneuvered about tables, speaking over one another. She did not want to go inside.

Henry was suddenly tugging at her arm. "There's Timmy! Can I go see him? Please?"

And before she could stop him he'd slipped away from her and was racing down the hall to meet his friend.

Emma looked up at her, her face echoing Vera's thoughts.

Vera took a deep breath and just as she was about to step into the chaos before them, a figure rounded the corner of the main hallway, stopping Vera in her tracks.

An elegant hand was poised at the back of her neck, a tense look wrinkling her forehead. Her eyes were hidden behind dark-rimmed glasses. They did not seem to register Vera at first, but once they blinked open again a look of recognition dawned upon a tired visage, followed by the slightest curl of a smile at the corner of her muted, red lips.

Emma was looking at Vera curiously, wondering what had detained her.

Joan.

Joan was here before her.

Joan in a prim and proper black pencil skirt, a simple white button up tucked into its band, feet encased in simple black kitten heels. A gold necklace wrapped about her neck.

Simple, neat.

Vera ran a hand over her A-line dress.

"Vera, isn't it?" Joan spoke, her voice low and mellifluous.

Vera could only nod.

"And who might this be?" Joan smiled and leaned down to acknowledge Emma pressed against her side.

"I'm Emma." Emma held out her hand bashfully.

"It's very nice to meet you, Emma." Joan's elegant hand enclosed her daughter's hand, shaking it.

Vera envied her daughter.

"What are you doing here?" Vera had not expected to find Joan here. Of all places. She did not remember seeing her with a husband or child.

Joan straightened and smiled. "I teach. Fifth grade."

Vera felt a smile tug at her lips. So she was a teacher. "It's very nice. To see you here."

Joan looked at Vera, something curious crossing her features. "It's very nice to see you here, as well. Is this your only child?"

"No. No, I have a son as well. He's run off somewhere."

"How old are they?"

"She will be eight in a few months, and he is six."

"Pity," something playful bounced across her lips. "I won't have either of them in my class. But perhaps someday."

Vera smiled, feeling warm. Wishing that perhaps Joan could have been Emma's teacher so she would have a reason to keep in touch.

"Joan! Mrs. Richardson wants a word with you about her son." Someone called from the noisy gymnasium doorway.

"Oh." Joan hummed. "I'll be right there, Cheryl." And then she looked at Vera again. "You must excuse me, but I do hope to see you again. Very soon." And she lightly touched Vera's arm before brushing past her, leaving a trail of perfume in her wake.

Vera inhaled deeply. The place on her arm where Joan had touched her throbbed.

"Who was that, mommy?" Emma asked at her side.

And for the briefest moment she had forgotten she was a mother and that her daughter was beside her, watching her every motion.

"Just a woman. No one." Vera muttered and reached for Emma's hand, turning to follow Joan into the too warm and too loud gymnasium. She fought her way through, all the while overly aware of Joan's whereabouts. Always finding her out within the room.

And at one point when she looked up to seek for her, their eyes met.

Joan smiled at her and turned away.

Chapter Eight

Joan was everywhere and nowhere at all.

She appeared at church and sat a few rows ahead, her hair tightly pinned at the nape of her neck, little white pearls adorning her ears.

She saw Vera at the end of the service, but their paths did not cross long enough to utter more than a hurried greeting.

"It's nice to see you." Joan smiled.

Vera bowed her head, feeling her cheeks coloring. Then a small hand slid into her own, tugging her away.

"Mommy, mommy, mommy! Daddy said we could get hamburgers on the way home!" Henry's excited voice.

She looked up and offered Joan an apologetic smile, wishing.

Joan's rosy lips had curled into a reciprocal smile.

Vera searched for Joan furtively the first day of school. As if the older teacher might be waiting to receive her and her children on the front steps of the school.

But she was nowhere to be seen. Likely tucked away in her classroom somewhere, greeting her new wards.

The second day Vera lingered, but saw no sign of Joan.

She drove aimlessly away from the school. Free in the car.

She ended up a town over, a diner emerging in the midst of the small downtown. She parked in front and walked inside. She felt eyes on her. Watching her every move.

In the city she'd stolen away to the little café down the road for a cup of coffee in the middle of the day when Emma and Henry had been at school. She had been no one, and they had not paid her any mind.

This was a freedom denied to her in suburbia.

She sat near the back of the room and the waitress greeted her gruffly. "What'll you have?"

"A coffee." She spoke softly, itching at the back of her neck.

The waitress returned with a mug and a pot of coffee. She roughly banged the mug down before Vera and poured the brown liquid into its recesses. Vera could feel her eyes upon her as she did so. The waitress smacked a piece of gum. Her eyes were small and tired. She did not like Vera. Something about her presence made her uncomfortable.

Vera was grateful when she went away.

She lit a cigarette and looked about the room.

Two old men sat at the counter, one reading a newspaper, the other shoveling food into his mouth. Both men's eyes were fixed upon her.

She did not like the way they looked at her. Hungry gazes.

The coffee was horrible, but she drank it down. After her third cigarette she stood, placing two quarters on the table. More than enough for the coffee and tip.

The waitress hardly looked at her as she left. The men blatantly watched her retreating form.

She returned home and poured herself a bourbon, kicking off her heels, stripping out of her dress and bustier and slip. She put on slacks and smoked while she cleaned the kitchen and vacuumed the carpet.

She fell on the chair in the corner of the room and lit a fresh cigarette. She was exhausted.

Her eyes slid shut, her mind wandering to Joan standing in front of a classroom.

It was only when she smelled something burning that she opened her eyes and realized the cigarette had burned a hole in the arm of the chair.

"Shit." She smothered it before it could catch fire. "Shit." She admonished herself, wondering if Roger would notice. Perhaps if she could cover it somehow...but it was useless.

She looked at the clock and realized time had passed all too quickly. She was late to get the children. She got back in the car and went to the school. Emma and Henry were standing docilely on the curb. A teacher stood behind them, looking disparagingly at Vera as she apologized for her lateness.

Emma and Henry did not seem to mind but fought with one another in the backseat of the car and her head started to hurt, and she ended up vomiting when they got back home.

She made dinner then rushed to the station, determined not to be late for Roger.

Roger, fortunately, did not notice the cigarette burn in the chair arm. He watched television raptly while downing a drink.

Vera put the children to bed and then found Roger undressing in the bedroom.

He was handsome. They looked very nice together, everyone had always told Vera this. They made a very attractive couple.

He had stirred something inside of her when they had first met, something she had never felt for anyone else. So she took it for love and had given herself to him.

He looked at her through the bathroom mirror as he brushed his teeth.

There was a lack of recognition. He did not look at her as he once had. He seemed to just see through her anymore. As if she were an apparition.

And she wanted desperately for him to recognize her, for him to see her as he once had.

She slid from her slacks and shirt.

He turned off the bathroom light and came to sit on the edge of the bed to take off his watch.

She laid on her side of the bed, half-naked.

He laid back on the bed, shutting off his light.

She reached out for him, putting her hand between his legs, but he grabbed her hand and pushed it away. "What are you doing?"

She sat up. Wordlessly she got up and went to the bathroom to put herself together for bed.

When she emerged a while later, Roger was asleep.

Kitty was to host the weekly party that Friday, but Junior had come down with a terrible flu and then John had gotten sick. Vera took chicken noodle soup over to try and help, and Kitty had looked relieved at her presence.

They'd smoked on the back porch together. Her tired eyes showed the same displeasure Vera knew all too well.

"Where the hell's the medicine?" An angry, low voice had called out from the kitchen, startling Kitty. She'd quickly stubbed out her half-smoked cigarette.

"He doesn't like it if I smoke." She explained apologetically. "I'm very sorry."

"No, go on." Vera walked through Kitty's backyard and back to the main road, inhaling freely on her cigarette.

A car came roaring down the road, halting before Sharon and Bill's house.

Billy got out and Vera wondered if she should acknowledge him in the light of day.

But she was being ridiculous.

He met her at the side of the road. "I haven't seen you around."

"Well," she inhaled on her cigarette, tilting her head to the side, glancing about to see if anyone was pressed against their front windows, watching. She had gone to the supermarket one afternoon instead of the morning, and Billy had not been at his normal post.

He looked handsome that day. Still dressed up from the store minus the apron.

"I go back to school in a week." He said as if this might affect her somehow.

"I'm sure Mary will miss you." She took the last drag of her cigarette and crushed it out atop the pavement.

He looked flustered and then began to laugh. "Sure." He smoothed his hand over his hair.

She took a step to leave him.

"I heard my parents will be hosting the weekly party since the Morrisons are otherwise disposed of."

"Is that so?" Vera shielded her eyes from the sun and looked up again at Billy. "And will you be there?"

Billy shrugged. "If I haven't got anything better to do."

Vera laughed, stepping to take her leave. She had lingered far too long. "Perhaps I'll see you then."

She went back home and tried to pick up the chores she had left, but ended up pouring herself a glass of bourbon. It made her feel heated. The sun pouring in through the picture window warmed her skin.

The children were at school.

The house was quiet.

She slid her hand up her skirt and touched herself.

The clock ticked and time suddenly sped up so that she had to quickly finish cleaning, race to get the children, feed them, and then retrieve Roger from the station and feed him his dinner.

Chapter Nine

Margaret was glowing in her pregnant state. There was something that made her look deliciously appealing, the outward curve of her stomach an insinuation. Her brunette hair was swept up attractively from her neck, her lips a pointed shade of burnt red accentuating her rosy cheeks.

Vera couldn't help but notice her as she was that evening.

Ken pointedly ignored Vera now. He talked instead to Darlene, who looked radiant that evening with her décolletage hanging out on display for all to see. Vera wondered why Ken couldn't see how attractive his wife was, why he needed to pursue every other woman in the room instead of Margaret.

"I mean, it's a relief to have half of them out of the house now that school's begun again." Margaret was saying.

Vera was lighting a cigarette. She perked up at the mention of school. "Your oldest...he's in fifth grade now, isn't he?"

Margaret looked at Vera. "Yes. Why yes, he is."

"Who's his teacher?" Vera's hand shook as she tapped off ash.

"Why it's Ms. DeBoer." Margaret was looking at Vera curiously.

"Joan? Joan DeBoer?" Vera felt Judy – who was also sitting near them - looking at her then.

"Why yes." Vera's heart leapt foolishly. "Do you know her?" Margaret inquired.

"No...well, only a little I suppose." Vera sipped her drink and met Judy's eyes.

"She goes to our church." Judy offered.

"Do you know her well?" Vera dared to ask.

Judy laughed stiffly. "Well? No, I wouldn't say so."

"She's the one who lives off in the woods all by herself, isn't she?" Sharon had entered the conversation. "I'd be careful with her. I've heard...things."

Vera's brow furrowed. "What do you mean? What sort of things?"

Margaret shifted. "Oh, just rumors. I'm sure none of it is true."

Judy looked uncomfortable at the insinuation. "I don't believe any of it. She's always been very kind. And she's absolutely devoted to the church and the school."

Sharon shrugged, "I think she should have married back when she had the chance." Her hand fell on Vera's shoulder. "Don't you get mixed up with her. No, I'd steer clear of her if I were you."

Sharon and Judy floated off to mix with the husbands, and Margaret smiled at Vera. "Well, I think she's very lovely. And Kenny absolutely adores her. I'm sure it's no more than some idle gossip."

Vera tried to smile in return, but felt something inside of her twist.

She excused herself for another drink.

She looked for Roger and found him dancing with Judy.

He looked at her over Judy's soft red hair and then looked away from her.

She did not go toward the bar to freshen her drink. The drink was half-full anyway.

Instead, she stumbled her way down a hall, searching. The powder room was on the left. There were stairs on the right.

She went up the stairs clumsily.

A light was on down the hall.

She moved toward it, hesitating for only a brief moment before she pressed open the door.

Billy was laying on his bed, smoking and reading a magazine. He looked up at her with wide eyes, as if surprised by her appearance.

Vera closed the door behind her. The sound of the party downstairs faded away into the background.

Billy sat up, putting out his cigarette.

Vera moved to sit on the edge of his bed, sipping back the rest of her drink before settling it on his bedside table. She inhaled at the end of her cigarette and crushed it out beside Billy's, her lipstick mark contrasting the white ends of his butts.

It did not belong.

She reached under her skirt and pulled at her tights.

Billy began undoing his pants. He moved to kiss her, but she stopped him.

"Lay down." She instructed.

He did as he was told.

She slid from her heels and pushed her tights and under-garments off. She bunched up her skirt about her hips, the slip itchy against her thighs, and she straddled Billy. He was large against her.

"Do you...what about a rubber?" He asked.

"Forget it." She snapped and positioned herself atop him.

He slid inside of her and she rocked forward. "Oh God." She bit her lip.

"Jesus." Billy kept saying, reaching up to cup her breasts through the material of her dress.

It was frenzied, she panted and felt a release building up. It shook her, the surprise that she could be brought to the edge so easily. She was still panting when he came inside of her. Warm and hot.

And what did it matter that he had?

She already knew she was pregnant.

She slid off of him, careful not to mess up her dress.

He lit a cigarette and they lay breathless side-by-side, passing it back and forth.

The sound from the party downstairs swelled, startling her.

She had been gone too long.

He handed her tissues and she cleaned herself and redressed.

Billy opened his mouth to say something, but she shook her head.

She lifted the tumbler from his nightstand and left, making her way down the stairs, legs wobbly and loose.

After a stop in the bathroom to put herself back together, she sneaked her way to the kitchen where Bill, whom she did not wish to see just then, complimented her on how beautiful she looked and refreshed her drink. "Roger's looking for you." He whispered before she went back to the hazy living room.

Roger was across the room. Their eyes met and he nodded for her.

She went to him.

"Where did you go off to?" He asked her.

"I just...needed to get away." She shrugged.

He looked at her with disbelief.

"I went outside...I walked, I..." she tried.

"Stop disappearing." He admonished her harshly beneath his breath. And she felt her shoulders tighten. "Just stop."

She went to the doctor the following week. He saw patients on the second story of a building in the sleepy downtown. A nurse took down notes, made her urinate in a cup in the adjoining bathroom, and then had her undress to put on a gown before the doctor came in. He regarded her with gentle indifference.

"So, Mrs. Wilson. What brings you in today?" He looked at her chart.

"I'm pregnant."

He looked at her over his glasses. "Is that so?"

She nodded.

"How far along?"

"Two months." She felt as if she knew the exact night it had happened.

"Well let's have a look, shall we?" He put down her chart and had her scoot down on the table. He parted her legs and stuck his hand inside of her. She felt at once violated but uncertain as to why. His finger lingered for a while, she could hear his breath, felt it on her thigh.

"Everything seems perfectly normal down there." He emerged after a moment.

She felt wetness pooling between her legs and her cheeks colored in embarrassment.

He washed his hands and then moved to inspect her breasts, rolling them about in his clumsy hands as if they were dough. "How have you been feeling?"

"Quite ill."

"Cramps?"

"Somewhat."

"You smoke?"

"Mmhmm."

"I'd keep it up. The menthols of course. It will help with the nausea."

She felt nauseous as he spoke and fondled her.

The nurse came into the room again, and he released her breasts.

"It's positive." She announced, her young face masking any sign of approval or disapproval at this result.

The doctor smiled at Vera. "I believe some congratulations are in order then."

Vera eased her way up on the table and reached for her cigarettes. Her head was beginning to pound.

Chapter Ten

She'd spilled a glass bottle of milk all over the floor. The white substance had splattered and then seeped its way across the linoleum. She'd cut her foot on the glass, a small trail of blood and a sharp pain making the process of cleaning it all up that much more difficult.

By the time she'd bandaged up her foot, cleaned the blood, gone over the floor again with cleaner so it was sparkling and no errant glass shard might snag someone else's toe, she found that she was, again, late to get the children from school.

She felt tears threaten to fall as she slammed the car door shut and lit a cigarette to calm herself, to stop the pain pulsing in her heel each time she pressed on the gas pedal.

As she pulled up to the barren looking school, her heart thudded in her chest. To both her delight and dismay, Joan stood just off from Emma and Henry. Speaking with them, a gentle smile on her lips. There was no look of anger or disapproval in her eyes as she chatted gaily with the children. They stared up at her with rapt attention.

The children hardly even noticed when Vera pulled the

car up alongside them. It was Joan who turned and eyed her, offering a slight wave and welcome smile.

Emma and Henry bounced into the backseat of the car as Vera rolled down the passenger side window.

Joan leaned against the window frame. The aroma of her, florid and earthy, came to Vera in an intoxicating wave.

"Hello there." Joan smiled.

Vera wiped stupidly at her cheeks, knowing she looked a fright, wondering if the tears had actually fallen or not. Her cheeks were dry as she touched them. She had forgotten lipstick. She felt naked beneath Joan's gaze.

"I'm...I'm so sorry. I dropped...well, I'm so clumsy." Vera stumbled over words.

"Are you all right?" Joan had leaned ever so much further in, her voice soft and low.

Vera felt a tear quiver in her eye and she looked away, smoking at her cigarette. She wiped at her cheek delicately. "Yes. I'm fine. I'm...fine. Thank you." And she collected herself enough to turn and smile at Joan.

"Listen," Joan spoke quickly, as if afraid Vera might drive off and away, but that was the furthest thing from her mind. "The school has its annual Fall Festival every year in October and somehow I got wrangled into heading the committee. I thought, well, I thought you might like to be the parent volunteer. You know, you could assist me in planning. It's not so very difficult, I –"

"Yes." Vera spoke decisively.

She was suddenly acutely aware of her children silently regarding her, absorbing the conversation.

"Oh." Joan's prepared speech died out. Her lips quirked upwards with a pleased smile. "Well then, I'll let Principal Nelson know he needn't look any further." She tapped the leather of the car door with her hand, pleased. "I'm very glad you agreed. I was hoping you would." She spoke, winking at Emma when she noticed the girl watching her intently.

Vera felt herself smiling. The prospect of working with Joan stretched out before her.

"Why don't you give me your number, and I'll call with the details." Joan asked.

"Of course." Vera put her cigarette between her lips and reached for her purse, fumbling about inside its recesses for the fountain pen she knew to be inside. And there, waded up, was an old receipt. She pulled it out, flattened it, and neatly scrawled her name and number on the blank side. "I hope this will do."

She handed it over to Joan, hoping the older woman would not notice the shake of her hand.

Joan smiled as she received the paper, holding it carefully so as not to smudge the drying ink. "I'll call you soon." And she righted herself, moving away from Vera's car. "It was nice to see you again. I look forward to our little project."

Vera smiled at her.

"Mom, can we go home? I told Jack we could play in the forest!" Henry whined.

"We're going, we're going!" Vera groaned and looked apologetically toward Joan.

Joan simply waved her off. Vera waved back as she rolled up the window. She put out her cigarette in the dashboard ashtray, watching as the dark-haired woman waved kindly to her children from her spot on the sidewalk. Vera pulled reluctantly away from the curb.

She maneuvered the car back around on the main road, all the while furtively glancing back at Joan who looked after the car and then turned back toward the school. Vera's number dangled from her red-tipped fingernails as she made her way gracefully back inside the building. She disappeared in the rearview mirror as the car descended down the hill.

Vera lit a fresh cigarette at the stoplight, heart pounding so deafeningly in her ears that she could not hear her children's raised voices coming from the backseat of the car as they fought about something.

She stopped at the grocery store. "Stay here, I'll be right back." She did not listen to their protests as she stepped out of the car and onto her sore foot. She winced as she walked inside and made her way to the back to fetch a fresh gallon of milk.

She thought to also purchase another loaf of bread, a bottle of wine, and a carton of cigarettes.

Joan would call her.

She stood at the register and saw Mary, but the boy who stood at the end of the counter bagging her items was a freckle-faced teen who did not even look at her twice. He offered to help take the bags to the car, but she declined the aid and hobbled out of the store.

She walked about as if in a dream as she made dinner that evening. She made it to the train in time to collect Roger, greeting him with a kiss. He looked at her surprised.

They sat across from one another at the dinner table that evening, the children off in their rooms.

Vera watched as smoke floated off her cigarette, food forgotten. Light jazz music came from the radio in the kitchen.

"Why are you smiling?" Roger had noticed a change in her.

She had not noticed she was smiling. She tapped off the ash of her cigarette before it could fall on the tablecloth. "I've been asked...well, they'd like me to help organize the Fall Festival at the children's school." She toyed with the corner of her placemat, lifting the cigarette to her lips to inhale.

Roger regarded her as he masticated the steak she'd made between closed lips. Finally he swallowed, eyes still trained on her but something gentler showing in them. "I think that's good for you. Very good for you to get involved."

She nodded and felt the smile that overcame her. She had pleased him at last. "Yes. I think so."

She washed the dishes in a daze, pausing to stare out the back window at the dark forest that stretched out and away for miles behind them. She thought of the little house in the woods, and wondered at the inhabitants of it.

She thought of Joan, of where she might live, of what she might do in the evenings, of when she might call her. And how she looked forward to the phone ringing and hearing the other woman's gentle, reassuring voice on the other end. She had never before been given the task of organizing school activities, but it sounded exciting. A challenge, a new endeavor, something that was not the home and the children and Roger.

And it involved Joan.

"Goddamnit! Vera! What the hell is this?" Roger's voice bellowed out from the living room.

Vera dropped a plate in the sink and it shattered. "Shit." She wiped her hands on a towel, walking toward the stairs to the living area.

"Don't you forget that I *let* you smoke in the house, but my God can't you be more careful about it?" He snapped.

Oh.

He had discovered the hole she'd burnt in the arm of the chair.

Her blood ran cold, fear coursing through her veins.

"Do you know how much I paid for this chair? Do you know how hard I work to provide you with this life? This house? These nice things? And this is what you do to thank me?" He was upon her, grabbing her arm tightly so she couldn't get away. And he would have slammed her back against the living room wall, but she stopped him with a simple sentence.

"Roger, I'm pregnant."

And he released her slowly, eyes blinking rapidly. And

then he was putting his hands carefully about her center, looking down upon her stomach as if he could see the child before him, his demeanor docile and childlike as he had once been with her. He looked her in the eyes, a smile creasing them. "A baby? You're going to have my baby?"

She nodded slowly up and down. "Yes."

"Oh, Vera." He wrapped her up in his arms, the anger and hatred had gone out of him but remained a stain upon her. Her heart raced as he held her close and pressed kisses against her forehead, the crown of her head, holding her so lovingly.

She wanted to push him away but she gave in to his arms.

"Oh, baby. We're going to have a baby." He kept whispering against her ear.

Chapter Eleven

itty's eyes watched intently as Vera held the lighter to the end of her cigarette. The paper caught and she inhaled.

"My goodness." Vera exhaled a cloud of smoke and held up the pack for Kitty.

"Oh no, I shouldn't." Kitty ran a hand across her forehead.

She'd come over for a coffee and had ended up staying through lunch, unloading her burdens, and Vera found she quite liked the woman after all. Kitty's polished exterior had cracked, come undone and Vera found beneath the façade was a woman much like herself.

Vera rolled her eyes and made for the refrigerator. "Then have a drink with me."

"It's the middle of the day." Kitty sighed.

Vera shrugged and pulled out the bottle of wine, reaching for two glasses. "It won't hurt." She said around her cigarette.

Two days.

It had been two days since Joan had said she would call.

Vera poured a generous helping of wine into the glasses and placed one before Kitty.

"I really shouldn't."

"Well, what should you do?" Vera took her seat at the table, tapping ash from her cigarette.

Kitty flushed at the question. "I left the wash in the dryer and the kitchen is in a dreadful state. John likes everything in its place - just so - you know."

"Then why doesn't he do it?" Vera snapped.

Kitty gave her a curious gaze and then laughed. "I couldn't imagine it." And she lifted the glass to her lips and drank.

Vera smiled at her approvingly.

A smile curled its way across Kitty's lips as she settled the glass back on the table. "I know he has a drink or two at lunch so I don't know why I should feel so guilty about it." She almost laughed.

"Certainly not." Vera agreed.

And then there was the ringing of the telephone.

Shocking.

It rang again.

Vera felt warm.

"Aren't you going to answer it?" Kitty asked.

Vera rose from her seat and took the receiver from the wall, hand unsteady as she did so. "Hello?"

"Why hello. Vera?" The voice rang through the phone. Crystal clear. As if the woman on the other end was there beside her, speaking against her ear.

It was a jarring sensation and Vera wished Kitty were not sitting at her kitchen table to witness it.

"Y-yes." Vera cleared her throat.

"It's Joan. I...well, I had intended to call you the other day but time escaped me. Please, forgive me."

"It's all right, quite all right." Vera assured her. Eyes catching on the clock. It was only twelve forty-five in the afternoon. "How do you have the time now?"

Joan laughed. "Teachers do have lunch breaks. Occasionally."

Vera laughed under her breath.

"Listen, I wondered if we might be able to meet about the Fall Festival, say Saturday?"

Saturday, well Roger would be rather miffed with her if she were to be absent that day, but it sounded like the perfect excuse to get away. He had wanted her to get involved, and so she would.

"Saturday would be just fine." Vera brought the cigarette to her lips, inhaling unsteadily.

"Would you be amiable to meeting at my place?" Joan's voice asked tightly.

"Yes. Yes." Vera spoke a bit too quickly.

"Oh. Well then." Joan gave her detailed directions which she jotted down on the back of a magazine along with Joan's personal phone number.

"I'll see you Saturday then."

"I look forward to it." Vera pressed the receiver close against her ear.

"As do I."

The line disconnected and Vera listened briefly to the dial tone.

"Who was that?"

"Oh!" Vera nearly dropped the phone, having forgotten she had a guest. She hung it up rapidly and put out her cigarette. Her heart was pounding when she sat back down across from Kitty. "I was asked...well I was asked to help plan the Fall Festival. At the school, Joan...Ms. DeBoer, is in charge. We're meeting this weekend."

Kitty was looking at her strangely when she dared to meet her gaze.

Vera fiddled with her lighter.

Kitty's cheeks had flushed from the alcohol. She looked

very pretty then. Pretty, yet there was a look in her eyes Vera did not understand.

Kitty drank her wine. "Joan DeBoer?"

"Yes." Vera drank.

"Well, I would be careful." Kitty cautioned as she took a cigarette from Vera's pack.

Vera leaned forward with the lighter. "Careful. But why?"

Kitty placed the cigarette between her lips.

Vera held the lighter steady and Kitty leaned in toward the flame.

Sitting back in her seat, Kitty exhaled a stream of smoke from between her pretty pink lips. "She's a certain type of woman you wouldn't want to get mixed up with, is all."

"She seems perfectly normal to me." Vera insisted. If anything, the older woman seemed lonely. And it was no wonder, the way the women of this town went on about her, like she was a pariah.

Kitty's eyebrow rose. "Perhaps you haven't been around long enough. Listen, I like you and I don't want to see you get mixed up with the wrong sort of people. You just listen to me and steer clear of her."

Vera's brows furrowed.

She was grateful when Kitty left around two.

Roger called to tell her he would not be home that evening. An important dinner meeting or something.

Vera felt a curl of pleasure seep into her bones when she hung up. A weight lifted. She did not finish the chores she had neglected during Kitty's visit.

She drove to the school to collect the children, arriving ahead of the dismissal bell. She smoked and watched the front door, as if waiting to see Joan emerge from the throng of elated children making their escape.

But Joan did not appear in the flesh. She remained an elusive voice on the other end of the phone that day.

The children were happy to see her and clamored into the car, telling her of their day, of the things they had done and seen. And she listened attentively as she drove them home. Asking questions, genuinely able to listen to them, to hear what their little minds were thinking.

They arrived home. She looked around and did not wish to be there. The kitchen revolted her, made her long to wreck it so completely that she would never be able to use it again. She contemplated what might happen if she were to leave the stove top burning. She saw the whole place charred and burnt and shuddered at the image.

She went to the living room and poured herself a drop of bourbon.

She sat atop Roger's chair. She examined the hole she'd burned into its surface, letting her finger pass over it mindlessly.

The days were growing shorter, so by five the sun hung low on the horizon.

"Where's daddy?" Emma's shy voice inquired from the foot of the living room stairs.

Vera had not noticed her. Was she drunk?

She held out her hand for her daughter.

The girl walked cautiously toward her, then allowed Vera to take her into her lap. She buried her face in Vera's chest. Vera stroked her hair. "He's not coming home this evening." She kissed her sweet-smelling forehead.

"Why not?" Emma asked.

Vera sighed. "Work. He's terribly busy with work."

"Oh." Emma simply sighed.

Then she sat up and looked at her mother, her eyes so bright, so terribly smart.

"I'm glad."

Her little hand tangled in Vera's hair, twisting a curl about her delicate index finger.

Vera smiled at her.

"Go get your brother. Let's go out tonight."

The girl's eyes sparkled with excitement at the prospect. She slid from Vera and raced away to find Henry.

Vera drove them to the diner downtown. She let them order whatever they wanted and sat sipping a Coke and smoking, stealing a French fry here and there. She watched as her children happily ate up burgers and onion rings and fries and sipped milkshakes.

She found them beautiful and realized she could almost appreciate them in that moment.

She took them home and Henry crawled onto the couch with her while they watched some Western show. She held him close to her, stroking his sandy blonde hair. He seemed to like her best when Roger was absent. As if he could own her then.

He cried when she tried to take him to his room, so she let him curl up in bed with her. Emma was suddenly too afraid to sleep in her own room, so Vera laid awake between them, feeling suffocated.

Once she could hear the evenness of their breathing, she carefully slid from the bed.

She went to the kitchen to light a cigarette and pour herself a glass of wine.

She took the glass and an ashtray and the pack of cigarettes and lighter quietly to the bathroom, where she went about cleaning the tub until it shone and then she drew herself a bath with fragrant oils.

She stripped down to nothing and slid into the warm recesses of water, letting her head fall back against the tile as she blew smoke streams up to the ceiling and drank back the wine, hand mindlessly caressing her stomach.

She laid there until the water went cold.

Drunkenly, she climbed from the tub and wrapped herself

in a robe. She cleaned her face, brushed her teeth, lotioned her skin.

Her body was loose and relaxed. And she thought of the curve of Joan's neck in stained glass filtered light.

What could be so terribly horrible about her that everyone told her to stay away?

She had learned long ago that other's perceptions of a person could be so terribly biased.

What did anyone truly know about anyone else anyway?

Vera pulled on her nightgown and shut off the bathroom light. She emerged to find her children's bodies draped across the bed so she could not have slept with them even if she had wanted to.

So, she went across the hall to Emma's room and slid between her rosy, pink sheets which smelled of youth and closed her eyes.

She was exhausted and yet sleep was fleeting.

Saturday would be in two days.

She slid her hand between her legs and touched herself. The release overcame her, pulling her into sleep.

Chapter Twelve

Friday evening had been spent at Louise and Dale's in a drunken stupor.

Roger had awoken wanting and had pressed himself inside of her and she'd let him despite the pain in her forehead.

She cursed herself for having drunk so much the previous evening, stumbling to the bathroom to relieve her stomach. Her tolerance was slipping, as it always did when she was pregnant. She knew she couldn't go on as she was.

She took an aspirin and then looked in the mirror.

She hardly recognized herself. She was still beautiful and yet older than she had once been.

There was make-up smeared beneath her eyes from the previous night, her hair was a bit wild, but her skin was golden, and her eyes shimmered back at her.

Her body was still supple, despite two pregnancies. She let her hand trail down from her neck, parting her robe so that she could see the rose of her pert nipple.

Her stomach was beginning to round, only slight enough

that she might notice. She let her hands wander over the stretched surface.

Her body was still alive, lacking the release it needed.

Something about this thrilled her.

That she would see Joan today and her body was throbbing.

Roger came into the bathroom and did not look at her.

"I'll be out today. For a bit." She said, pulling her robe back into place, wetting a washcloth to clean her face.

He looked at her then. "Out? What about the children?"

She looked at him amused. "They'll likely play outside. Kitty's just across the street if you need anything, and I'll leave the number of where you can reach me just in case."

Roger's brow was creasing. She wasn't sure if he was angry or frustrated with her.

"And just where is it that you're getting off to?"

She rubbed at the make-up stain beneath her eye. "Planning. For the Fall Festival at the children's school. Remember, I mentioned it."

"On a Saturday?"

"Yes."

He would not interrupt these plans. She would give him no choice.

He hummed in response as he lathered his face in shaving cream.

She felt as if she'd gotten away with murder.

She made breakfast and then jumped into the shower before piecing herself together meticulously. She pressed perfume to her pulse points, placing simple pearl earrings into her earlobes. She smoothed her hands down her dress; it fit tighter than it had only weeks before.

She jotted Joan's number on a pad of paper where Roger might find it, and left before anyone could detain her.

She followed the meticulous directions that Joan had given to her. She had committed them to memory, gone over it a hundred times so that it felt as if she were traveling a familiar path.

Joan lived out of the town but, Vera realized, only down the road from the neighborhood. She followed a winding road about, admiring the tall, strong trees that lined it.

And then there was the blue mailbox Joan had instructed her to look out for. She turned the car off the road and angled it down the graveled drive. The car skirted in and out of shade cast down by leaves overhead.

The house revealed itself slowly, unfolding like a mirage off in the distance.

She was not certain if she was dreaming it or if it were real.

It was *the* house.

The very home she had stumbled upon in the forest, appearing now before her.

It frightened her.

That they should live so near and yet so far from one another.

The home that had looked so invitingly aged, so homey and warm - of all people, it belonged to Joan.

Vera killed the ignition and slid from the car.

She found her hands were shaking and she was nervous.

The front door opened, and Joan appeared.

A fluffy, orange cat wound itself about her legs.

The image threw Vera off kilter, her hip pressed against the warm hood of the car.

Joan in slacks and a loose-fitting shirt. Her hair pulled back without her usual pressed and pinned precision, as if she had carelessly done so. And Vera liked the way it framed her face.

It was very attractive.

And Joan with a cat before the home made a pretty picture.

She was smiling.

Vera tucked her purse and a folder beneath her arm and walked the short distance to Joan's porch. The lovely home was open and welcoming to her.

The cat meowed at her, and she stooped down to hold out her hand so it would come nearer to her.

"That's Lucille." Joan introduced the cat. "But I call her Lulu."

Lulu pressed her face against Vera's hand and Vera delighted in the feel of her soft fur. "It's a pleasure to meet you, Lulu."

The cat meowed back at her.

"I miss having a cat. Roger, my husband, doesn't believe in keeping pets in the home." Vera sighed, righting herself to find Joan smiling at her. "She's lovely."

The cat meowed her approval and they laughed.

Joan stood back and held the front door open for her.

"Thank you for coming. I hope I didn't spoil your day with this dreadful task." Joan spoke apologetically.

"Not at all." Vera hummed as she stepped inside the home, taking in the piney, cinnamon scent of it, the dark wood that lined the walls, the fireplace in the corner, the warm, comfortable looking chair beside it, a worn leather couch leaning against a wall. It was a place she wanted to simply disappear inside, to sink down upon the inviting furniture, to curl up atop the rug before a blazing fire with a mug of hot cocoa, the rest of the world forgotten...

"Are you all right?" Joan had caught her arm.

Had she nearly fainted?

"I'm fine...I'm..." Vera warmed at the tenderness of Joan's touch.

"Why don't you have a seat here? Let me get you a glass of water." Joan led her to the leather couch and helped her down atop it.

Lulu jumped on the couch and curled up beside Vera, peering up at her with curious green eyes.

Joan disappeared into what could only be the kitchen and returned with a glass of water. "Here, drink this." And Joan settled atop the couch, a respectable distance away.

Vera sipped the water and tried to smile. "I'm...I'm so sorry."

"Please, you needn't be."

Vera took another drink and then settled the glass atop the table before them. "I was a little surprised. I've seen your home before. I live just through the forest. Over there."

Joan marveled at this. "Ah, you're in the new development, aren't you?"

"Yes."

Joan leaned back as she looked her over, as if searching for something. "You know, my family owned that land for many years. It was all farmland."

Vera smiled at this. To know Joan's family had once owned the land upon which her new home sat. There was a comfort in it. "Really?"

Joan nodded. "Well, I suppose we're neighbors then."

Vera laughed. "I suppose we are." Joan's eyes were the most beautiful shade of mahogany Vera had ever seen. Deep and haunting.

They stirred something within her. A thought, a memory. "Perhaps you might know...there was a well."

"A well?" Joan asked.

"Yes, the children - they found a well in the backyard."

"Ah," Joan nodded. "That was the old homestead."

Vera tilted her head.

"It burned." Joan said simply. "The rest of the farm has been sold off and disassembled to build other properties. Unfortunately, only this house remains." She tried for a smile.

Vera swallowed. "Burned?"

Joan smiled tightly. "Yes." She brushed imaginary lint from her pants. "Would you like some tea? Cookies?"

Vera could sense she might not get more information from the woman. "Yes, thank you."

Joan smiled and stood up. Though something detained her. She turned back to look at Vera. "The well...it was uncovered?"

Vera nodded. "Yes."

A worried look crossed Joan's brow.

"My husband thought it was unsafe. He had it covered up and sealed."

"Perhaps I should offer to pay him..."

Vera waved her off. "It was nothing."

Joan did not seem put at ease by this.

Vera sat up. "It's all right now."

Joan appeared to resurface from a trance. "Yes. Yes, I suppose so." She shook her head and her smile returned. "I'm glad nothing happened."

"Oh, no. I kept the children away." Vera smiled, wanting to pull Joan back to the present moment.

Their moment.

"I'm sorry...I'll be just a moment with the tea and then we can get on to this pesky business of planning." Joan offered her a pleasant smile.

Joan disappeared around the corner.

Vera pressed her shaking hands between her knees. Had she displeased Joan?

But when Joan appeared again with a tray of cookies and a pot of tea, their eyes met and Joan's soft smile struck her.

She had to look away, glancing down to find the folder next to her on the couch. The Fall Festival. The reason for this afternoon. "Well, shall we?" Vera could not look again at Joan's eyes.

Joan sat the tray of refreshments atop the coffee table and

went about pouring tea into cups while Vera began laying out the numbers and figures and outreach she had accomplished already. The strangeness of before dissolving as she spoke. "... and if you account for inflation the amount the school has allotted for the event will hardly cover the cost of the booth rentals, but I do think that with some of the higher priced items I've been able to procure we shouldn't have any trouble making it all back. I've got pearl earrings committed by Thompson Jewelers that will surely rake in a high fee. Everyone will be vying for them. And I had a talk with Judy – you know, Kenny's mother - about arranging the cakes for the cake walk. I thought she could take a list to the PTA and the mothers could sign up for what they'd like to bring. I hear everyone has a specialty so I wouldn't want to presume as I hardly know them..."

Joan was looking at her with wide, rapturous eyes. "Christ." And then she looked embarrassed. "I mean, you've done all of this?"

Vera blinked. Had she over done it?

"You got Thompson Jewelers to donate for the raffle? How on earth..."

"Do you mind if I smoke?" Vera asked.

"Not at all." Joan turned and pulled an ashtray from a side table drawer.

Vera fished out her pack of cigarettes from her purse. "It wasn't so terribly difficult. I simply got the list of items from last year and when I was downtown the other day I noticed the jewelers and thought I would give it a try."

"Mitch Thompson is the most impossible man in town and you got him to donate?" Joan watched as Vera placed a cigarette between her lips.

"You know his grandson is in kindergarten at the school now." Vera lit the cigarette. Joan's eyes were upon her lips as she exhaled.

"I hadn't a clue." Joan marveled. "You clever woman."

Vera feigned hurt. "You didn't know I had it in me, and yet you asked me to help?"

Joan looked flustered. "Oh, well I certainly thought you would be competent and I had hoped...but...how on earth?"

Vera tapped off her cigarette in the ashtray coyly. "I studied accounting in college." She inhaled at the cigarette. "Useless really."

Joan was looking at her in amazement. "But..."

"Well," Vera tilted her head. "It was war time and I had thought, hoped really, my father would take me on at his firm. You know, women were doing things then and I wanted..." She sighed. There was no point in rehashing it all now. And she had only just met Joan. She didn't wish to bore her.

"But what happened?" Joan was leaning forward, looking far from bored with her.

Vera shook her head, daring to look into those enchanting eyes. There was a genuineness in her gaze, a want to know. "I met Roger." She stated simply.

Joan's gaze faltered.

"My father hired my brother after the war. He was in the reserve out in Colorado. He never even saw war, nor did he have a degree." Vera tapped ash angrily. A sardonic smile twisted its path on her lips.

"Oh." Joan's lips formed a pretty circle.

"Well, it's all in the past now, isn't it?" Vera shrugged.

Joan sat speechless.

Vera put out her cigarette. "I shouldn't have..."

"No." Joan shook her head. "I'm...well, I'm sorry it happened that way."

Vera nodded. "No, I was foolish to think..."

"You weren't." Joan assured her.

Vera felt the prick of tears in her eyes and turned away from Joan, feeling childish. She couldn't think about it. There was nothing to do but to go forward. There were the children to care for, Roger, the house...

"I'm sorry. I shouldn't go on about myself. I've spoiled the afternoon." She wiped at her cheek flippantly.

"You haven't." Joan insisted. "But, I do fear we've planned the whole festival."

Vera laughed then. When she turned she could see the pretty smile spread out on Joan's face. "Perhaps I shouldn't have revealed my hand so soon."

"No, it's a relief." Joan assured her, pouring them both more tea. "But I must admit I was looking forward to weekly afternoons working together." The mirth in Joan's voice had faded to something less certain as she spoke.

Vera felt her breath catch in her chest. Her hand shook imperceptibly. "Perhaps we still might have more to discuss. I quite like your company."

Joan smiled then, her dark eyes alighting. "Shall we reconvene next Saturday?"

Vera looked at the golden watch about her wrist and found time had elapsed far too quickly. Roger would be cross if she did not return soon. "Yes." She agreed, finding she did not wish to leave this home.

It was the sensation of having been out to sea and only just finding solid ground to stand upon again.

"I should..." Vera began collecting up her things, afraid if she didn't set herself into motion she might never leave.

Joan walked her to the door, Lulu tagging along behind. "I look forward to getting to know you better." She said as they stood on the porch.

Vera hugged the folder to her chest. Her eyes flickered over the Cupid's bow of Joan's lip. "I feel as if..." She swallowed, looking away past Joan, out to the forest.

"Feel what?" Joan crossed her arms over her chest.

She hadn't a clue what she had been about to say.

"It's...it's nothing." Vera tried to laugh. "I must go. Thank you, thank you for the lovely afternoon." She reached down to pet Lulu who meowed up at her, and then escaped before she could say anything more.

She got in the car and watched Joan standing on the porch – arms still crossed, a curious look on her face – as she started the ignition and turned the car around to make her way back down the shady drive.

Joan remained a lone figure in her rearview mirror until the house disappeared from view.

Chapter Thirteen

oger had called to tell her he wouldn't make it home that evening. She had smiled to herself as she'd continued sweeping the floor. "...and I've made reservations for the weekend."

At first she had thought she hadn't heard him correctly. "Reservations?"

"Jesus, Vera. Are you not paying attention? I've just told you they expect us in Lake George for Labor Day weekend. Buddy wants me up there to wine and dine a prospective client. He wants it to be a family affair. I thought you'd be happy for a vacation."

She wasn't sure why she wanted to cry.

"We'll leave Saturday morning."

She could hardly hear a word he said after that.

After he hung up, she leaned the broom against the kitchen counter and sank down at the kitchen table. Tears trailed down her cheeks. Damn him. "Damn." She cursed, slamming her fist against the table.

She reached for her cigarettes.

The kids wanted to stay up since Roger wasn't there so she

let them watch the television while she sneaked off to the kitchen with a refreshed glass of bourbon. She lit a cigarette to steady her nerves then lifted the phone from the cradle, listening to the dial tone on the other end.

The number was seared into her memory.

She sipped the bourbon and then dialed.

The phone rang in her ear.

She hoped it wasn't too late, that she hadn't put it off for too long.

But there was the click of the phone picking up on the other end and then *her* voice through quiet static. "Hello?"

"Joan...it's Vera." Vera pressed her head against the kitchen wall. She errantly traced the flower pattern of the wallpaper with her ring finger. "I'm sorry if it's late..."

"Not at all. Why it's nice to hear from you."

Vera drank again. "Well, I don't know if I have such nice news."

"Is everything all right?" There was concern in Joan's voice on the other end.

"Oh yes, yes...it's only that I won't be able to see you this weekend. I had forgotten it was Labor Day weekend. Roger wants us to go away. He's already made the reservations. A work thing...a..." Vera hated that she wanted to cry again. She could only think the pregnancy was altering her, making her act ridiculously. For Joan would not mind if this should come between them.

"Oh, I see." But she sounded a bit deflated on the other end of the line.

The cigarette made a shaky ascent to her lips. "I'm very sorry, I...I should have thought..."

"No, these things happen. We can put it off a week. Would you like that?"

"Yes. I would. Very much." She wiped at the tear that had slipped down her cheek, pressing her eyes shut so she might see the inside of Joan's home again, to imagine Joan sitting beside her, speaking as they were now.

But when Vera opened her eyes she felt terribly alone.

She did not wish to disconnect from Joan, but there was no reason to prolong the conversation.

"You're all right?" Joan spoke carefully.

Vera sniffed. "Of course." Of course she wasn't.

She heard Joan's breath on the other end of the phone.

Neither spoke for what seemed like ages.

"Where will you go?"

"Lake George." Vera turned to lean against the wall.

"Well it is nice this time of year."

"You've been?"

"A time or two. A long while ago, though. I'm sure it's much different now." Joan laughed.

"It can't have changed that much." Vera smiled at Joan's laugh.

"I do happen to be a great deal older than you." Joan pointed out.

"Are you now?" Vera felt something twisting tight and warm low in her stomach.

"Uh-huh." Joan hummed playfully.

"I don't mind it." Vera spoke soberly.

Joan did not respond immediately.

Vera turned to press her head against the wall again. "What will you do this weekend?" She suddenly needed to know, desperately.

Joan laughed again, the mood lightened. "A friend of mine has a place on the beach. I had planned to go there."

It sounded so idyllic. A friend...well. "I hope you hadn't rearranged to meet me." Vera suddenly felt horrified that she had inconvenienced Joan.

"Oh no, I wasn't going until Sunday." And Vera was not sure if she meant it or not.

Vera turned from the wall and nearly dropped her cigarette in fear.

Emma was standing in the doorway.

Looking at her.

"I should...I'm terribly sorry, but I should go." Vera spoke hastily, heart pounding in her chest.

"Of course, have a good night, and I'll see you next week." Joan spoke politely.

Vera hung up the phone and drank back her bourbon while eyeing her daughter.

"Who were you talking to?" Emma asked sleepily.

"No one." Vera lied poorly. "You're exhausted, let's get you off to bed."

They slept piled atop her that night.

She dreamt of Joan's home, of a fire roaring in the fireplace, of the forest out beyond the window panes, of the well in the woods, of a figure standing beside it, dark and distorted.

The image startled her. She awoke drenched in sweat, the children's bodies pressed tightly against her. Henry's legs draped over her thighs, Emma's head resting uncomfortably on her shoulder.

The children were ecstatic at the prospect of a weekend away. Vera, however, had spent all of Friday packing for the weekend and was rather exhausted by the time Saturday morning rolled around. Roger helped load the car and she was grateful to sit in the passenger seat, smoking cigarettes listlessly while trees and cars raced by on their way upstate.

She dozed off a time or two, hot from the sun.

They stopped on the way at a small park where they ate sandwiches Vera had made and drank lemonade, and the kids ran around while she reclined on the picnic blanket smoking and Roger sat reading something.

As she stared at the blue, blue sky overhead she wondered if Joan would have gone to see her friend. She wondered what kind of a friend this person might be, trying to conjure up some kind of an image of Joan with anyone else.

She couldn't see her with anyone. There seemed to be no one who matched Joan.

"Let's get going. There's a dinner tonight." Roger was getting up, disrupting her daydreams.

Some time later they pulled into a motel with flashing neon sign. The children raced from the car, taking in the pool and further down, the lake that stretched out beneath the dimming light of day. Boats went floating by, the sounds of children yelling and laughing rang out from the beach.

Everything seemed happy and gay about her, but she was indifferent.

Roger led them to a cabin where the children bounced on the bed until he yelled at them. "We'll be expected at the Sagamore at six. Can you have the children ready before then?"

"Can we go swimming?" Henry was pulling at her skirt.

"All right, but only for an hour. Then you'll need to be showered so we can leave." Vera announced after she checked her watch.

Roger made quick work of unloading the car as the children put on bathing suits for the pool and raced outside. He showered and changed into a rather attractive suit while she unpacked. "They'll pick me up early. You'll drive to the Sagamore. It's just up the main road there, you can't miss it on the right."

A car honked outside and Vera watched him go. He was always surprising her with plans, as if he just assumed she might go along with them at every turn.

Vera took her cigarettes and went to the pool to sit in a lounger and watch the children.

The sun made her lethargic and lazy. She hadn't the will to move, to do Roger's bidding.

Until a woman appeared. Vera's heart sped up at the sight of her.

Dark, wavy hair, sunglasses hiding away her eyes.

Vera watched her through the shade of her sunglasses.

The woman walked towards a lounger on the opposite side of the pool and removed her caftan. Vera's eye traveled the length of her exposed skin. She was perhaps only a few years older than Vera, but her body was taut and lean and round in all the right places.

She flipped her hair over her shoulder as she took her seat and then seemed to look right at Vera, as if she could feel her eyes upon her.

Vera looked sharply away.

She busied herself with her cigarette.

She looked at her watch and realized time had slipped away.

She called for the children, cleaned them up, put on a fresh dress herself and then they piled into the car.

She was only five minutes late to the Sagamore.

Roger caught her elbow roughly when she entered.

It was a tedious affair. The children did not like their meal, but were too afraid to say anything. The other wives were all dull. Vera spoke kindly to Susan Hawthorne because she was the wife of Roger's boss, but otherwise remained aloof. Smoking cigarette after cigarette despite Roger's disapproving gaze.

It was a relief when he told her to take the children back, that he would come later, there was still business to deal with.

She drove the children to a diner and ordered them a real meal, and they ate happily.

They passed out watching the television and Vera laid in bed feeling light headed from smoking too much.

The walls were too short, the room too small. She could hardly breathe.

Panicked.

She slid into her moccasins and slipped quietly out of the cabin.

She began walking with no destination in mind. Simply moving toward the bright neon of the main strip. She inhaled the Lake George air as she walked aimlessly.

People passed her on the street, but she did not seem to notice their curious stares in her direction.

There was a bar down the road.

She went inside and ordered a rye. The bartender looked at her with interest.

A couple of men sitting down the bar from her kept their eyes on her, watching her hungrily. She drank back the whiskey, ignoring them. She placed cash on the bar and left, heart pounding.

She wanted to run, to get away, but to where? Where was there to go?

Her only escape was back to the motel. Back to the children.

They were still sleeping when she returned.

Roger was still gone.

It was nearing midnight.

She showered and put herself hazily to bed.

Roger was next to her when she awoke the next morning.

Chapter Fourteen

On Monday they stopped at a little gift shop on the main strip and Vera noticed a postcard of the town as it was.

She purchased the postcard and scribbled a note on the back.

So you can see if it's changed any.

-Vera

She dropped it at the Lake George post office before they left for home.

Chapter Fifteen

The phone was ringing when Vera came back from having coffee with Kitty and Judy. She picked up the receiver hurriedly, heart racing.

"Hello?"

"Mrs. Wilson?" But it was a strange voice on the other end.

"Yes?"

"I'm the school secretary, Nancy Schmidt. Your son, Henry, has been brought to the principal's office for hitting another boy. The principal would like for you to come to the school immediately."

Vera's palms were sweaty. "Henry hit a boy?" She repeated, voice tight.

"Yes, I'm afraid so."

"He's never hit anyone before."

"These things happen, Mrs. Wilson. You know how young boys are."

She did not.

Nervously, she drove to the school with a cigarette between her teeth.

Henry was sitting outside the principal's office swinging his legs innocently. He looked at Vera blankly, as if he hadn't a clue what he had done or why he should be sitting there.

"Mrs. Wilson, Principal Nelson will see you." She looked up from Henry to find a round woman gesturing toward a door. This was Nancy Schmidt.

Vera looked at Henry again.

He did not look at her.

She passed into the office and found Principal Nelson seated at his desk smoking a pipe.

He stood to greet her. "Mrs. Wilson."

"Principal Nelson." Her voice wavered.

He pointed toward the chair and she sat obediently, as if she were the one in trouble.

He sat down again behind his desk and leaned back with his pipe. He looked far too young to be smoking a pipe.

"Thank you for coming." He adjusted his tie, puffing on his pipe.

"Do you mind if I smoke?" She asked, not certain of what the proper protocol for such a situation might be.

He waved his hand, and she pulled a cigarette from her pack and lit it.

"It seems your son has gotten himself into a little bit of trouble." Principal Nelson seemed to delight in telling her this.

"What did he do?" Vera blew a stream of smoke, fidgeted with the hem of her skirt.

Principal Nelson sat forward. "Well, it seems that while out on the playground some words were exchanged and the next thing the teachers saw was your son punching Jack Harding."

Vera's brow knit in confusion. "But Jack is his best friend. They play all the time at home. Aren't you sure it wasn't just some..."

"Jack has a bloody nose. He's in the nurse's office as we speak."

Vera's eyes widened. "I'm...I'm sure it was all some miscommunication."

"Be that as it may, we must take disciplinary action against your son."

Vera nodded, smoked with an unsteady hand. "What does that mean?"

"We're suspending him for the rest of the week."

"The rest of the week!" Vera cried. "But he'll miss school. He'll get behind...you can't..."

"We'll have his teacher send this week's work home with you."

Vera tapped ash off in the ashtray atop his desk. "I don't believe this is the right punishment for him. He's only a boy..."

"A boy should learn how to control his impulses, wouldn't you agree?"

Vera very much did not see how he might learn about it this week. Roger would be furious.

She stood on unsteady legs and put out her cigarette. It seemed there was no say in the matter.

She felt shame creeping into her cheeks.

"Oh, and Mrs. Wilson." Principal Nelson spoke as she put her hand on the doorknob.

She paused, turned to look at him, hoping he had changed his mind.

"I must say you look very beautiful today. That dress is very flattering."

She did not smile.

She turned the knob and returned to the waiting room where Henry sat. "My God, what did you do?" She muttered under her breath.

"I'll send for Ms. Rainer. She'll bring you his books and

homework." Ms. Schmidt informed her. "It will only be a moment."

Vera sank into the seat beside Henry.

Henry leaned against her.

"I didn't mean to." He finally whispered against her ear.

"What happened?" She asked in return.

Henry turned closer to her, whispering in her ear conspiratorially. "Jack was going to try to look up Valerie's skirt."

Vera turned to him. "You were trying to protect her?"

Henry nodded up and down. "I didn't want him to see."

Vera was beginning to get the picture.

"Then I think it's good what you did."

Henry folded his hands in his lap. "Yeah, but I didn't want the teacher to know. I didn't want to embarrass Valerie."

Vera sighed, then noticed the scent of a familiar perfume sweep into the room. Her eyes traveled to the doorway and she felt lost.

"Can I help you, Ms. DeBoer?" Ms. Schmidt asked.

Joan's eyes were upon Vera.

"I was just dropping this off for Principal Nelson." And she sat a file atop the secretary's desk, offering a quick, serene smile in the secretary's direction.

"Do you need to speak with the principal?"

"No." Joan shook her head, eyes flickering to Vera again.

Ms. Schmidt looked from Joan to Vera.

Vera was acutely aware of the secretary's gaze.

"What are you doing here?" Joan asked, moving toward Vera.

Vera moved to stand, but suddenly became lightheaded, so that she lost touch with the world and everything faded to a dull gray.

"You're all right, I've got you." A voice spoke hypnotically to her.

When she came to, she found herself in Joan's arms.

She could smell the soap and perfume on the woman's skin, she was so close.

"You're so pale. Come with me." Joan supported her and led her to a restroom around the corner from the principal's office.

Joan sat her on the toilet seat and wet a paper towel, pressing it gently against Vera's forehead.

"Are you all right?" Joan asked as she held the paper towel in place.

"Oh, yes. It's nothing." Vera waved off her concern. "I'm... I'm pregnant."

Joan's hand went slack against Vera's forehead, as if she might pull away. "Congratulations."

Vera hummed but did not respond.

"Let me get you a glass of water." Joan urged her to hold the towel and went out of the bathroom.

Vera closed her eyes, delirious.

Joan returned with a glass of water.

"I'm so sorry. Thank you." Vera slumped atop the toilet feeling warm and humiliated.

"There's nothing to be sorry about." Joan leaned against the wall opposite her.

A big wet tear slipped down Vera's cheek and she wiped angrily at it.

"What happened?" Joan asked.

Vera shook her head. "They're suspending Henry for the rest of the week. He told me that his friend, Jack, was going to look up a girl's skirt, so Henry tried to stop him. He shouldn't have punched Jack, but...he was too embarrassed to tell the teachers on Valerie's behalf. And now they're suspending him!"

Joan shook her head.

"Roger will be so angry." There were tears falling down her cheeks. She felt ashamed.

"Let me talk to Principal Nelson."

"Oh, no. I don't think there's anything to be done..." She tried to reach out, to stop Joan.

"Well, I think he's being unreasonable."

And Joan was out of the restroom before Vera could stop her.

Vera wiped at her eyes, looked herself over in the mirror, reapplied her lipstick, powdered her nose, and then dared to leave the bathroom.

The secretary was standing, waiting for her to return. "He would like to see you." She spoke, her eyes scrutinizing every detail of Vera, seeking something out in her.

Vera stepped into Principal Nelson's office and found Joan standing off to the side. Her arms were crossed over her chest, her eyes hard-set and determined looking.

Principal Nelson cleared his throat. "Ms. DeBoer has brought to my attention some rather... upsetting details that were left unmentioned. In light of this, I will reduce his suspension to the rest of the day. He can return tomorrow."

Joan walked with Vera and Henry to the main entrance of the school.

"I...thank you." Vera's heart was pounding a mile a minute.

Joan waved her off. "It was nothing. He should know the truth of it." And then she turned to address Henry. "It was very brave of you to stand up for Valerie. I'm sure she is grateful to have such a good friend."

Henry nodded up and down as he clung to Vera.

Joan turned to face her again. "I have to get back to my class, but I look forward to seeing you. Saturday."

Vera felt her lips curl into a smile. "Yes, Saturday."

She watched as Joan turned and disappeared down the hallway.

It was Henry's insistent pulling at her hand that broke her out of her reverie.

She took Henry to the diner and got him a hamburger and told him not to mention it to his father that evening. "And don't punch anybody ever again. I mean it. Do you hear me? Don't you ever hit anybody for any reason. You go and tell a teacher next time someone might do something bad."

Henry nodded in agreement and shyly ate another bite of his hamburger.

Chapter Sixteen

They arrived at Darlene and James's home a little past seven. The room was already filled with smoke, the drinks conservatively poured, the music still soft for the weekly chatter to commence before the dancing and the touching and the loss of formalities.

"Well, well, well." James walked toward Roger with a swagger to his gait. "Guess you should get your son signed up for boxing lessons. He's got a real mean jab, hasn't he?"

Vera felt her cheeks flush bright red.

She watched the confusion pinch Roger's eyes for the briefest of moments and then it was gone. "Why I suppose so."

"He really gave it to my little Jack. Guess my son needs a lesson from yours."

"Guess so." Roger nodded, still in the dark.

"Kind of queer, wasn't it? The boys just wanted a little peek under that girl's skirt. You know how boys can be. Always curious about what's down below." And he ruffled his wife's skirt as she passed by.

"Will you cut that out?" Darlene pushed his hands away.

Roger nodded. "I'm sure it was only a bit of fun."

"That's what I said. I told Jack he'd better learn to give as good as he gets, too." James made a mocking fist.

"Now you stop it." Darlene rolled her eyes to the ceiling.

But James was laughing. He slapped Roger on the back and the two began walking toward the kitchen, Roger not giving her another glance as he went.

Vera was frozen in place.

He was upset with her.

Darlene eyed her warily before turning back to the party.

Vera opened her mouth to say something, anything, but faltered.

Darlene hardly spoke or looked at her the rest of the night.

She could feel the eyes of the other women upon her, whispers behind her back.

She drank until it all started to blur together and she stole away to a quiet patio off the back of the house.

Kitty appeared behind her, stumbling and intoxicated.

Vera lit her a cigarette and they stood side-by-side, blowing smoke into the night air.

"Ignore them." Kitty finally said after some time. "It's a good thing what Henry did."

But Vera had a sinking feeling in the pit of her stomach.

She threw up in the hallway bathroom. When she emerged, she nearly fell into a wall. She leaned against it and stared into the living room, watching as Roger danced closely with Louise.

He looked up and their eyes met, and she thought she might be sick again.

Her head was beginning to pound. She would have had another drink, but her stomach twisted at the thought of it.

She stood, leaning against the wall. The outcast, invisible.

Roger finally came to her after several couples had left. She'd watched him kiss Darlene on the cheek, allowing Louise to plant her lips against his stubbly chin. "Let's go home." His soft demeanor with others had faded, his voice held contempt for her.

She stumbled along the street.

He did not help her.

He did not seem to register her presence again, had no words for her as they walked into the front foyer of the home.

She kicked off her heels, reaching for the zipper on her too tight dress. She could hardly breathe.

He went to the minibar and poured himself a drink.

She slumped down on the couch and lit a cigarette.

Waiting.

He slammed his fist on the minibar and she jumped in her seat.

"How long?"

"What?"

"How long has everyone else known that our son got suspended?"

She tapped off the ash of her cigarette. "It happened Tuesday."

"And you didn't think to tell me?" He was looming over her.

Vera swallowed, smoking with an unsteady hand. The strap of her dress slid down her arm. "I spoke with him."

"I am his father, damn it." Roger drank back the glass of liquor, slammed it atop the minibar. "I have to talk to him."

"Roger, no! He's asleep." She got up and reached for him, but he pushed her. She stumbled backwards, leg catching on the coffee table. "Christ." She cursed in pain.

Roger came to her then. "Are you all right?"

She cursed again, sinking down to the ground to hold her banged knee, placing the burning cigarette in the ashtray so she wouldn't burn a hole into any more of Roger's precious items. "It's fine." She spoke through clenched teeth. "Please, I spoke with Henry. He knows what he did was wrong."

"He should hear it from his father." Roger was leaning down, inspecting her leg in the dim light of the lamp in the corner. "I don't know why you kept it from me." He was trying to sound angry, but there was a childish hurt to his tone.

"He was trying to protect his friend." Vera reasoned, the pain keeping her from censoring herself with Roger.

Roger sat on the floor across from Vera. He shook his head. "I'm not raising a...he's a real boy. He should act like it. He's not a sissy and he doesn't need his mother protecting him."

Vera recoiled from Roger. "Well." And she reached for her cigarette and leaned back against the couch. Smoking.

Roger watched her for a moment.

He was drunk and irritated.

He climbed to his feet after a while. "I'm going to bed."

She watched him go and lit another cigarette, pulling her dress down so that she could breathe fully again, sucking smoke into her lungs.

She coughed and felt ill again.

She crushed out the cigarette and crawled out of the dress so she was only in her slip.

Standing again, she hobbled to the kitchen and pulled a pack of frozen peas from the fridge. She wrapped it in a towel and pressed it against her leg, wondering if it would bruise.

She stared out the back window, out to the quiet forest that laid just beyond the manicured yard.

The moon was full, casting its silvery light upon the earth beneath. The trees shimmered, the path illuminated in the darkness, calling to her.

She slid into her moccasins, leaving the frozen peas atop the counter, and went out the back door.

It was chilly in the cool night air, but after the heat of all the bodies and the noise and the too tight dress, it was a relief to move airily through the grass and out, out to the trees.

She walked the path she had come to know, marveling at

the way the light of the moon illuminated everything so brilliantly before her. She could see for miles through the trees and she was not afraid.

The air became cooler as she approached the clearing in the woods.

The well rose up to greet her, the moonlight casting a spotlight upon its covered surface.

The cover hid its identity, its depth.

She shivered.

The air was stagnant.

And she felt terribly alone.

If only...

Her gaze turned to the horizon. She peered out through the forest, seeking.

She walked further into the woods.

The house would be just over there and yet she saw only forest for miles and miles stretched out before her.

She walked until the pain in her leg became unbearable and she stood in the midst of the forest lost.

Where was it?

Panicked tears came to her eyes.

She stumbled upon a branch, but when she looked down she found that it was stone. Perfectly laid stone. In the light of the moon she could see the stones stretched out in a line, disappearing, rising again, and then disappearing into the shape of a rectangle. A stone foundation.

The remains of something.

Her heart raced, panicked.

She turned away and half-ran, half-walked back the way she had come, afraid.

Grateful and relieved when the sight of the backyard rose up before her.

Chapter Seventeen

The winding driveway curved through tall, overgrown trees until it finally opened up to reveal the house in the woods.

Her heart leapt at the sight of it. Warm, inviting.

She parked the car and looked into the rearview mirror to check her eyes were not too swollen and that her complexion was even.

Joan and Lulu were waiting for her on the porch when she looked back at the house again.

Vera felt her lips tug upward at the sight.

She reached for her purse and the tinfoil wrapped bread, fresh from the oven. It was still warm in her grasp. She tottered in her heels over the gravel of the road, acutely aware of her bruised leg.

She'd traced her finger around the black and blue mark as she'd sat on the toilet that morning.

She tried to walk steadily, evenly to mask the discomfort.

She'd worn cigarette pants that day and a simple pink blouse with puffed sleeves.

She could feel Joan appraising her warmly as she made her way onto the porch.

She liked seeing Joan in her trousers and button-up. A far cry from the sheath dress she'd been wearing the day they'd met at the school.

Somehow the pants suited her more.

"You didn't need to bring anything."

"Oh, yes I did." Vera smiled as she petted Lulu who had jumped up onto the porch railing and meowed her welcome.

Joan opened the door for her to enter.

She felt the muscles in her shoulders relax as she stepped inside.

"Well, whatever that is, it smells divine!" Joan exclaimed.

"It's a recipe I thought to try for the Fall Festival. It's pumpkin bread." She handed it off to Joan. "It's the least I could do."

Joan waved her off and nodded for her to follow her into the kitchen. "Paul Nelson was a mischievous little boy in my fifth-grade class years ago. He did much worse than your Henry, believe me. Can you believe I helped him write his college thesis? He came home during his college break and begged me to help. Personally, I think he had a little crush on me." She winked as she unwrapped the bread from its tin foil casing.

Vera felt her cheeks go warm.

"Now he's the principal. I can't believe it." Joan nodded in disbelief as she cut into the loaf.

Vera was caught off guard for a moment by the familiar image of Lake George hung up on the refrigerator. It was a split image of boats on the lake and a strip of the bustling downtown at the bottom.

"It does seem very different now." Joan said.

Vera turned to find her looking at her.

"I was very happy to find it in the post. Did you enjoy the lake?"

Vera leaned up against the counter. "Not particularly."

Joan's smile faltered.

Vera took a deep breath. She laughed uneasily. "It was a work thing for Roger mostly. I watched the children play at the pool." She shrugged.

"I see." Joan arranged the bread on a tray with some tea. "Come." She lifted the tray and led them back to the inviting living room.

Vera sank down on the couch, allowing its comfortable curves to consume her. Lulu curled herself nearby and Vera let her hand tangle in the cat's soft fur, the vibration of her purring soothing.

Joan sat on the other end and poured them each some tea. Vera watched, anxiously, as Joan tried a bite of the bread. Her face lit up in pleasure. "It's delicious." She concluded. "Really, you must give me the recipe."

"Oh, it's nothing." Vera bashfully sipped her tea, delighted Joan should like it so well, that she had pleased her. She looked up at the older woman and suddenly needed to know everything she possibly could about her. "And your weekend? Did you have an enjoyable time at the beach?"

Joan placed her teacup atop its saucer. "In fact, I did. It was nice to get away and be surrounded by friends."

So it had been a group, not just one.

For some reason that pleased Vera.

"I don't get to see them very often so it was nice to spend time together. I knew them when I lived in the city." Joan spoke succinctly.

"You lived in the city?" Vera asked.

"Yes, for a number of years."

"Where did you live?"

Joan eyed her curiously but smiled. "The Village."

"We lived on the Upper East Side." Vera smiled in turn.

"Did you like it there? In the city?" Joan asked.

"Oh, yes."

"Do you miss it?"

Vera nodded. "Yes."

A bird called out somewhere in the distance.

"It's so quiet here." Vera folded her hands in her lap. She looked down to observe the skin of her fingers. The wedding band about her finger.

Joan stopped as if listening for something. "I suppose it is."

"Do you miss it?" Vera looked up at Joan's handsome face. "The city?"

Joan's features hardened, and Vera felt afraid that she had said the wrong thing.

"Of course." Joan finally said after a moment.

Something shifting in her faraway gaze.

Vera reached for her purse at her feet. "Do you mind...?" She held up her cigarettes.

Joan shook her head, watching intently as Vera placed one between her lips and lit it.

There was an ashtray already placed on the table before them. Vera smiled at the sight of it.

"I didn't mean to go morose." Joan apologized suddenly. "It's only that I didn't return here of my own accord. It was my father. He was very ill toward the end and I...well, I came back to help out and then just...stayed." She shrugged, tried to laugh.

Vera nodded encouragingly. Wanting to know.

"I had a nice enough job here and my father left me the house. It was much better than the tiny one bedroom I was living in. A walk-up at that!" Joan laughed, but there was something missing in her smile. "And when the war came and disrupted the whole market it was just easier to stay put."

Vera blew a stream of smoke away from Joan. "It's nice here. This house, it's beautiful."

Joan looked around, as if seeing it all for the first time. Vera watched a smile form on her lips, pleased. "Yes, I suppose. I've redone it over time. It's a little more to my taste than it once was anyway."

Vera liked her taste.

"Would you like to see the rest of it?" Joan was studying her curiously.

"Oh, yes. If you wouldn't mind." Vera nodded.

She put out her cigarette and followed Joan, Lulu trailing after them. "Well, you've seen the kitchen. It was my latest project. I just finished painting the cabinets before school started. I was just drawn to this particular shade of green." She explained as she led Vera towards a room behind the stairs. "This is my office here." And she opened the door to reveal a neat little room with a desk tucked beneath a window and several walls of bookshelves, a window seat wedged between two of them. "Lulu likes sunbathing here best, don't you?" Joan bent to pet her head and she meowed her agreement.

Suddenly, a daydream overcame Vera. A fantasy that made her falter, an image in which she, sitting upon the window seat, would be curled up with a book and Lulu would be purring on her lap as the sun shone in through the window while she lazily watched Joan, who would be seated at the desk, marking up papers.

Joan touched her arm lightly.

The touch startled her from her delusion.

They went out of the room, the illusion shattered.

There was a little powder room beneath the stairs, and then Joan was leading her up those same, wooden stairs.

Vera's heart was hammering in her ears.

They ended up on a landing and Joan pushed open a door to the front room. "This is a guest room. Occasionally my city friends come to visit. They call this place their country retreat." Joan was smiling at the thought of it.

Vera looked at the made-up white bed, the floral wallpaper that adorned one wall, the painted white shiplap of the other walls. It was so calm, so serene. She wanted to be one of Joan's friends who had the privilege of staying in this very room.

"And over here is my room." Joan's commanding voice sounded suddenly soft and shy as she turned the doorknob.

Vera's heart hammered in her ears. She stood in the hallway, staring in at the bedroom. A voyeur, peering into something secret, forbidden.

It was simple, tasteful. Darker than the guest bedroom and yet more inviting. It was here that Vera had the strongest urge to lay down upon the welcoming bed and never leave again.

She turned away from the sight of it, drawn to it.

"Perhaps...might I use your restroom?" She fumbled.

"Of course, there's one here." Joan opened the door to the second-floor bathroom. "I'll be downstairs." She smiled as Vera moved past her, into the space smelling intensely of Joan.

A claw foot tub, a shower in the corner, a counter of perfume, powders, lipsticks, little bottles of creams, the little intimacies of the woman all lined up for Vera to peruse.

She leaned against the wall, placing a hand over her chest to stop the racing of her heart. She wiped a hand over her brow.

She stumbled toward the sink, wetting a tissue, patting at her cheeks, her neck, her chest.

When she looked in the mirror she found herself flushed. Her cheeks piqued with redness.

Her hands came to rest at either side of the sink basin.

She gazed over the perfume bottles, memorizing the names of the scents.

She lifted one, held it to her nose to inhale, eyes closing as she did so.

It smelled warm and heady. Like Joan.

She placed the bottle back exactly as it had been and let her finger trail over the countertop.

She sat on the edge of the tub, examining the bottles of shampoo, a bar of soap, and the little bottles of bath oils the woman used. She lifted each, inhaling the scents.

What was she doing?

She got up, staring again at herself in the mirror.

She caught sight of her watch, noticing it was growing late. Remembering that Roger was still upset with her; he had yelled at Henry that morning for trying to help her bake the bread for Joan. She shouldn't have left the children for so long.

But she was held there suspended, unwilling to move, to leave this euphoric utopia.

There were the chimes of a clock that started up somewhere downstairs. Time. Time passing too quickly. It was getting late. Too late.

She flushed the toilet, washed her hands, and then descended back to the living room where Joan was sitting atop the couch petting Lulu. Waiting for her.

The sight of her stopped Vera at the foot of the stairs.

Her dark hair loosened about her face, those deep eyes so bottomless and enchanting.

Vera wanted to kneel before her, to bury her face in her chest, and forget Roger and the children.

The thought frightened her.

"I...I should be going."

Joan rose from the couch. "Are you all right?"

Vera's lips turned up at the corners. "Yes. Yes, I'm fine." She collected up her purse. "I have to go home...I have... Roger...the children..."

Joan understood.

She walked her to the door.

They stood on the porch, Lulu winding about their legs.

Near but far from one another.

"Thank you for the loaf of bread." Joan smiled. "I really do want the recipe."

Vera looked up into Joan's eyes. Lost. "I'll bring it next time."

Joan's face brightened. "Yes, please do."

"Thank you for...everything." Vera breathed.

Joan nodded. There was a look in her eyes, in the way she stood that made it seem as if she might just embrace Vera but she drew no closer.

They stood looking at one another until Vera had the overwhelming urge to kiss Joan goodbye.

Fear welled up in her chest. She looked down at her feet. "I...I must go. Thank you...thank you...but I'll...I'll see you next weekend, then." Vera felt her cheeks grow red again.

Joan was smiling. "Yes. Next weekend."

Vera looked down at her feet, forcing them back to her car. Lulu trailed after her until she got to the edge of the porch.

The cat stood meowing sadly as she went over the gravel, away from Joan.

She got in the car and tried not to look back because tears clung to her lashes. Foolish, silly, childish tears.

She paused at the end of the driveway to light a cigarette, pulse beating rapidly.

Chapter Eighteen

She awoke to sticky wetness between her legs.

The sun was only beginning to peek over the horizon.

Roger was still asleep beside her, turned away.

She went to the bathroom and turned on the harsh overhead light.

Pulling down her underwear she found a red stain.

Her heart pounded unsteadily, breaths shallow and shaky.

Her hands came to rest on her stomach, still taut but slightly distended. She felt for a sign but could not tell if it was any different than it had been the day before. She felt the same as always in the morning: nauseous, and slightly lightheaded when she stood to turn on the shower.

She washed herself clean. She found a sanitary pad and secured it between her legs.

Her hand shook.

She sat on the edge of the tub and lit a cigarette.

She placed her head in her hands, wrapping a wave of her hair tightly about her finger.

Tears came to her eyes.

The bathroom door twisted. Roger came in.

She watched his bare feet come to a halt, his eyes upon her.

"What the hell's the matter with you?" His voice was rough in the morning.

She wiped at her cheek. "Nothing." And she stood up and slipped past him to dress and to make his breakfast.

She took him to the train station, saw him off, and then returned home to find the children already up and racing about. She settled them down and fed them.

Emma watched her curiously as she sat smoking at the breakfast table. The food made her stomach churn and she raced to vomit in the downstairs bathroom.

She took them to the school, eyes glued to the front of the building. But everyone was a stranger to her.

She dropped the children off and returned home.

She went to the bedroom and pulled back the covers.

There was a small blood stain on the sheets.

She stood staring down at it, mesmerized.

She ripped the sheets from the bed and carried them to the bathroom. She scrubbed at the spot in the sink, watching as the blood dispersed and flowed away, leaving a light pink stain. She carried the sheets down to the washing machine.

There was a sharp pain in her side, and she doubled over.

She took an aspirin and then cleaned the kitchen.

She went to the bathroom and pulled down her underwear.

The sanitary napkin was red.

After smoking a cigarette at the kitchen table, she rose and put herself together, collecting her purse and car keys, and drove downtown. She parked before the building and walked up to the second floor.

She waited, patiently smoking a cigarette, until a nurse called her name.

They told her to undress, gave her a robe, took some blood, and then the doctor appeared.

Her body shook.

"Are you cold, Mrs. Wilson?"

She shook her head.

He smiled at her, patted her knee, and moved between her legs.

The exam went much as before.

He touched her stomach, and then was inside of her.

She closed her eyes.

Finally the doctor removed his large, warm hand.

His cheeks were flushed.

He pressed a cold stethoscope against her stomach and stood there listening. He kept repeating this same, uncomfortable process, lifting the cold implement and placing the frigid surface to another spot, listened, and then moving again.

He nodded, looking pleased.

"Well, Mrs. Wilson, the baby's heart is pounding away. I wouldn't worry about the bleeding. Give it a few days and if it doesn't go away then you come right on back and see me again." He patted her knee again and winked.

Her chest expanded. For the first time that day she felt as if she could breathe.

A nurse came in to bring her a fresh sanitary napkin.

She dressed and made her way back down the stairs of the building and out into the fresh afternoon air.

She did not know what to do with herself.

She looked at the car parked before her but did not wish to get inside, to return home.

Instead, she put on her sunglasses, lit another cigarette, and walked aimlessly down the main strip of town. She walked and walked until she reached the park and she sat on a bench and watched as the little children ran about.

A young mother, holding a child to her breast, called out to her son who was about to jump off the edge of the play set. Vera studied her, the frustration and apathy etched in her features, aging her. Was she like Vera?

Vera pulled at smoke from her cigarette, letting her hand come to rest against her stomach.

She tried to envision herself holding a baby again, watching it grow and race about the playground...but she could not see it.

Out of the corner of her eye she noticed a figure standing off in the distance.

Startled, she turned to get another glimpse, but when she looked again, no one was there.

A chill came over her.

She caught sight of her watch.

It was nearly three in the afternoon.

She would be late to the school.

She put out her cigarette and walked briskly back to the car.

As she pulled up to the school, she felt her heart contract at the sight of Henry and Emma on either side of Joan.

Vera came to a stop and rolled down her window as the children climbed into the backseat.

"I'm so sorry." She apologized, looking over Joan's smart dress, stretched attractively over her frame as the woman came to lean against the passenger window.

"Is everything all right?" Joan asked, her perfume floating into the interior of the car.

Vera's lips turned upwards, hoping for something akin to a smile. "Yes. I...I just had a little doctor's visit. Nothing serious."

Joan's dark eyes raked across her, lips twisting downward in concern. "You're sure?"

Vera nodded up and down. "It was nothing to be concerned about. I was silly to think...well, it's all right now. Everything's all right."

Joan did not believe her. "I hope you aren't going to that doctor in town. He's...well I must recommend a friend of mine. Just a town over. I'll give you his number the next time I see you."

Vera glanced at Joan.

She knew.

Vera's cheeks flushed. She fumbled for her cigarettes. "That would be very nice."

"You're sure you're all right?" Joan's eyes shone with something fierce.

Vera nodded as she lit her cigarette. She turned and smiled at Joan. "Yes." Smoke escaped her mouth as she spoke in a hazy cloud.

Joan's brow furrowed, but she nodded. "I'll see you Saturday, then?"

Vera nodded and smiled. "Saturday."

Joan said goodbye to the children.

Vera drove away from the school, eyes glancing backward, seeking out Joan. But it was the sight of Emma's eyes in the backseat, firmly fixed upon her, that made her uneasy.

When they got home, Vera made quick work of putting the freshly cleaned sheets back on the bed.

And when she looked up, she found Emma standing in the doorway. Watching her.

"Are you okay, mommy?"

Vera sighed, sat on the edge of the newly made bed, exhausted from her efforts. She patted the spot beside her, holding out her arms to the girl.

Emma came to her, allowed her to press her tightly against her breast. "I'm okay, baby." She whispered against Emma's soft, brown hair. "I'm okay."

Tears slid from her eyes.

She held Emma closer so she would not see.

Something was bothering Roger that evening when he came home. He did not take it out on her, simply sat drinking as he watched the television. He ate the dinner she made and then returned to the television while she cleaned up.

She went upstairs to the bedroom, exhausted.

He came into the room behind her, closing the door.

He grabbed her about the waist and put his hand between her legs.

She pushed at him.

He pulled her tighter, landing them both on the bed. "I want you." He kissed her cheek, her neck, her shoulder, pawing at her house dress.

"Roger..." she gasped.

His hand slid up inside her dress and she twisted, fighting him off.

"What the hell's the matter with you?" He demanded.

"Roger, I'm bleeding." She whimpered, caught off guard by his assault.

He lifted her dress and peered between her legs as if he did not believe her. "Is that normal?"

She felt blood racing in her ears. "Yes, the doctor said so."

"The baby..." A tenderness returned to him.

"It's okay." She assured him, pushing her dress back into place.

He looked her over.

She could see his arousal.

He got up and went to the bathroom, slamming the door shut.

She laid on the bed and closed her eyes, waiting for him to take care of himself.

In the darkness of her mind, she saw herself inside Joan's bedroom. Each detail floating back to her in technicolor.

And Joan lying beside her.
Quiet, serene.
Roger grunted.
She heard the shower start.
She rolled onto her side and lit a cigarette.

Chapter Nineteen

Joan was laughing, eyes closed, head thrown back so Vera could see the long straight line of her neck.

Her finger itched to trace the exposed skin.

She petted Lulu as a strange feeling washed over her.

She leaned forward for a cigarette.

"Well, it wasn't that hilarious." She felt her lip quirk upward as she lit the end of the paper, inhaling.

Joan wiped her eyes. "I can see it now; I imagine he was a very attractive girl."

Vera tilted her head, exhaled a stream of smoke. "He was." And she smiled at the thought of Henry all done up in her make-up.

Emma had taken it upon herself to give Henry a makeover on Thursday when it had rained all afternoon and they hadn't been able to go outside. Vera had stumbled upon them in her bathroom. She'd stood admiring her son along with her daughter, who had looked so very proud of herself.

But then Vera had hurriedly cleaned him up which made her late picking up Roger.

Roger had been so uneasy around her.

Joan caught her eye, and she felt her heart leap.

Vera sat back, crossing her legs. "You're lucky."

Joan broke off a piece of a cookie. "Why's that?" She asked, placing the piece between her cherry red lips.

"You don't have the responsibility of a family." Vera placed the cigarette between her lips.

Joan's eyes fell to her trouser clad legs.

Vera felt her pulse quicken, worried she had said the wrong thing.

"I suppose you might say that." And she brushed an invisible crumb off her lap.

Vera bit her lip. "I'm...oh, I didn't mean..."

Joan waved her off. "No, I suppose I am lucky. I can do as I please. You're right." And she looked again at Vera, but her eyes were no longer alight with mirth from before. She reached for the rest of the cookie.

Vera leaned forward to tap off ash. "Did you ever want..." She was teetering on the edge of something. A line being crossed.

But a selfish need had arisen in her.

All those nights she had spent trying to puzzle it out – who Joan was and what her past looked like – had left her curious.

Joan had finished the cookie. "For a time, I suppose I thought I wanted that."

Vera leaned back against the couch, smoking. "I never did."

Joan eyed her curiously.

"Oh, I shouldn't say that, but I..." She shook her head.

Joan patted Vera's hand. "I know many women who never wanted it."

Vera enjoyed the feel of Joan's hand against her own. She could still feel the weight of it after the hand had been removed from her person. "I'm sorry...it's none of my business." She smoked again before putting out the cigarette.

Joan's lips parted. She looked at Vera, something different in her expression. "It's quite all right. I don't mind."

Vera rubbed her hands over her skirt, not knowing what to do. "Do you have something real to drink?" She finally asked.

Joan laughed. "Are you sure you should be drinking?"

Oh. Vera looked down at her stomach.

The bleeding had stopped.

"Yes, it's all right."

Joan considered it a moment and then got up to retrieve a bottle of wine and two glasses from her kitchen. Vera had lighted a fresh cigarette and gratefully took the wine offered to her.

Joan settled onto the couch beside her again, sipping the drink. "I nearly married twenty – oh, twenty-five years ago. It would have been an awful mistake." She extended the information. A peace offering.

Vera smiled at her. "Why?"

Joan laughed. "Why? Well, we were very dear friends, but I wouldn't have been a good wife to him. He deserved someone who could give him what I couldn't." She swirled the wine about in her glass. "I don't usually drink during the day." She admitted into the surface of her drink.

Vera chuckled. "I don't think I can say the same."

Joan sat back, a playful smile on her lips. "Is that what you mothers get up to while I'm slaving away at the school?"

Vera mirrored her body. "Oh, yes. It's all fun and games. Whiling away the day with a bottle of wine."

She drank again.

Joan was watching her closely.

"I was resolved to never marry. You know," Vera laughed, "when I asked my father what I should study in college he said it didn't matter. I'd just end up married and pregnant anyway."

Vera paused to smoke, almost laughing at herself. How resolute she had been. So single-minded in her focus. How she'd graduated near the top of her class – honors denied to her because of her sex – and how she had been so determined to take the job at her father's firm. "I met Roger at a bar in the city after I graduated. I was clerking for a firm out of school, quite promising really. Roger was back from the war. We spent one drunken weekend together." She shrugged. "Emma was conceived, and that was that." She laughed bitterly. "I suppose I proved my father right."

Joan was not laughing. "No."

Vera drank the wine, smoked, wiped at her cheek, and then hung her head. "I'm sorry."

Joan took her hand, holding it gently. "There's nothing to be sorry about."

Vera found she enjoyed the feel of Joan's hand in her own. She studied the veins that ran beneath Joan's soft skin.

She felt ridiculous, the wine had made her sullen.

She'd said too much.

She could hear a clock ticking somewhere off in the distance.

Joan's hand remained clasped in her own.

Ash dropped from her cigarette.

She did not want to lose the contact, but she sat forward to put out the cigarette.

Joan's hand came away from her hand in the process.

"Tell me something." Vera's voice was a whisper in the quiet home.

"What do you want to know?"

Vera's eyes fell upon a framed picture. A young woman with dark, enchanting eyes. "You went to school here? In the town?"

Joan looked at the image of her younger self. "Yes. There was a small schoolhouse up the road." She looked lost in the memory of it, a faraway smile in her eyes. "I don't know how Miss Wiley did it. One teacher for the whole town." She shook her head.

"Did you always know you wanted to teach?"

"Oh, no. No, I don't know." Joan shrugged. "I admired Miss Wiley, that she didn't have a husband. But back then you weren't allowed to be married if you were a teacher."

"Perhaps I should have gotten a teaching degree." Vera mused, reaching for her cigarettes.

She caught Joan eyeing the pack.

"Do you smoke?" She asked shyly.

"Oh," Joan rubbed a hand over her thigh, laughing. "Here and there. You know, maybe one in the evening."

Vera held out the pack.

"No, I shouldn't...I..."

Vera smiled and placed two cigarettes between her lips. She lit both, passing one off to Joan who took it between her fingers before placing it between her lips.

Vera watched her inhale expertly, a cloud of smoke streamlining beautifully from her lips as she leaned back to exhale.

"I think you're a bad influence." Joan sighed.

Vera's lips twitched upward as she smoked.

Joan swirled the wine about in her glass, watching as smoke rose from the cigarette in her hand. "I had to sign a contract to never touch a drop of liquor or be seen out in public after eight in the evening when I first started." She laughed.

Vera smiled. "And smoking?"

"Oh, strictly forbidden." Joan put the cigarette between her lips and inhaled again. "It's not like it once was."

"When did you start teaching?" Vera leaned her arm against the couch, cradling her head in her hand.

Joan smiled intriguingly. "I think I know what you're getting at."

Vera stared at her innocently. What was she trying to get at?

"Miss Wiley told me about Adelphi College in Brooklyn when I was sixteen. When I was seventeen my father agreed to pay for me to attend and I got accepted, but the pandemic of nineteen eighteen happened, so I stayed home and helped him on the farm for a year. I graduated in nineteen twenty and started teaching at a school in the city. You like working with numbers – I assume you can figure out the rest." Joan stated coyly, lifting an eyebrow as she smoked again.

Vera's mind put the numbers in order.

Joan was fifty-three.

"And yourself?" Joan asked pointedly. "Young, I imagine. Not even thirty."

Vera laughed at this. "Your math skills must not be that sharp. Thirty-one."

Joan was laughing. "Math was never my favorite subject in school."

Vera was warm all over. She drank the last of the wine, the room about her going just a bit hazy, Joan's features soft and warm, and she wanted...

A clock chimed.

Lulu stretched herself long across the couch.

Vera looked down at her watch. "Oh, God."

Joan sobered, smoking at the last of her cigarette before crushing the stained red end out amongst Vera's pink tipped butts. "I wish you..." Joan caught herself.

Vera stubbed out her cigarette, placing her pack and lighter into her bag, moving as if to leave. Because if she stayed a moment longer...

They stood together from the couch, walking toward the door. The walls that had tumbled went back up into place.

Vera stood before Joan on the front porch. Lulu sat atop the railing, watching. "The festival is in another two weeks."

Joan nodded. "You've handled the cake sign-up sheet with the PTA?"

"Yes."

"Then I think it's all in order." Joan crossed her arms over her chest.

Vera's whole body ached. She felt as if she might be sick.

The feeling overtook her violently.

"Are you all right?" Joan had caught her arm gently.

Vera sighed at the contact. "I'm all right, I'm...I'm fine." And she righted herself and she smiled and she stepped away from the reassuring touch. "Next weekend then?"

Joan did not look reassured but nodded up and down. "Next weekend."

Chapter Twenty

Vera lifted the coffee pot and watched as the black liquid splashed into two coffee cups.

A symphony was playing quietly on the radio.

Kitty sat listlessly across from her at the table.

To the untrained observer she was as pieced together as always, but Vera could see beyond the make-up to the red-rimmed eyes and dull complexion.

Vera watched her from across the table as she clasped the refreshed cup of coffee between her hands and stared into the steaming black surface.

Vera sipped her coffee. Waiting.

"He hasn't come home the past few nights." Kitty toyed with the handle of the cup, a long red fingernail pinged against porcelain.

"I'm sure it's only work..." Vera offered.

Kitty shook her head. "I found a letter." Her hands were shaking. A hint of tears shown in her eyes. "In a woman's hand in his coat pocket. She signed it 'XO – P'."

Vera reached for her cigarettes, placing one between her lips.

"Oh, God. I don't know what to do." Kitty whispered.

"But you can't possibly know..."

Kitty fixed her with a pointed gaze, a harsh, broken laugh escaping from between her lips. "He hasn't touched me in weeks. I think I would know..."

Vera tapped off ash, looking at Kitty. She wanted to tell her it would be all right, but they both seemed to know the truth of it. "He'll come home." Vera said instead.

Kitty reached for the cigarettes. The sleeve of her dress rolled upward as she did so, and Vera noticed an angry gash in the porcelain skin of her wrist.

Kitty gasped when Vera clutched her arm, holding it suspended in air.

"What are you doing?" Kitty tried to wrestle her arm free, but Vera held tight.

She clutched the cigarette between her teeth and rolled Kitty's sleeve up further.

It was not only one gash. It was an array of slashes that ranged from fresh to faded.

Kitty pulled her arm forcefully away from Vera's grasp, pushing her sleeve back into place, standing as if to leave. "You have no right." Kitty hissed, reaching to collect up her purse.

"What the hell happened to you?" It unnerved Vera. The sight of those angry lines, as if the woman had gotten stuck in a metal fence.

"It's nothing." Kitty was shuffling away from her.

Vera seemed to understand then. The embarrassment that rose in Kitty's cheeks.

She rested her burning cigarette in the ashtray and stood up. "You've done this? To yourself?"

Kitty shook her head, crossing then recrossing her arms over her chest. "Please, please...don't say a word...don't..."

"Shh," Vera pulled her into her embrace, holding her as she fought at her.

"Get away." Kitty was whispering, pushing until she was whimpering her protest against Vera's chest uselessly. "Oh, God." She collapsed into Vera.

Vera tried to sooth her, stroking her back in calming circles.

But the consolation felt hollow.

Kitty sobbed.

"Why do you do it?" Vera cautioned.

"You don't understand." Kitty breathed.

They ended up on the couch. Kitty's hand in her own as she sobbed. The tears flowed messily, smearing her make-up beneath her eyes, undone.

She cried until she was simply humming a low, guttural hum. "I thought we would be different."

"That is not your fault." Vera assured her.

Kitty laughed darkly. "It is. All the magazines say it. If you let yourself go then he'll stray."

"You're beautiful and he's a fool."

Kitty looked at her strangely, removing her hand from Vera's.

Vera shifted on the couch, leaning forward for a tissue to hand to Kitty.

Their legs had been touching, but now there was space between them.

"You've been busy." Kitty stated after she'd dried her eyes.

Vera's brow furrowed. "What?"

"I see you going somewhere. Saturday mornings."

"Oh," Vera's heart was pounding, and she wasn't sure why this should upset her. "Yes, planning the Fall Festival."

"With Ms. DeBoer?"

Vera nodded her head slowly up and down.

What was it everyone seemed so suspicious of when it came to Joan?

Kitty wiped beneath her eyes. "You like her?"

"Yes." Vera rested her elbows on her knees. "Why is everyone so afraid of her?"

Kitty was smiling now. "Oh, dear." She wiped at her eyes again. Strength returning to color her cheeks. "She's not like us."

"No, she's not." Vera could see that clearly enough.

Kitty looked hesitant, as if afraid to say more than was absolutely necessary. "Joan's family used to own half the land this town was built upon. They were early Dutch settlers and as the story goes, they lived harmoniously with the natives who took up residence in the nearby woods. Apparently, Joan's father fell in love with one of the Native women and he took her as a bride. It wasn't ordained by the local church or anything, but they lived together, and she gave birth to Joan."

She thought of Joan's strong, dark features and seemed to understand then.

But what of that made Joan so different? It only enhanced her beauty. Why should everyone avoid her because of what her mother was?

"My grandfather was one of the first policemen in the area, you see, and the relationship between Joan's parents was quite difficult, as you could imagine. There was an incident one night in the woods. Her mother disappeared and no one knew what became of her."

Vera sat wide-eyed. "They never found her?"

Kitty shook her head. "She just...disappeared."

"Did Joan's father..."

Kitty shrugged. "He was a very kind man, but after that he...well, he started drinking away their fortune. Joan was in quite a pinch when she moved back here and had to sell all this land. It was for the best, though. My brother helped develop all these houses." She said with a sense of pride in the community.

That everything had been taken from Joan so now they could live here. Vera didn't like it one bit.

"Besides, it's rather strange, isn't it? That she came back here and never married?"

Vera was caught off-guard.

"There was a wealthy banker interested in her, but she turned him down. Can you believe it? Could have saved all her land if she'd married him, but she flat out refused." Kitty laughed. "Rather queer, isn't it?"

Vera didn't know what she was getting out, but she didn't like the implication.

Joan had been strong to refuse a marriage of convenience. She should be commended for her actions.

Besides, hadn't she saved things with the sale of the land? Surely, she would have made some kind of a profit...

The phone started to ring.

Vera startled from her trance, pulling herself up from the couch.

She went to the phone in the kitchen, picking up the slow burning cigarette in the ashtray on the table as she answered. "Hello?"

"Vera."

It was Roger.

She hoped he would tell her that he wouldn't make it home that evening, but instead he said, "I'll be on a later train tonight. The seven-fifteen."

Oh.

"All right." Vera exhaled a cloud of smoke.

"I've got to go."

The line disconnected.

Vera stubbed out the cigarette and turned to find Kitty fixing herself up in a handheld mirror. "I should be going. John will be home tonight, and I haven't a clue what to make for dinner."

It was as if the last half-hour had not existed at all.

The sun was pouring through the picture window in the living room.

Vera leaned against the wall.

"You won't..." Kitty began but her voice faltered.

Vera shook her head. She would not tell her secret. "Only I wish you wouldn't..."

Kitty laughed. "It's nothing, dear." Kitty came toward Vera, patting her on the arm. "Don't you worry about me."

She walked Kitty to the door then returned to the kitchen table for her cigarettes. She sank down onto the chair in the living room, feeling the press of her stomach against her too tight housedress.

She let her hand trail over her taut middle, knowing she would start showing soon.

Lighting a cigarette, she sat listlessly in the living room.

The things Joan had suffered...

A Mahler symphony was playing in the background.

She put out her cigarette and dozed off in the warmth of the sun.

But her dream was dark and damp and crowded, and she awoke sometime later feeling a tight, suffocating pressure on her chest.

She coughed and coughed until she lit another cigarette.

Chapter Twenty-One

The gym had been transformed into a haunted apple orchard. Tall paper trees had appeared with the help of Mac, the custodian who moved about on a ladder to affix things to the ceiling. Booths were erected beneath the branches of the trees, a pumpkin patch littered the corner of the gym, glistening orange pumpkins waiting to be 'picked' and carved for the carving contest.

It had all come together over the course of a hectic afternoon in preparation for the festival the following day.

Joan was at the center of the mess, instructing and constructing and picking up the slack.

Vera watched her furtively from beneath a pile of paper she was cutting and gluing and stapling together. She wrapped and folded and twisted the colorful card stock into branches and leaves and delicate red apples.

The afternoon had gone long, Vera exhausted but content for the work. To be outside of her home, to have *something* constructive to do.

"Vera, do you have any more staples?" Jannie, the mother

of one of Emma's classmates, asked. She was sitting near Vera, finishing up a rather complicated looking tree branch.

Vera found she only had one block of staples left. "Let me see if I can find some more." And she pulled herself up, brushing off scraps of paper from her trousers, and walked toward where Joan stood next to Mac, staring up at the ceiling.

Joan turned as she approached, as if sensing Vera's presence. Her face relaxed into a welcoming smile. She crossed her arms over her chest. "There you are. I wondered what you'd gotten up to."

Vera smiled, looking uneasily at Mac and then back to Joan. "I've been playing the role of mother nature."

"Ah, crafting I see." Joan laughed.

"And we've run out of staples." Vera crossed her arms over her chest, mirroring Joan.

"Oh dear." Joan scowled playfully. "I may just have some in my classroom." And she nodded for Vera to follow her.

Vera followed.

But as she went, she happened to notice Kitty's curious gaze upon her.

Kitty, who had avoided her from the moment she arrived. She had taken to working as far from Vera as she possibly could.

Vera looked away, continuing out of the gym and down the hall.

Her stomach knotted as if she were doing something wrong.

But what was wrong in retrieving a box of staples with Joan?

She focused on the back of Joan's head as they went, on her long, trouser clad legs and the way her perfume floated along after her.

Vera followed Joan up a stairwell. The only noise between them the click of their heels on the linoleum.

Her room was down the second-floor hallway and on the right.

Joan pushed open the door, turning to face Vera as she held it for her to enter.

Vera was shy as she slipped past her, pausing just in the doorway to take in the scent of chalk and books and children. The sun was setting on the horizon, casting a bronze hue over the room.

Joan did not turn on the overhead lights as she moved toward her desk in the corner.

The room was just as Vera had imagined it to be. Perfectly lined rows of desks. A chalkboard erased after a day of use. A globe atop a long shelf full of books.

Vera could hear Joan rummaging about in her desk, opening and closing the drawers.

She turned to look at her in the pink light of early evening.

Roger was riding with John back to the house that night.

She'd left dinner in the fridge for him to heat in the microwave oven.

She did not have to rush back to him.

The children were with Judy.

Judy had offered to feed them.

For a brief, fleeting moment, she was beholden to no one but herself.

"I saw some here the other day..." Joan opened the center drawer of her desk and triumphantly extracted a box from its depths. "Ah ha." She smiled.

There was a tightness in Vera's chest.

She hadn't had a cigarette for hours.

Her hand shook so she held it against her side.

"What is it?" Joan was looking at her with concern.

Vera shook her head, trying to break out of the trance she found herself in.

"Are you all right?" Joan was moving closer to her.

"Y-yes." Vera swallowed.

"The baby..."

"It's fine. I'm fine." Vera bit her bottom lip.

Joan was before her, eyes two deep wells of worry.

Vera's hands went about Joan, pulling the taller woman against her.

Joan bent her head down and their lips crashed together, Joan's hand resting on the small of Vera's back, the other, still holding the box of staples, stuck awkwardly between them.

Their lips parted.

It was only the sound of their breathing and the distinct click of a clock in the otherwise silent room.

They stared at one another.

"We -" Joan started and then swallowed. "We should get back."

Vera nodded and followed her out of the room.

A tightness knotted itself low in her stomach.

She followed Joan back down the hallway, to the stairwell. They descended together wordlessly.

They came upon a girl's restroom and Vera paused. "I'm going..."

Joan nodded. "I'll deliver these." She turned to continue on down the hall.

The restroom was all pink with terribly bright fluorescent lights hanging from the ceiling. The mirrors were lower than normal, the toilets somehow dwarfed for the children who used them.

Vera caught sight of herself in the mirror and startled, as if having just seen a ghost.

She went into a stall and pulled down her pants. She was wet.

She sat back so that she could reach her hand between her legs and caress the ache that throbbed.

With the pregnancy it seemed to take no time at all before she felt a release.

She leaned back, panting, hoping no one had heard what she had done.

There were no sounds in the hallway. Everyone would still be in the gym.

She relieved herself and then sat on the closed seat smoking a cigarette to calm her racing pulse.

She blew smoke lazily, watching as the gray clouds swirled about her, dirtying the pristine elementary school bathroom.

It took her back to another time, a time she had hated. When she had stolen away for a smoke in the restroom between classes in high school. Careful to never get caught so her parents might never know their little girl had been smoking since she was fourteen. Persuaded to try it by a fellow class-mate and then it stuck. The only stain on her otherwise pristine exterior.

Well, she marveled, appearances could be deceiving.

She flushed the butt of the cigarette then washed her hands in the small sink and left the overwhelmingly pink room.

Joan did not look in her direction when she walked back into the gym.

She resumed her spot next to Jannie and began cutting a piece of red paper to form it into an apple.

By the time they were finished, the gym looked better than she could have imagined.

Everything was in place, every detail meticulously executed to Joan and Vera's specifications. Vera heard the other mothers marveling at how nice the festival would be that year.

She felt good. She had done this. She was capable of something other than the daily chores, the caring for the children, for Roger. The banalities of life.

She stayed right until the very end to make sure things were neat and tidy and ready for the following day as the others began to leave to return home to their husbands and children.

And she found she was soon alone with Joan.

Vera waited on the front steps of the school smoking while Joan shut off the lights and locked the front door.

The autumn night was cool and smelled of far away bonfires.

The moon was a small sliver in the sky so that, apart from the lights on the front of the school, they were shrouded in darkness.

Joan came to sit next to her.

She took the cigarette from Vera and inhaled deeply.

"The kids will like it." Joan said as she blew smoke out the side of her mouth.

"Yes." Vera agreed.

They sat in silence. Passing the cigarette.

They did not look at one another.

"Something like this could be very dangerous." Joan spoke carefully.

"I don't care."

Joan scoffed. "Well, you should."

Vera took the cigarette from her, their fingers brushing for longer than was necessary.

"I'm sure you've heard about me by now." Joan whispered.

"I'd have to hear it from you." Vera looked at Joan and saw the strong profile of her face. How beautiful she was. How Vera wanted to take her into her arms just then.

But instead she looked away and put the cigarette out against the concrete of the step beside her.

"You should be going home." Joan stood up, brushing invisible dirt from the back of her trousers.

She held out her hand for Vera, who took it. Joan pulled her up and they stood staring at one another.

"Not here." Joan cautioned, then turned and walked down the stairs and toward the parking lot at the side of the school where their cars were parked.

Vera followed, not sure what was happening. She supposed that they would leave and perhaps never speak of it again and the thought of that made her heart pound terribly, painfully in her chest.

It was agony.

But before they reached the parking lot, she felt Joan's hand wrap about her wrist, pulling her into an alcove away from the main street, out of the lights illuminating the school. A bush brushed against Vera's cheek when Joan pulled her to a halt, turning her around to face her.

Joan cupped Vera's cheeks in her hands, looking into her eyes.

Their lips met. Hungry, wanting.

When they parted Joan took a deep, shaky breath. "Oh, God." She sighed.

"Are you okay?" Vera whispered, even though no one else was around to hear them.

Joan shook her head. "No."

Vera's heart sank again. "Joan, I..."

Joan rubbed her eyes. "I don't know if I can do this..."

"Please." Vera whispered before she could stop herself. Needing.

Joan looked at her warily, frightened.

Her head slowly bobbed up and down. "Okay. But don't look at me like that in public."

"Like what?" Vera frowned.

"Like...like you want to take all my clothes off."

"But I do."

"Vera." Joan stepped away from her. "Oh, Vera." And then she was laughing.

Vera did not find it particularly funny but preferred Joan laughing to the panic that had overcome her only seconds before.

Joan finally sobered and wiped at her eyes. "You have a husband to get back to. We should...we should go home. I'll see you tomorrow."

Vera did not want to go home like a good girl to her husband. She wanted to go to the home tucked away in the woods with Joan.

But she nodded. "Yes. Tomorrow."

They began walking toward their cars parked several spots away from each other. "You promise?" Joan asked before she got into her car.

Vera nodded up and down.

Joan smiled at her and then got into her car.

Vera followed her out of the school parking lot, pulse beating rapidly, lighting a cigarette when Joan turned left at a stoplight and she lost her to the night.

Chapter Twenty-Two

Relegated to the raffle room, Vera had sent Roger off with Emma and Henry to explore the festival.

Vera sat smoking at a teacher's desk, monitoring as parents and children walked about the items up for auction. She was particularly pleased with herself that the pearl earrings drew a great deal of attention. She watched as two fathers meandered in and out in a silent war against the other to claim the earrings for their wives.

They always looked at her, conspiratorially, as they bent over to place a higher bid. As if wanting her to see, to know what they were doing.

She found it tediously amusing.

She was just about to light another cigarette when Joan appeared in the doorway.

She carried a clipboard and looked rather quite official, hair all swept up and neatly sprayed into place.

Their eyes met and Vera lowered her lashes to focus on the end of her cigarette.

Someone was talking to Joan. Vera hadn't a clue what was

being said, only that Joan looked utterly enraptured in the conversation.

She had scarcely seen her all afternoon. Hardly a moment alone and her skin crawled with want.

And what could she say? That she'd awoken in a sweat from a rather erotic dream of the dark-haired teacher and had had to slip her hand beneath her underwear to ease the ache of it next to her sleeping husband?

It was hardly idle chat fit for an elementary school festival.

Vera re-crossed her legs beneath the table and attempted to not follow Joan's every move with her eyes.

Until Joan appeared before her.

"And how is everything going in here?" Joan came to stand beside her.

She basked in her warm scent.

"I see we have quite a bidding war going on the pearl earrings."

Vera picked ash from her tongue and laughed. "I told you they'd be a sure bet."

"You certainly know your stuff." Joan conceded.

They did not look at one another as they spoke.

They stared at the families walking about the room, oblivious.

"And the rest of the festival? How is it?"

"I do hope you can get out from behind this desk and find out. Your enchanted forest idea is a big hit. The kids can't stop talking about the décor." Joan fingered an errant pencil atop the desk.

"Judy will come to relieve me soon." Vera assured her.

"That's good. I have to make my rounds. Next stop, the cake walk." Joan lightly touched Vera's shoulder.

It sent a shock coursing through her.

She watched Joan walk away but tried to make it seem as if she weren't watching at all.

One of the dueling husbands was hovering over the pearl earrings, looking at her again.

She smiled at him and then tapped off ash to smoke again.

Judy arrived several minutes later.

They exchanged a cordial greeting, Judy talking on about something inane, Vera half-listening. She finally escaped and went off to relieve herself in the little girl's room. As she washed her hands she noticed the curve of her pregnancy beneath her dress.

There was something disturbing yet relieving to know the baby was still developing.

She set out to locate her family in the mess of the festival.

She wondered where Joan had gotten off to.

Vera wandered in solitude down the hallway, children brushing past her in excitement, wary parents chasing after, balancing cakes and pumpkins and toys in their arms.

The gym was quite enchanting. The overhead lights shut off in favor of colorful lights hanging about. She walked, looking, taking in the booths as she went.

There in the corner was a fortune teller.

She hadn't remembered it in the initial plans. Perhaps something she had overlooked.

She peered in and saw a woman who looked only a few years older than her with unruly red-hair curled about her face and a scarf tied over the top of her head. She was seated before a rather fake looking crystal ball.

She caught Vera's eyes and smiled. "Come in, won't you?"

"Oh no..." Vera laughed, shaking her head.

"I can sense you're seeking something."

Vera rolled her eyes. "Yes, my family."

"No, it's not that." The woman's voice stopped her cold. "Come. Please, come in."

Vera looked about. She did not see Roger or the children, nor Joan, anywhere near.

Hardly anyone was around this little corner of the gym.

She stepped into the booth.

"Sit down." The woman gestured toward the chair across from her.

Vera sat.

The woman smiled at her then reached behind her, pulling out a deck of cards.

"What are you..."

"Let's let the cards speak, shall we?" The woman winked at her.

They looked like a pack of playing cards.

The woman shuffled.

Vera leaned forward, watching as the woman moved the crystal ball to the side of the table then spread the cards out in a long straight line.

"Pick three."

Vera hesitated.

Was this a test?

What would they reveal?

The woman looked at her encouragingly.

She chose one from the right, the left, and the middle.

The woman placed the three chosen cards in the order they were picked onto the center of the table and cleared away the rest.

She slowly flipped each card over.

Vera watched with rapt attention.

A yellow card with a woman wrestling a lion, the word 'strength' printed upside down.

Animals looking up at a shining moon in the sky above.

A forceful knight on the back of a glorious white horse.

Each one a colorful scene, a puzzle to be solved.

"Very interesting." The woman mused.

Vera looked up at her. "What does it mean?"

The woman considered the cards carefully.

"This first card here, you see, has appeared to you upside down. Strength. The opposite of strength is giving into weakness or desire. There's a relationship about to form that could bring about destruction if it continues on its current trajectory. If the people involved give in to their desires."

Vera took out a cigarette and with an unsteady hand lit it. She exhaled a cloud of smoke, eyeing this fortune teller.

What did she know?

"Well, what about the rest of it?"

The woman bent her head and regarded the next card. "The moon has a dark, powerful energy. Our fears come out and are exposed in the night. It's hard to know who to trust or what to believe. But, there's a pond here at the bottom," she pointed with her long red fingernail. "This is your subconscious mind. It can help guide you and teach you to tap into your intuition if you listen to it."

Vera tapped with the cigarette between her fingers at the last card. "And what is this? My knight in shining armor?"

The woman laughed a little. "Perhaps. The knight of swords comes to clear the confusion around you. Someone is coming into your life to help you better understand what is unclear. If you let them in."

Vera sat smoking.

Oh, this was all nonsense, wasn't it? Utter ridiculousness.

They were only cards after all.

What did they know?

The woman raked the cards back into the pile and moved the crystal ball back into place.

Vera reached to take money out of her pocketbook, but the woman stopped her.

"It's on the house." The woman assured her then looked past Vera at a little blonde girl at the booth entrance who stood peering inside curiously. "Would you like your fortune told, little girl?"

Vera stood, practically tripping backward, in her rush to be away from the fortune teller.

Who was she to tell Vera anything about her life?

She walked blindly through the crowd until a man walked in front of her and she ran into his chest.

He put his arms about her.

"What's the matter with you?" It was Roger's voice.

She shook her head. "Nothing...it's nothing. How are the children?" She asked stepping out of Roger's embrace to wipe at her cheeks, her forehead, to lift the cigarette to her lips to inhale again.

Roger motioned toward the pumpkin patch where Emma and Henry were carving their pumpkins. Emma looked up at Vera and smiled shyly.

She smiled back and felt queasy.

Everything upside down.

She looked up at Roger and felt as if she did not know him.

Joan appeared at the gym entrance.

Their eyes met and Vera's knees went weak.

Roger must have thought she looked unwell. He forbade her from staying to help clean up. And Joan - when she happened upon her again - agreed she should go on home, that she looked pale.

Vera's stomach sank. She wanted to stay.

Roger took them all out to the burger joint downtown. She picked at her food, not hungry, feeling sick to her stomach.

Roger seemed happy that evening. He was kind to the children. He read Henry a bedtime story.

She let him press himself inside of her that night before he drifted off to sleep.

Chapter Twenty-Three

"Go on ahead, I'll be right in," Vera had awoken ill again that morning.

She stood near their parked car in the church parking lot, lighting a cigarette she would need to make it through the next insufferable hour and a half church required.

The kids raced ahead, meeting up with their friends as they clamored into the church.

Roger followed after, leaving her to smoke.

She stood beneath the shade of a tree in the lot, the October day warmer than normal. Or else she was warm.

She wiped a hand over her forehead, pearls of perspiration gathering at her brow.

A familiar car turned into the parking lot. She watched as it moved down a row and then pulled into a parking spot.

The ignition died.

People passed by, nodding at her in greeting.

Vera smiled back distractedly.

She emerged slowly, eyes covered behind black sunglasses. Hair covered by a crescent cap, body encased in a simple black dress with a maroon cape.

Vera's heart beat wildly beneath her plaid dress bodice.

She smoked slowly at her cigarette, not wanting it to end.

Joan saw her. She walked toward her as she tucked her handbag beneath her arm.

"How are you feeling?" Joan asked as she approached.

"I've been better." Vera blew a stream of smoke into the sky above. "I'm sorry I couldn't stay to help last night, I…"

Joan waved her off. "You did enough. It was a great success."

Vera smiled as she placed the cigarette between her lips again.

Joan removed her gloves and waved at someone passing by.

She did not look back directly at Vera before she said, "I was thinking you might like to join the church's ladies auxiliary group. We're always looking for someone who can handle the budgets and deal with the church treasury." Joan was peering at her through her sunglasses. Vera could feel her eyes upon her, appraising her favorably.

"Yes." Vera found herself agreeing. "When do they meet?"

"Thursday evenings. I do hope you can make it." Joan slapped her gloves idly against the palm of her hand.

"Roger did say he wanted to see me more involved in the community. I don't think he would object." Vera puffed at the end of her cigarette and longed for another, but the church bells were tolling.

"Then there shouldn't be an issue." Joan's lip had curled upward in the corner.

Vera could viscerally feel Joan's lips against her own.

"We should get inside." Joan lowered her gaze.

Vera looked at the toe of her heel as she crushed out her cigarette.

They turned and walked towards the church doors together. Vera could feel the heat of Joan's body beside her as they greeted Reverend Johns at the door.

And then Joan went to her pew several rows ahead and Vera climbed into her seat beside Roger.

"What took you so long?" He asked against her ear.

Henry sleepily nudged at her, so she allowed him to press himself against her. Roger would no longer let him climb atop her lap. He felt he was too old for that, but he had the habit of wanting to be near to her when they were out. She put her arm about him and stroked his blonde hair from his forehead. "They want me to be a part of the ladies auxiliary group here at the church."

Roger nodded in approval, looking quite pleased with this sudden interest in outside activities.

He did not object when Vera left a plate warming for him on the stove Thursday evening. John drove him back from the station. It was all set so Vera could attend the church meeting at five-thirty that evening.

It was a group of older women. Joan was perhaps the youngest of the whole bunch.

They appeared to highly value Joan's input and deferred to her on a variety of points.

They were to have a November fundraiser and Joan looked to Vera. "Perhaps you might want to take on this project?"

Vera was delighted to be given another task. To look at the numbers and see what she could do about raising more money than the year before. It became a challenge to her, a need to do well.

The ladies enjoyed tea and cookies at the end of the meeting.

The older women were very grateful to Vera for coming, very happy to see someone so young, so interested in the health and welfare of the church community. They shook her hand and gratefully left a little past six that evening.

Joan had asked if Vera might stay a bit longer to help her clean up so no one else need to worry about washing up.

Joan was cleaning off plates in the kitchen when Vera came in with some teacups.

"They leave quite early, don't they?" Joan commented, as Vera came up beside her to place the teacups on the drainboard.

"Well, they're rather old, aren't they?"

Joan looked playfully hurt by this. "Ethel is only a few years older than I am."

Vera bit her tongue.

Joan laughed. "Well, us elders have to take on the tasks the younger women don't want to assume."

Vera leaned up against the counter, marveling at Joan. "I don't understand it."

"What?" Joan looked up from washing out a teacup.

"Your interest in the church."

Joan's eyebrow sunk. "And here I thought you were a devout Christian."

Vera laughed. "It's Roger's family that is devout."

"Ah," Joan said.

"But you..."

Joan placed the last of the teacups to dry on a towel and grabbed another to wipe off her hands. "Call it survival."

Vera frowned.

"They're all gone, aren't they?"

Vera nodded.

Joan moved closer.

She placed the dish towel on the counter beside Vera so her arm was touching Vera's arm.

Their eyes locked.

"I think I understand." Vera whispered.

Joan's eyes were upon her lips as she nodded up and down.

Vera's hand reached up and cupped Joan's cheek, pulling her close. Their lips melted together. The hum of the church's refrigerator, the sound of their labored breathing, lips moving together.

Vera's hands found their way between their bodies, working at the buttons on the front of Joan's shirt. She got to the fourth button - Joan's skin warm against her hand - before Joan broke apart from her, clasping her shirt tightly shut against her chest.

"We shouldn't be doing this." Joan's chest heaved as she looked wildly into Vera's eyes.

"Why not?" Vera breathed, her body on fire.

Joan shook her head. "I'm just..." Joan inhaled then exhaled, laughing uneasily. "It's been so long. I..."

Vera leaned forward and kissed her again. "It's not something you forget."

Joan allowed herself to be kissed, Vera amused by her waning bravado.

"Have you...have you ever done this before?" Joan laughed hoarsely.

"Yes." Vera replied as she nipped at Joan's neck.

"Oh God." Joan sighed as Vera gently removed the hand clutching her shirt closed so that Vera could kiss her way down Joan's sternum, shifting the shirt aside to reveal a breast covered by a white bra. Vera pressed the material downwards to reveal a dark nipple that she sucked between her lips.

Joan gasped above her.

Vera shifted so Joan was pressed against the kitchen island. Her hand found Joan's pantyhose-covered thigh. Her skirt was tight, but Vera managed to wiggle it upward with Joan's help and then they were fighting the pantyhose down, the material ripping against Vera's fingernails and rings. But it didn't matter; all that mattered was pressing her lips to Joan's as her hand finally sank into the band of Joan's underwear.

Joan whimpered against her, leaning back against the island as if to keep her balance.

Vera held her about the waist, keeping her knee steady between her legs, pressing kisses against her chin, her neck, her chest, hand moving over slick folds as Joan's hips responded beautifully to her motions.

It was a throaty, low gasping that told Vera she was close.

Vera's fingers moved deftly until Joan was grasping at her and moaning as her body rode out the orgasm.

The hum of the refrigerator and their labored breathing followed.

Joan finally stumbled forward, unsteady on her feet. "I need...I need to sit down."

Vera helped get Joan's skirt back into place then wrapped an arm about her waist, leading her back to the meeting room and sitting her down at the table, ripping off her torn pantyhose as they both laughed.

"What a mess." Joan wiped at her eye as she held the destroyed garment.

Vera sat down in a chair beside her and took out her cigarettes. "I hope they weren't expensive."

They shared a cigarette, using a teacup saucer as an ashtray. Vera could see Joan's hand was unsteady; she was shaken by what had just transpired between them.

Vera's body was burning as Joan buttoned up her shirt.

It had been too hurried, too rushed. She wanted more time, she wanted...

Joan looked at her watch after she crushed out the cigarette. "It's nearly seven."

"Roger will be expecting me." Vera toyed with her pack of cigarettes.

Joan rested her elbow on the table, cupping her chin in the palm of her hand. "I always made it a rule to not get involved with anyone in town. This rather complicates things, doesn't it?" She spoke uncertainly.

Vera shook her head. "I hope it doesn't because I'd like for it to continue."

"Well then," Joan shyly glanced downward. "I know you know as well as I, but we have to be careful." Joan tapped her fingers against the table top. "Very careful."

Vera let her hand fall over Joan's hand. Their eyes met again, and Vera found she liked the way in which Joan's irises were vibrantly alive. "We will be. Very careful." And she stood, leaning down to place her finger beneath Joan's chin, to lift her head so she could press a lingering, longing kiss to her lips. "Good night."

Chapter Twenty-Four

The moon waned in the sky, falling into blackness.

For a moment, when she looked up between the tree branches, she saw three moons shining brightly above.

But it was only a trick of the eyes.

The pure white light of the lone moon began to wilt, a stain appearing at the center, bleeding outward.

And there before her, the well.

Illuminated in the ghastly light.

She watched closely, waiting.

The wind picked up, whipping up dust, tossing her hair about her face. Fog wound its way through the trees, obscuring the world around her.

There was suddenly a figure somewhere off in the woods, but when she looked again it was not there.

Something was inside the well, but when she looked again, it was nothing.

It was the feeling of someone watching, of something...

There was a flash, the sensation of being beckoned forward, forward, closer to the well. As if pulled by an invisible force until her toes touched the stone and she was looking down into the bottomless pit.

Jump.

"No!" She cried as the brilliant red light of the moon grew brighter, bursting around her into flames.

She flailed, trying to run away, but an arm wrapped tightly about her, holding her in place. She couldn't move.

"Damn it, Vera! Wake up!"

Vera's eyes came open and she found herself face-to-face with Roger. He was pinning her down against the bed.

Above him there was the flash of a red light on the ceiling. It appeared and then disappeared and then appeared again.

"What the hell's the matter with you?" Roger was saying.

"Roger, something's happened." She pushed at his shoulders, and he slowly rolled away from her.

"What are you talking about?"

She got out of the bed and went to the window.

The red lights were brightly flashing away, a beacon in the usually dark night.

She reached for her robe and darted out of the bedroom, down the stairs to the living room to peer out to the street.

She knew before she saw it.

Roger was calling to her from atop the stairs as she raced to the front door. She ran across the grass barefoot, over the asphalt of the road, until she reached the police car parked before the house across the street.

"You can't go in there, ma'am." Someone was saying, but she didn't stop.

She pushed forward, racing towards the porch steps when the front door came open and the medical workers appeared hauling a stretcher between them, Kitty's lifeless face pale and fragile, her arms bandaged in white.

Vera saw her eyes flicker, fighting to stay in the land of the living. She was whisked away into the ambulance.

Her husband appeared in the doorway in his pajamas, a jacket over his arm and hat in hand. Lost.

"Go...go with her." Vera coaxed.

He looked angry and hurt and lost.

She shoved at him. "I'll take care of it. Just go."

He nodded, heading for his car parked in the driveway to follow the wagon as it raced off into the night, siren blaring so all the neighbors could hear, could see, could know what had transpired in the early morning hours.

A policeman tried to stop her, but she shoved her way inside.

Eleanor and Junior stood at the top of the stairs. The girl clasped at her brother protectively. The boy had tears of confusion in his sleepy eyes.

"Come here." Vera held out her hands for the children.

They came toward her, frightened and afraid.

She picked Junior up, taking Eleanor by the hand, and led them out of the house, away from the flashing lights of the police car. She had to set Junior down when they returned to her home. She couldn't carry him up the stairs, but she held both their hands as they climbed the steps to the front door where Roger stood watching.

He held the door open, allowing the three of them entrance.

Vera took the children to the guest bedroom in the basement. She tucked them in, handing them some of Emma's forgotten stuffed animals.

She sat with them for a long time, until their breathing evened out and she knew they were asleep.

She climbed the stairs and found Roger drinking in the living room. "We can't take in those kids."

"We will until Kitty comes home."

Roger looked doubtfully at her. "I wouldn't be too sure about that."

"What are you talking about?" Vera lit a cigarette.

"He's leaving her, you know."

Vera sank onto the sofa.

So it had happened.

"He said she's been like this for months." Roger said.

He blamed her for the split, did he?

Vera blew a stream of smoke to the ceiling. "I see."

Roger finished his drink. "I'm going back to bed."

Vera did not move.

She smoked slowly at the cigarette.

She went to the bathroom.

She walked down the stairs to make sure Kitty's children were still asleep.

She checked on Henry. She looked in at Emma.

Roger was asleep when she slipped back into the bed beside him.

She could not sleep.

She thought of touching Joan. She thought of touching her naked in her bedroom in the house in the woods, and of Joan touching her in return.

She touched herself.

She stared at the ceiling in the dark.

Roger woke, in the darkness, to his alarm and groggily got out of bed.

She got up after him, relieved herself, brushed her teeth, examined how her stomach was growing, then dressed herself, leaving Roger shaving to start his breakfast.

She took him to the train station then returned home to start breakfast for the children.

Once it was ready, she awoke Henry and Emma and quietly explained to them that they had guests and they were to be kind to them. Then she went down to the basement and gently woke Eleanor and Junior.

They sat at the table with her children, eating stoically.

Vera found some clothes for them to wear and after dressing the children, she took all of them to the school, telling them not to pay any mind to what any of the other children might say.

Emma promised to look out for them, kissing Vera gently on the cheek before darting away toward the school.

Vera searched vainly for Joan, but knew she would not see her.

She drove back home and gathered her cleaning supplies in a bucket before making her way across the street.

She heard birds chirping. She noticed how cold it had become, how winter would arrive soon. The trees were fading to brown.

She lingered on the front porch, contemplating the quiet suburban world around her.

The door was unlocked.

She let herself in.

The house was silent.

It mirrored her own, so she knew the bedroom would be up the stairs and to the left. She followed a trail of dirty shoe prints through the house.

Her stomach knotted.

She looked at the broken wood of the bathroom door where it had been forced open the previous night.

It fell open when she lightly pushed, and she had to turn away from the sight before her.

She tried to steady herself by looking at the bedsheets in disarray atop the bed, the clothing draped about the room, the books and glasses on the bedside table, the little messy details of life.

Closing her eyes and then opening them again, she turned back to the bathroom and pulled on her rubber gloves.

The blood and soap swirled together, turning pink as she scrubbed the floor, the toilet, the bathtub, the walls.

She had to stop, to sit back on her aching knees to put her forearm against her mouth, trying to keep the bile down.

She tried not to think about what she was doing and finally, when it was over, she stood up and gazed upon the spotless bathroom.

Not one drop of red remained.

She pulled off her gloves, collecting up her bucket and supplies, and made it to the living room before she had to race to the bathroom on the main floor, vomiting up the little she had in her stomach.

She sank down on the cool tile floor, bracing her stomach with her hands.

She let her palm trace over the curve of it, seeking the sensation that something was alive beneath her skin.

She had yet to feel the baby move inside of her as Emma and Henry both had.

She tried not to think about it.

She pulled herself up, grabbed the cleaning bucket, and stepped out into the welcome autumn air.

Chapter Twenty-Five

itty did not return home with John.

John did not come to collect the children. Instead Sharon told her he was drinking himself silly.

The other women brought extra food, offering to take Kitty's children, but Vera knew they needed consistency just then.

They invited her for lunch. It was some days after the incident that they sat smoking in Judy's kitchen over coffee when Louise told them John had had Kitty committed.

"Committed? To an asylum?" Judy cried.

"She's a danger to herself." Louise tapped off her ashes. "What else was he going to do?"

"I heard he was going to divorce her. That's what started it all." Sharon boldly stated.

Vera looked at her through the smoke of her cigarette. "I heard he was having an affair."

Sharon laughed. "Please, honey, it's not so shocking, is it? She didn't have to go and try to off herself over it."

Vera put out her cigarette and got up to leave.

"What's the matter with you? Too good for all of us, huh?" Sharon eyed her.

Vera collected up her cigarettes and lighter. "No, I don't suppose so. I have dinner to make."

She walked down the street smoking idly.

Kitty's house looked as it always did.

Yet, she was not there so it was not the same.

She looked out between the houses to the forest and felt a chill race through her.

The branches of the trees were all brown and dry. The lush greenery of summer had vanished.

She longed to slip into the woods, to wind her way down the familiar path that would bring her to the house in the woods...

Her knees weakened, and she nearly fell over at the thought.

It felt like a distant memory, something that happened in another lifetime millions of years before.

She could see the outline of a dark nipple in the too-bright overhead lighting of the church's kitchen.

The thought sent her shuffling quickly inside and promptly up to her room where she touched herself into oblivion, trying to take the edge off, but there was no relief in sight.

An older, wary looking couple appeared on the front porch that evening.

Roger was not home. He had called her earlier to let her know, so she had prepared a feast for the children and had delighted in watching them laugh together.

The merriment dwindled down at the unexpected arrival of Richard and Mary Bennington. They were Kitty's parents and had come to take the children with them for the time being, until Kitty was well again.

The children cried and clung to Vera, but she helped them pack their bags and assured them they would be okay.

Junior held tightly to her leg until Richard picked him up and carried him crying and flailing in his arms to the waiting car. Eleanor went quietly and Vera pitied her, longing to pull her back and protect her.

Instead, she watched the car drive away down the street, disappearing around the corner.

Emma and Henry were looking at her curiously as she walked back up to the living room. She sat on the couch and lit a cigarette.

"Will we see them again?" Henry asked quietly.

Vera shook her head. "I don't know, baby."

Henry came to her and laid his head on her lap.

After the kids fell asleep in bed with her, she slid from the covers and went to the kitchen.

She poured herself a glass of wine and lit a cigarette before lifting the receiver of the phone from its cradle. She listened to the dial tone, staring at the clock on the wall. It was nearly ten. It was terribly late and yet she could not stop herself from putting the call through.

The voice she wanted to hear answered on the third ring.

"Vera, is that you?" Joan's voice flooded over the line.

"Yes." Vera sank down to the kitchen floor, tears pulling at her eyes. "Roger's away...he's not home tonight...I..."

"Oh, darling. Oh, I can't believe what happened. Are you all right?" Joan's concern was a solace.

Vera sniffed, reaching for the ashtray on the counter. "No."

"I wish I could...I...I feel sick about it..."

"Their grandparents came this evening. I guess they'll go to stay with them...but I...oh, they were so upset." Vera wiped at her cheeks as she smoked her cigarette.

"It was very kind of you to put them up like you did."

"There wasn't another choice. I couldn't just leave them there. She was my friend." Vera choked on her tears. "I can't believe...my God."

"It's all right. It's all right." Joan whispered.

"Is it?" Vera drank back the wine.

Joan did not respond.

Vera listened as Joan exhaled on the other end of the phone.

She was smoking too.

The thought aroused Vera.

"I can't stop thinking about you." Vera whispered.

Joan hummed on the other end.

"What are you doing?" Vera desperately needed to know.

Joan lightly chuckled. "What do you mean? Like right this minute?"

"Yes." Vera responded soberly.

"I'm sitting on the couch with Lulu."

Vera could picture it all. A fire glowing dim in the fireplace, Joan with her hair undone, wearing plaid pajamas, smoking a cigarette, Lulu curled into her side. It was so real to her that if she closed her eyes she could feel herself there, curled on the other end of the couch.

Vera leaned her head back against the wall, blowing a stream of smoke toward the ceiling.

"You frighten me." Joan's voice was hardly above a whisper.

"Why is that?" Vera pressed the receiver closer to her mouth.

"I'm losing my reason."

Vera laughed. "It's not as bad as all of that."

"No." Joan agreed. "Far from it."

And they sat in silence, knowing.

"It's not as if you're innocent in all of it." Vera spoke, lighting a cigarette with the end of her burning one.

"I didn't say I was." Joan laughed again.

"How did you know?"

"How did I...well, you have no idea how you looked at me that day at church."

"You were the most beautiful woman I'd ever seen." Vera smiled; the image seared in her mind.

Joan tutted at that.

"I wanted to know you. I still want to know. Everything." Vera held the phone close, cradling it like a lover against her cheek.

"Everything? Well, that might take more than tonight." Joan deferred.

"Have there been others?" Vera asked forwardly.

"Others? Oh, here and there. I did live with a woman in the city. It was very much like a marriage, I suppose. We were both teachers and had to be very careful."

"What happened?"

"My father. He got himself into an accident and lost the use of his arm. When I came back to take care of him, she stayed in the city and that was that." Joan said shortly.

"She didn't want to be with you?"

"Of course she did, but she didn't want to leave the city and come to a small town where it would have been worse for the both of us."

Vera felt both sad and jealous. That Joan had lived with a woman, had shared such small intimacies with someone else before.

"And you..." Joan asked gently. "I hadn't expected you..."

"Ah, you thought I hadn't a clue. Would you have preferred it that way?" Vera twirled the cord of the phone in her fingers.

Joan shifted on the other end. "No, it was very...attractive. Just unexpected."

"I suppose I've always had an interest. In college I had crushes on other girls, professors, house mothers...but I never acted upon it until - " Vera tapped off her cigarette, remembering it all as she so often tried not to. "I was twenty-six. Roger's work had a summer business retreat in the Berkshires. We took Emma; she was three at the time. There was another wife there, several years my senior. She took an interest in me, and we ended up rolling around together while Emma was napping and our husbands were working, or doing God knows what."

Joan's breathing was audible on the other end of the phone.

"I saw her a few years ago at a Christmas party. She acted like she didn't even know me." Vera brought the cigarette to her lips to inhale deeply.

"It's a shame." Joan sighed. "Always having to hide."

"I wish..."

"I know."

Vera put out her cigarette, dizzy from the smoke. She coughed. "I haven't felt this way before. About anyone."

Joan inhaled shakily. "Nor I."

Vera smiled at that.

Chapter Twenty-Six

She'd smoked too much, was down to nearly her last cigarette that morning, so after she dropped off the children, she drove to the drug store on the corner for a fresh carton. She browsed the shelves, picking up a new bottle of aspirin and some vitamins for the kids.

There was a rack of little books with tawdry covers. She had seen them before but had never dared to pick one up.

It was, however, the image on a cover of two women that caught her eye.

One woman stood smoking, her hand on the other who sat on a couch before her.

A tension between them.

Vera looked around her.

There was an older gentleman who had walked in and was taking a seat at the counter.

The soda jerk dipped his head at the man and did not seem to pay Vera any mind.

There was a woman picking up her medicine at the pharmacy counter; the pharmacist in his white coat gave the woman a quick smile and friendly welcome.

They also paid her no mind.

Vera's finger skimmed the corner of the book, cheeks warming.

Her curiosity won out.

She plucked the book from the shelf and blindly reached for another, as if to hide it.

She took the items to the counter calmly. A woman in a white coat stood at the register.

"And a carton of Chesterfields." She spoke evenly.

"Well aren't you glowing?" The woman smiled fondly at her. 'Doris' her name tag read.

Vera warmed at the compliment, clutching the books against her chest.

"How far along are you?"

"Oh," Vera smoothed a hand over her dress. The bump was visible now. There would be no hiding it. "Four months." She spoke as she laid the items on the counter, trying not to look at the books as she did so.

"It's very exciting. Is it your first?" The woman continued on, and Vera realized her luck as the woman was far too distracted by her to care what it was she was ringing up.

"No. I have a daughter and a son." She explained.

"It will be a full house then." Doris winked as she placed her items into a brown paper bag. "That will be $4.35."

Vera fumbled with her pocketbook, thrilled to have gotten away with it. She handed over the bills and tucked the brown paper bag beneath her arm, pulling her jacket tighter about herself as she left the store.

She drove home without delay.

She carried the bag inside, settling it atop the dirty counter.

There was breakfast to clean up from.

The book sat at the bottom of the bag, tempting her.

She went to work, putting the carton of cigarettes in the

fridge, the aspirin and vitamins away in the medicine cabinet, washing up the dishes, loading them into the dishwasher, wiping down the table, the counters, mopping the floor. It was the day she should wash the windows. She inwardly groaned and made quick work of it.

As she stood at the front window wiping it, she gazed across the street.

There was Kitty's home.

Or was it really her home anymore?

Vera thought to ask about the address of where she was staying so she might write to her. But who would she ask?

John had put the house up for sale.

It looked forlorn and gloomy.

It made her feel sick.

She stood back from the window.

It was crystal clear.

She put away the cleaning supplies and went for the book.

She had hidden the books in a top drawer in the kitchen, in case Louise or Judy were to stop by.

She glanced at the cover of the other novel she'd chosen at random and found a young male gazing at a salacious woman.

She took both into the living room and sank onto the couch, pulling her feet up as she tossed the male covered book onto the table and held onto the one with two women.

She became absorbed in the story, feeling warm and liquid as she read. A familiar pull in her chest, a hunger rising in her.

Until the phone began to ring.

She nearly dropped the book like a hot frying pan, startled at the noise.

She left it folded open atop the couch and got up to answer the ringing device, warm between her legs.

"Hello?"

"Vera, dear, I hardly hear from you."

Vera had not expected to hear the voice on the other end, feeling the way she was feeling. "Mother, what a surprise."

"Well, if I didn't call you, I don't think I would ever hear from you."

"We spoke a week ago." Vera reached for her pack of cigarettes.

"It's not enough, you know. Vivian's daughter calls her every day."

"It sounds like they're too dependent on one another. They always have been."

"You were friends with her daughter once."

"Yes, mother. But she lives in Vermont now." Vera sighed, bored already, itching to get back to the story in the other room.

"You could still call her up."

"Is there something you need, Mother?" Vera pressed.

"I can't just call my daughter and ask about her day? You are peculiar, you know. Always have been."

Vera sighed.

"Well, tell me how are things? The children..."

"Are just fine. At school."

"I'm so anxious to see them for Thanksgiving. It's been far too long." Oh, Vera had tried to forget about Thanksgiving. "They're enjoying the new house?"

"I suppose so."

"You know you are very lucky."

"Why?" Vera blew a cloud of smoke before her face.

"Why? You have that brand-new house and you sound morose about it."

"It's quite a bit to manage."

"Manage! It seems as if you wish you'd stayed in that little cramped apartment in the city."

She did.

"What is there to manage, dear? You have a dishwasher

and a washing machine. Your father won't even consider putting in a dishwasher for poor Cora, and you know we have the money." Her mother went on and on about inane and idle things, Vera smoking while leaning over, forehead pressed against her hand, elbows on the counter. She made vague agreements.

"And I hope you aren't still smoking. It's very unattractive, Vera."

Vera rolled her eyes, head beginning to throb. "Mother, I have to start dinner."

They finally hung up, and Vera realized time had slipped by far too quickly. The book that was flattened on the couch would have to be taken up later.

At least the pulse between her legs had abated while speaking with her mother.

She took care to hide the book beneath the box spring mattress on her side of the bed.

When she went to pick up the children, however, she saw Joan standing outside speaking to another teacher. Her pulse quickened and she felt a foolish need to touch the woman, to press their lips together, to feel her trembling in her arms again. It was such a violent need that her fingernails left little half-moon markings in her palms from clenching them too tightly.

"Mommy, can we have ice cream after dinner?" Henry was asking as he got into the back seat of the car and Vera was deaf to him.

Joan glanced at her.

Their eyes met.

Joan smiled at her, let her fingers lift in a gentle wave.

Vera drove away from the school, face burning. It was two more days until the next auxiliary meeting, and it might as well have been a lifetime.

Chapter Twenty-Seven

She could feel the rapid beat of her heart as she stood beside Joan.

They were alone as they had not been for the past excruciating hour.

Joan placed the last dried teacup back into the cabinet.

Vera could hardly breathe.

Joan's hand fell about her wrist, clasping it, turning her about to face her. "My goodness, you're tightly wound."

"Well." Vera huffed.

"Come." Joan led her by the hand out of the kitchen, back through the meeting room, up some dark stairs, emerging out into the annex, and across to the church library.

Joan did not turn on the overhead lights.

It was only the light from the parking lot that filtered in through stained-glass windows, rainbow colored light illuminating the center of the room. There were two cushioned benches at either end, tucked away between bookshelves. Joan led her to one.

"I never thought I'd be doing this in a church." Joan whispered, taking Vera in her arms.

"I don't care." Vera stated, impatient.

Their lips crushed together, Joan's arms about her, intoxicating.

Joan was undoing the buttons on her dress, her fingers soft and imploring against her skin.

Vera ripped open Joan's blouse through fevered kisses. A button popped off, rolling away beneath a bookcase. Neither noticed nor cared as Joan guided them down to the pillowy top of the hard bench.

Vera wanted Joan's hand between her legs, to ease the dull ache that had been drumming there since the last time. She pulled Joan toward her, dress forgotten on the ground, Joan's exposed chest and stomach pressing against her own bare stomach. Skin against skin.

But it was not enough with pesky bras and Joan's skirt still about her waist.

Vera wanted to rip it all off, but there wasn't time. Never enough time.

Joan's deft touch left her breathless, wanting when fingers finally caressed her. She groaned in the quiet library, lips seeking Joan's, pulling her impossibly near as her body was overcome with sensations. For a while it was all too much, and she wasn't sure she could abate the need, so overwhelmed by it - but Joan struck just the right place and Vera felt herself falling.

She grasped at Joan, sighing contentedly, panting, body quivering at the force of it.

Joan held her, pressing her close against her neck until it washed over her.

She had hoped it would quell the dull persistent ache of the past days, but it only served to make it worse.

Joan seemed to sense this, holding her close. "There will be time."

"When?" Vera's voice shook.

"We'll find it, but we can't stay here too long." Joan kissed her again for good measure and sat up to straighten herself out.

Vera could hardly move, did not want to move, but Joan insisted, helping her back into her dress.

Vera put an arm around Joan, not wanting to be far away from her just then, as they walked back to the basement meeting room. She lit a cigarette, sitting perched atop the table before Joan, who sat in a chair before her. She leaned forward and shot gunned smoke between Joan's lips, before kissing her.

Joan took the cigarette from her, smoking at it as she adjusted her shirt. "Why are you so glum tonight?"

"I'm not glum," Vera toyed with the missing buttonhole on Joan's shirt. "It's just hell waiting to be with you again."

Joan laughed, blowing smoke before placing the cigarette between Vera's lips. "How do you think I feel?" And her hand went up Vera's skirt to rest on her thigh. The sensation was heavenly.

Vera gave her a sad smile as she puffed at the cigarette. "I bought a book."

"A book?" Joan's eyebrow rose at that.

"Yes, one of those cheap drugstore books." Vera let her finger trail down Joan's strong jaw line, kissing her again.

"A lesbian pulp novel?" Joan ventured to guess.

Vera nodded, tracing the outline of Joan's breast. Joan allowed it and Vera found it pleasing. "Yes. A lesbian one."

Joan took the cigarette. "Did you like it?"

Vera tilted her head to the side, "at first. But it was rather depressing."

Joan laughed. "They all either die, go for a man, or go insane, don't they?"

"How did you…"

"Oh," Joan squeezed her thigh. "Darling, those books are nothing but a man's fantasy. If you're a woman reading them you must read between the lines and know where the real story ends. I have a friend in the city who writes those, you know. They're heavily censored as to what they can and can't say."

Vera looked at her with big, wide eyes. "So not every lesbian hates herself?"

Joan laughed again. "Oh, no, not every lesbian hates herself. Perhaps because of how society views her, but I know very many wonderful, happy people who love someone of the same gender."

"And it doesn't all implode in the end?"

Joan looked at her with a sad little smile. "Well, I suppose that depends on the people involved."

Vera was overcome with foolish tears then. She leaned forward, wrapping herself around Joan. "I don't want it to end."

Joan held her close. "It's getting late." She kissed away Vera's tears.

"I hate going home to him." Vera whispered as she wiped at her eyes, getting out her compact to try and salvage her appearance.

Joan put out the cigarette in the teacup saucer, her hand removed from where it rested beneath Vera's dress, and she missed the touch terribly. "Believe me, it's no walk in the park for me, either."

"Oh." Vera felt as if she could cry again.

"You must get home, darling." Joan stopped her with a kiss then helped her to reapply her lipstick.

Roger was watching television and the children were running amok when she made it back that evening.

"You're awfully late." He said without looking at her, lifting a tumbler to his lips.

She felt her cheeks redden so that she had to turn from him. "The meeting went late. There's a fundraiser in the coming week..."

Henry came whizzing past her, nearly knocking into her. She grabbed him up. "You should be asleep, Henry."

"Daddy said we could stay up until you got back."

Or rather Roger hadn't wanted to be bothered with the children.

Vera took Henry by the hand and settled him down to sleep. She went to check on Emma and found her draped across her bed atop a paperback book. She pulled it from beneath her and tucked her in, kissing her forehead. The girl stirred, looked up at Vera and smiled, then drifted off again.

Vera went back down the stairs. Roger was watching her out of the corner of his eye.

She went into the kitchen to pour herself a glass of wine and light a cigarette.

She loosened her too tight dress and began cleaning the kitchen, trying desperately to not think about what had happened only moments before. Joan buried inside of her, touching her.

Roger had come up behind her. He put his arms about her, nuzzling her neck with his scratchy chin. He smelled of liquor.

"Roger," she whispered, wanting to slip into a steaming hot shower before he touched her.

"Let me have you." Roger whispered.

She wanted to claw at him, to scream, but she could only submit to him. She let him take her up to bed where he was enthralled by how ready she was for him.

But it wasn't for him, and it would never be for him again.

Chapter Twenty-Eight

Henry had been invited to Mitch's birthday party that Sunday, and Vera had forgotten to get him a present.

Perhaps there had been time that week, but it had dwindled and Saturday morning arrived all too quickly.

It was a simple enough premise.

Vera sat smoking at the breakfast table, having been ill that morning.

She folded her hands together, looking from Henry to Emma eating pancakes, to Roger absorbed in the newspaper, mindlessly eating bacon and sipping coffee.

"I'm going to run out to the store." She announced, tapping off her cigarette.

The corner of Roger's newspaper descended. He was looking at her. "What for?"

"A present. Henry has a birthday party to attend tomorrow. Judy and Phil's younger son."

Roger huffed at this. "Take him along then."

"No," Vera blew a stream of smoke as she crushed out her

cigarette. The children were watching her. "No, it will be easier if I go alone."

Roger shrugged and went back to his paper.

Henry whined that he wanted to go with her after Roger's insistence, but she wrapped herself up in her coat and told him that she would bring him home a surprise if he'd stay and be good for his father.

She stole away with the car.

She smoked herself dizzy as she turned the car away from the small downtown with shops, and toward the outskirts of town in the opposite direction.

She watched behind her, fearful someone might see. But the streets were barren.

The familiar driveway appeared and she turned in.

She hadn't a clue if anyone would be there, but it was an earnest need that consumed her. She could always leave and wait it out the few more days, but she had to know...

Her car came to a stop and she killed the ignition, feeling bolder than ever before. She got out, crushing the cigarette beneath her heel.

The door opened.

Joan appeared, white button-up shirt, hair loosely about her face, black-rimmed glasses slipping down her nose.

Vera leaned against the hood of her car.

Lulu came racing out, meowing excitedly.

She scooped the cat up into her arms, burying her face in the soft fur as she walked forward.

"It's chilly out today." Joan called out as she approached.

"Yes." Vera simply nodded, coming to stand before Joan on the porch.

"Get inside." Joan held the door open, pulling her in.

Vera allowed herself to be maneuvered, Lulu jumping from her arms and then Vera was in Joan's arms.

A fire was blazing in the fireplace, papers scattered over the coffee table. It smelled of pine and cinnamon.

Joan removed her glasses and their lips met.

"What are you doing here?" Joan whispered.

"I'm out shopping for a birthday present." Vera replied between kisses, hands sneaking their way beneath Joan's shirt.

"I see." Joan smiled, flattered.

"I have to be with you."

"You have to?" Joan laughed, but led Vera up the stairs to her bedroom.

Vera's coat was abandoned on the stairwell, shoes kicked off in the hallway. She managed to get Joan out of her shirt once they were inside the room. She sent it flying into a corner. "I have to." Vera insisted, helping Joan to undress her, the two of them ridding her of her dress, her tights, her slip. She sat on the bed and unbuttoned Joan's pants, pushing them to the ground.

She wanted to feel Joan desperately.

Joan was glorious. Her body tight and taut and muscular. Vera pulled off Joan's bra, hands roaming over her breasts in praise, mouth pressed to a nipple as Joan let her hands caress and hold at her shoulders. She pressed Joan's undergarments to the ground, pulling her onto the bed with her as she rid herself of her own underthings.

Their bodies melted together, skin against skin.

Vera was burning wild and hot.

Joan's hand was between her legs, easing the ache.

They tumbled into one another, Vera intoxicated by the fantasy turned reality. Joan before her, Joan within her grasp, the wetness between Joan's legs, the way she smelled when she pressed her nose to the nape of her neck, the feel of her nipples hard in her hands, the taste of her on her lips.

She devoured Joan, consumed her with unbridled want

and Joan gave to her beautifully, allowing anything she wanted.

Exhausted, she watched as Joan lifted a pack of cigarettes from her bedside table and lit one, taking a puff before passing it off to her. She was still entangled with Joan's body, so that she kissed her exposed skin reverently, pausing only to smoke.

"Darling," Joan stroked her hair from her wet cheek.

"Hmm?" Vera's mind was cloudy.

"How long did you say you would be?"

"I didn't say." Vera let her hand wander between Joan's thighs and then back again. Never wanting to leave.

"God," Joan sighed as Vera trailed her fingers over her sternum.

"Don't make me go." Vera kissed Joan's stomach.

Joan groaned and twisted away from Vera. "Don't make this hard."

They dressed in relative silence. Joan fixed Vera's hair back into its curl.

Vera went into the bathroom to relieve herself, to reapply her lipstick with a shaky hand.

Joan walked her back down the stairs, reaching for Vera's coat as they went. Vera stared longingly at Lulu stretched out on the couch near the fire as Joan helped her into the coat.

The cat lifted her head lazily and smiled at Vera.

Vera pressed herself into Joan's arms.

It was the worst pain to part like this. Horrible, pain.

To get back into her car, to go back into town, to blindly purchase a present and two lollipops, and then to return home.

Roger was raking leaves in the yard and looked at her as she got out of the car.

"Did you go a town over to find something?" He asked her.

"No, I ran into someone in town." Vera said coolly. "I'll make some lunch." And she went inside to find Henry sitting quietly before the television and Emma off in her room.

Henry raced to Vera when she walked in. "Mommy, mommy! I was really good. I promise."

She hugged him close to her body and pulled out a lollipop from her purse.

His eyes enlarged at the treat and he happily took it as he went back to watching television.

Vera found Emma writing at her desk when she lightly pressed her door open. The girl closed her diary and looked up wide-eyed and frightened at her mother.

Vera wanted to know what she was writing.

"I brought you something." And she held up the other lollipop.

The girl took it from her and thanked her shyly.

"Are you all right, baby?" Vera looked at the girl.

Emma nodded.

"I'll make lunch. You come down soon."

Emma smiled shyly at Vera as she went.

She made lunch for her family. She watched them eat, picking at her food as she smoked. She caught Emma eyeing her surreptitiously as she ate.

The day progressed uneventfully. Roger watched a game and got drunk off beer. She knew he wouldn't bother her that night.

She put the children to bed, she cleaned the rest of the kitchen, she peered in at Roger dozing off in the living room.

She closed herself away in the bathroom and drew herself a bath.

She let her eyes close, images from the morning returning to her so vividly she could feel Joan there with her.

The water went cold.

She got out and put on her pajamas and went to peek in at Henry and then turned toward Emma's room.

Emma was a sound sleeper. She could hear her breathing evenly outside the door before she looked in.

Vera tiptoed inside her room and quietly rummaged through the top drawer of her desk. She found the diary on the right hand side.

She lifted it and closed the drawer, stealing out of the room without her daughter even stirring.

Across the hall, she lit a cigarette and settled atop her bed, opening the diary.

Emma was astute. Perhaps more astute than she had imagined.

"...it's different here. It's so quiet...I don't feel like the other girls. They're so pretty...They all know one another..." Observations about the neighborhood, the children, her teachers, her classes at the new school, the scary woods, the darkness at night.

And then the words she had feared.

"Mommy doesn't like it here. I can tell...She looks so sad sometimes...I don't think she likes Daddy. Sometimes I don't like Daddy either...I wish I could make her happy..."

Vera wiped at her cheek, tapped off ash, and brought the cigarette to her lips.

"She looked happy the other day when she came home. She was smiling. Until Daddy said something to her. She's so beautiful when she smiles."

Roger stumbled into the bedroom.

He looked at her and then went into the bathroom.

She closed the diary and put out her cigarette.

She got up and went back across the hall.

Emma was still asleep.

Vera opened the drawer and returned the notebook to its rightful place.

Emma turned in her sleep.

Vera settled at the edge of her bed, brushing her light brown hair from her face.

She was overcome with an awful surge of affection for the

girl. How Emma had no idea how she had ruined her life and yet she loved her despite it all.

Emma's eyes opened and she looked startled at Vera's presence.

Vera realized she was crying.

She buried her face in Emma's pillow and wrapped the girl up in her arms. Holding her close.

Chapter Twenty-Nine

The three rows of pews that separated Vera from Joan seemed as vast as the Pacific Ocean.

She heard nothing of the good word spoken from the pulpit.

She was inside Joan's room, in a world far removed from the sanctuary. Naked bodies and sweaty skin and swollen lips and hours of time, of nothing but time.

Afterward, she watched Joan furtively as she greeted her fellow congregants. Their eyes met briefly, before Vera watched Joan disappear into a corridor.

Vera told Roger she had to use the restroom.

There was a stairwell.

Vera slid inside and found Joan pressed against the wall.

She looked at her through wide, dark eyes.

"Your eyes could burn a building down." Joan said.

Vera couldn't help the slow smile that came to her lips.

Her hand reached out to wrap about Joan, to pull her close.

"We have to be careful." Joan warned as she allowed Vera a kiss.

"Aren't we always?" Vera hummed boredly.

"I wouldn't say always...not with a stunt like you pulled yesterday." Joan smiled at her as she caressed her arm.

"I don't know how else we accomplish it. You're busy when I'm free. And one night a week isn't enough for me."

Joan laughed. "I know." She sobered. "I know."

"I want to go away, I want to...I want to be far away from here." Vera ran her fingers over Joan's waist.

"Darling," Joan examined her. "Are you all right?"

Vera shook her head, trying to stop the tears from falling.

Her family was only a wall away. She had only a few precious seconds. "I'm fine. It's this...awful pregnancy." She took a deep breath to steal herself.

It had not been like this the past two times. But as the awful doctor downtown had mentioned, it was different the older a woman was.

"Is the baby okay?" Joan reached for her arm.

"Yes. I just wish..."

Joan kissed her. "I do, too."

Vera's stomach knotted at the impossibility of their situation, of the days that would stretch out unendingly before she could see Joan again.

Joan fixed her lipstick then shoved her out of the stairwell.

Vera lit a cigarette outside the church.

Roger and the children found her there.

Joan appeared, shaking Reverend Johns' hand in the doorway. She looked at Vera as she walked down the steps and Vera's heart pounded in her ears.

Roger turned as Joan descended the steps. He saw her.

It seemed inevitable that they should collide like this.

Joan smiled at Vera, friendly, aloof. "I look forward to the auxiliary meeting, Vera. It will be so nice to have an update on the fundraiser."

"Yes, it's coming along." Vera tried to smile, unable to look at Joan, so that she turned to her husband. "Roger, you know Joan? Joan DeBoer?"

Roger extended his hand and she watched as Joan's slender hand was taken into his rough one. "You must be the one I lose my wife to once a week."

Vera puffed at her cigarette.

Joan smiled warmly, not at all perturbed. "She's quite an asset to the church, I must say."

Vera found she was holding her breath.

He did not seem to place any importance upon meeting Joan and it irritated Vera.

He wanted to leave.

"I must be going, but it was nice to meet you." Joan spoke cordially.

Vera did not dare look her directly in the eyes as she said her goodbyes.

Joan walked away and Vera wanted to cry.

They drove home.

Vera made lunch then walked with Henry to Judy's house. Judy had asked her to come help set up the decorations. The success of the Fall Festival seemed to haunt her now.

Judy was relieved to see her and put her to work twisting and hanging crepe ribbons.

It was as she was standing on a step-stool, dangling in mid-air, that she felt a terrible pain in her abdomen, a horrible punch in the gut.

She staggered in pain, reaching for a nearby wall, stepping down from the stool.

Judy was at her side. "What is it?"

"I just...I need to sit down." Vera apologized.

Judy brought her a glass of water.

She lit a cigarette.

After a while the pain subsided. She apologized and

assured Judy she was just fine. She took up the task of opening lanterns and passing them to Judy.

The children came at two.

They raced about the house, wild and reckless.

Vera did her best to help Judy calm them into games.

But when it was time for cake, the pain came again.

Catastrophic pain. Unlike anything she'd ever felt before.

Judy told her to go lay down in her bed.

She was miserable, smoking cigarette after cigarette until the pain passed.

She was being ridiculous, she decided. It was only the baby shifting, perhaps. Nothing more.

But when she stood up to relieve herself, she felt a mess of liquid rush from between her legs.

She froze, afraid of what was happening.

It was too soon. Far too soon to be going into labor.

She dragged herself to the bathroom and cleaned herself up, the pain persistent.

When Judy came to knock on the bathroom door, to ask if she was all right, she could barely respond.

She managed to open the door for Judy and Judy immediately saw something was wrong.

It was all a blur after that.

Roger appeared.

He took her in their car.

There was the clean white, sterile hospital, the lights racing by on the ceiling.

The pain of labor, a doctor telling her she was doing well, that she should not worry.

And then after the pain had passed, there was silence.

Vera passed out, perhaps from the pain and shock of it or because of the drugs they had given to her.

Later - minutes, days, years later, she could not be certain - she awoke in a quiet, dark room.

Roger was in the corner.

His face unrecognizable.

He saw she was awake and he stood, unsteady on his feet.

He reached blindly for her hand.

When he came closer she saw the tears in his eyes.

"What...what happened?" She whispered, already knowing.

Roger shook his head.

There was the beeping of a machine.

"He didn't make it."

Chapter Thirty

The curtains were yellow.

She stared at them through thick clouds of smoke.

They kept the cigarettes well supplied and a doctor came to check her once in the morning and once in the afternoon.

It was the pain of labor without the result.

She had not seen the baby, but they had told her it was a boy.

Roger had not come back to see her again.

When she'd called home the previous day, Roger's mother had answered the phone and curtly informed her she was taking care of things and Roger was not home.

Vera leaned her head back against the pillow and exhaled a cloud of smoke to the ceiling. She watched it dissipate into thin air.

She was terribly bored, but they had insisted she stay for the week to heal.

She did not know if her parents had been informed. She hadn't even told her mother she was pregnant. She had planned to when she'd come for Thanksgiving. Vera wouldn't have been able to hide it then, but now…

She was confused by the relief and despair she felt. Both coming in waves. Crushing her and then freeing her with the realization.

She felt dirty in the hospital bed, despite the nurses coming to help wash and change her daily. There were residual cramps. She bled still. And the worst of it was that her breasts had swollen with milk. They ached. A nurse gave her a cold compress to help with the pain, but it did little to help with the feeling of fullness that only a baby could relieve.

When she closed her eyes, she imagined Joan's lips at her breasts, sucking at the milk.

The thought aroused her terribly, but the discomfort between her legs discouraged her from acting upon the impulse.

She longed for a drink, anything to take the edge off.

She had no idea what time of the day it was. She could not see out of a window and the lights remained constantly dim.

She smoked and fell asleep, then awoke coughing and reaching for her cigarettes, then a nurse would come to check on her, and then she would drift off to sleep again. It was a horribly mundane routine.

She longed to stand up, to move of her own accord again.

She had been dozing when she heard a commotion outside the curtains.

Her eyes came slowly open, and she was startled at the presence that appeared before her.

Joan.

Joan in the flesh.

"Joan." Vera hoarsely whispered, not trusting the veracity of the presence.

Joan was holding flowers, her smile betraying her concern

and discomfort. "How are you?" She looked as if she wanted to reach out but held herself rigid.

"Terribly bored and terribly uncomfortable, but better because you're here." Vera eased herself up in the bed, Joan's hand reaching out to assist her. The contact was warm and comforting, and she didn't want her to take her hand away.

But the contact was brief.

Joan stepped away, placing the flowers on the bedside table as Vera lit a cigarette.

Joan was looking her over, as if seeking something out within her.

Vera did not like the scrutiny. She wanted her to look at her as she always did. "How did you know?"

Joan sighed, "You know Judy's older son is in my class. I overheard him whispering to his friends about Henry's mother being taken to the hospital at his brother's birthday party."

"Oh God," Vera groaned. "Emma will be mortified."

"I put an end to it. Don't you worry." Joan assured. "Emma's just fine. She misses you." Joan's hand reached out to stroke Vera's forehead.

No one was around.

Vera took Joan's hand in her own.

Vera wanted to grasp her and press their lips together, but it would be far too risky. The nurses always in and out.

Their eyes danced together. The thought coming and then going again.

Joan straightened.

Vera smoked to busy her lips.

"I would have come sooner, but I wasn't sure if you would want me..."

"Of course I do." Vera spoke firmly, tapping off ash. "Roger hasn't been here since..." She smoked irritably. "He probably blames me."

"How could he?" Joan looked at her incredulously.

"He knew I didn't want another child." Vera whispered.

"You didn't do this on purpose." Joan's response was firm.

She hadn't?

Vera played with her fingernail. The polish was chipped. She picked at it. "It was a boy."

Joan patted her leg.

Joan stayed with her until a nurse came to let them know visiting hours were over.

They could not say a proper goodbye, the nurse lingering.

Joan left.

Vera cried like a child, emotions all haywire and confused, unable to keep anything in. The nurses gave her an extra dose of medicine and she slept without dreams throughout the night.

They released her on Sunday.

Roger came to take her home.

His mother was there with the children, who rushed to her.

"Be careful, be careful with your mother. She's only just come from the hospital." Eileen cautioned, but Vera swept the children up in her arms atop the couch and held them close.

"I'm all right." She insisted, kissing Emma's sweet-smelling head, holding Henry close even though he pressed roughly against her sensitive chest. "Oh, I've missed you both."

They gave her cards they had made and Eileen served them all dinner and even cleaned up afterward.

Vera put the children to bed and then, with dread, returned to help Eileen in the spotless kitchen. She could tell everything had been reorganized according to her mother-in-law's specifications and it all shined in the overhead light.

"Thank you, for helping." Vera said as she dried a pot.

"It's the least I could do." Eileen spoke with a stiff upper lip.

They finished cleaning the kitchen in silence.

"I'll be leaving tomorrow morning. I expect you can handle it from here." Eileen announced.

Vera nodded. "Yes, thank you."

Eileen paused before she left the kitchen. She turned only halfway back around. "I am very sorry about what happened." The words sounded difficult to enunciate.

"Thank you." Vera whispered and felt a terrible weight on her chest. That everyone would pity her now.

She watched Eileen descend the stairs to the guest room.

She lit a cigarette and walked into the living room where Roger was watching television.

He did not look at her.

She left him, moving up the stairs to their bedroom. She closed herself in the bathroom and drew a bath, happy to be able to move about freely, to do as she needed. She sank into warm, perfumed water and let it cleanse her aching body.

She brushed her teeth, eyes catching at her rounded stomach.

She felt a horrible emptiness consume her.

She tried to lay in bed, she tried to sleep, but she was restless.

Roger came to bed a few hours later. He did not say much to her.

She laid smoking, listening for his breathing to even out, before she slipped from the bed.

She moved to the living room quietly, uncapping the bourbon to pour herself a glass. She drank it while standing at the window, staring out at the desolate street.

She liked the way it made her feel. Loose and warm.

It all wasn't so terrible after the first drink.

She poured herself another and roamed about the house like a ghost.

A third glass and she sprawled out on the couch, blowing smoke rings to the ceiling, dizzy and elated.

"Mommy." The little voice frightened her; she nearly dropped her cigarette.

She looked up to find Emma at the bottom of the stairs watching her.

Everything seemed a bit sideways as she tried to sit up. She was certainly drunk.

"Come here, baby." She slurred as she crushed out her cigarette.

Emma approached her cautiously.

She held out her arms and the girl folded herself into her, pressing her face into her shoulder. "Are you okay, Mommy?"

"I'm okay, baby. I'm okay." She kissed her daughter's forehead and held her close, not sure whose tears dampened her cheeks.

Chapter Thirty-One

Her parents arrived from Boston Wednesday evening.

She had been drinking steadily throughout the day.

Joan had called her briefly at four thirty to let her know she was going away, but would be reachable at such and such number.

Vera had jotted it down on a piece of paper and shoved it into the pocket of her handbag where no one would think to look for anything.

They had hardly a second to speak to one another, but Joan had told her she would miss her terribly, and it had brightened her dismal mood for the briefest of seconds.

She picked Roger up at the train station at five and he seemed in a nasty mood. Upset with her from the minute he got into the car.

Her parents arrived promptly at six, cordially greeting her.

Her mother marveled at the home. "How very modern." She mused, going up the stairs.

Emma and Henry were washed and done up in their finest

for the grandparents. Neither seemed to recognize Vera's parents, but she nodded for them to give their grandmother a hug and saw her mother enjoyed the show of affection tremendously. "Why it's been far too long since I've seen you." She pinched Henry's cheek and he giggled.

Her father and Roger shook hands and started up a conversation Vera was pointedly excluded from. Roger went out to help her father bring in their overnight bags.

Her mother took off her coat and Vera hung it in the coat closet. "Well, shall I help with dinner? I'm famished. Your father never wants to stop on the way."

"It's nearly ready." Vera said, as she led her mother into the kitchen, sending the children to wash up for dinner.

She lit a cigarette and felt her mother's disapproving gaze upon her. They were alone now. Her mother could see her up close. "You look exhausted, dear."

She puffed at the cigarette. "I haven't been sleeping." She said, daring her mother to find fault in her.

"No," her mother chose to ignore her cigarette smoking. "No, I wouldn't suppose you have been. It's terrible what happened."

Vera leaned against the counter, studying her mother.

She was hardly older than Joan, Vera realized.

They heard the men enter the house again.

"Shall we get dinner out, then?" Her mother offered her assistance and in no time they were seated about the table.

Vera poured the wine freely. Roger watched her drink over his dinner.

She smoked feverishly, as if needing to prove something. Her father turned a disapproving eye, but as he had ignored her for all those years before, he continued to ignore her then. Addressing Roger about work matters, things only men were supposed to know about, but Vera understood.

Afterward, her mother helped her clean up the kitchen.

Vera could tell she wanted to speak candidly to her, that she wanted to be a confidant, but Vera was being held together by a fine thread. The slightest thing could unravel her and, thankfully, her mother did not needle in the way she so often did.

Vera took the children up to bed, too sloshed to carry Henry so that she held his hand. She read him a story and kissed him goodnight, and then went to Emma.

Emma wrapped her arms about Vera and held her tight.

It was not until the girl fell asleep that Vera could tear herself away.

She descended the stairs into the living room where her parents and Roger sat watching the television.

She poured herself a drink from the minibar and sat beside her mother on the carpet and smoked until the end of the nightly news.

"We should be going to bed." Her father said. And her mother stood with him.

Vera saw them off to the basement steps, allowing her mother to give her a lingering kiss on the cheek.

She went upstairs after Roger.

The only consolation was that she had been instructed not to have sex while she healed. Roger, however, was on edge. She could sense it.

She went into the bathroom to conduct her nightly routine and when she returned, she found Roger sitting on the edge of the bed touching himself over his pajamas and looking at her.

She stopped cold in her tracks, surprised by him.

It was as if she owed this to him. For losing the baby, for having her parents come to stay with them, for any other number of things he felt towards her.

She wanted another drink before she did this.

She went toward her side of the bed for her hand lotion, but he grabbed her about the wrist before she could get it and pulled her before him. He held her tight, forcing her to her knees.

She gave what he wanted – his hands pressing her head down so she could hardly breathe, her gag reflexes flaring up when he came inside of her mouth.

He released her and she staggered backward, knees tired, face hot and moist. She pulled herself up using the side of the bed and fled to the bathroom, shutting the door behind her. She opened the toilet lid and started spitting until the thought of it made her vomit.

She stood, pale and listless, staring in the mirror as she brushed her teeth.

She felt shame creep across her skin.

When she came out of the bathroom, the lights were off and Roger was asleep in the bed.

She could not bear to be near him.

She went to the living room and poured herself a drink to wash it all away. She sat on the couch and lit a cigarette.

She thought of Joan – Joan who would be miles away from her now.

She thought of the phone number buried deep in her purse.

But it would be too risky. Someone could get on the line, someone could hear.

She smoked another cigarette and curled herself up on the couch.

When her eyes opened again, her mother was above her, perched on the edge of the couch, stroking Vera's cheek.

Vera startled, coughing until she reached for a cigarette.

Her mother watched her light it as she sipped her coffee.

Vera inhaled the smoke into her lungs, needing it.

Her mother picked up a cup of coffee she had made for her and extended it. She took it gratefully.

"It would be hard for anyone." Her mother spoke in the early morning light. "But you can't wallow in it."

A tear slipped down Vera's cheek.

She wanted, just then, to turn to her mother and embrace her and tell her everything.

A child confessing to a sympathetic parent.

It was not just the loss of the pregnancy, it was a million other things.

But her mother couldn't possibly comprehend the other things.

She wiped furiously at her eyes and smoked.

Her mother pulled her close to her, pressing her lips against her forehead.

"Your father will be up soon expecting his breakfast. Shall we?" Her mother was not one to give in to sadness. Vera had never seen her upset the whole of her childhood, as if she could simply turn it all off. She never let unpleasantness touch her.

It seemed inhuman.

But humiliation clouded her mind when she glanced up and saw Emma at the foot of the stairs, watching her cry.

Was she any better for allowing her children to see her sadness?

"Emma, darling. Come help us in the kitchen." Vera's mother was delighted by the girl's presence.

Her mother took the girl's hand and led her into the kitchen.

Vera stood on unsteady legs and moved soundlessly to the mini-bar. She poured a dash of whiskey into her coffee and then followed her mother and daughter to the kitchen.

Chapter Thirty-Two

Thanksgiving Day was spent in the kitchen.

Her mother forbade her from smoking in the kitchen, so she'd steal away for a smoke and a drink in the basement, away from Roger and her father drinking beer and watching a game on the television in the sitting room.

On her way back up the stairs after a smoke break, she happened upon her father coming from the downstairs restroom.

He looked at her and she was suddenly very sober.

"What's the matter with you?" His calm voice chilled her. "You walk around here like you're the only one who exists, just like when you were a child. You have a family now, girlie. Open your goddamn eyes." And he went up the stairs, leaving her pressed into the wall.

The tears collected in her eyes.

She stood frozen for what felt like ages.

She heard her mother calling for her.

She wiped at her cheeks as she went up the stairs and saw Henry playing atop the upstairs steps. He looked at her and

202

she wished she could wrap him up in her arms and hold him close and let the world fade away around her.

He smiled at her and she had to look away.

She helped her mother find a measuring cup that had been missing and then busied herself with the mashed potatoes.

They ate after the game ended. Far too much food for the six of them. A turkey, stuffing, hot rolls, cranberry sauce, green bean casserole, mashed potatoes, candied yams, a pecan pie, and a blueberry pie.

Vera was not hungry. She picked at the turkey, stirred the mashed potatoes about her plate, plucked at a roll.

She thought of what Joan would be doing, of what she would be eating, of who she would be with. Probably somewhere much better, with more interesting people.

"Vera?" Her mother was asking her something.

She looked up, dazed, confused.

"My goodness, I asked if you could pass the casserole. Henry just loves it." Her mother was looking at her with concern.

Vera lifted the dish but it was still hot and burned her hand. "Damn." She cursed, dropping it back atop the table.

The whole family looked at her.

She couldn't take it. Not a minute longer.

She excused herself from the table, grabbed up her coat and bag, and escaped the house.

She could hear her mother calling out to her from the front door, but she did not listen. She got into the car and drove.

She hadn't a clue where she was going, but she had to get away.

She pulled out of the neighborhood and drove into town. It was shuttered, closed for the holiday, eerily desolate.

She drove on, smoking furiously.

Her hand hurt where she had burnt it.

She drove out of town and down the windy country road toward the next town over.

It was on the outskirts of this town that a sad, sleepy roadside bar popped up. She could see it was open despite the holiday. A few cars scattered the parking lot.

She pulled in.

Her nerves stood on end when she stepped inside.

The few men who inhabited the place looked up when she arrived.

She did not belong in this place and she was afraid, but she hadn't a clue where else to go.

She sat on a barstool. The bar top was sticky. She nervously lit a cigarette.

The bartender eyed her. "And what'll the beautiful lady have?"

"A whiskey."

"Straight?"

"Yes."

His eyebrow rose in amusement.

He slapped a glass before her and poured with polished finesse.

She sipped the drink, wishing he would leave her alone.

"Shouldn't you be celebrating this colonial holiday with your family somewhere?" He asked.

She rolled the amber liquid about in the glass. "I should be."

"I see." He nodded.

She studied his face and saw he was a Native. It made her miss Joan terribly.

She remembered the number in her purse.

But Joan would be busy, wouldn't she?

Vera finished her drink and ordered another.

The bartender looked at her kindly, as if he understood something.

"Do you have a phone?" She asked him.

He nodded toward the back of the bar.

She found the number in her bag and slid from her seat. She stumbled into a chair and felt an arm go about her. "Whoa there. You all right?" An older gentleman asked.

"Just fine." Vera stepped away from him.

He released her and tipped his hat, assuring her he meant her no harm.

She walked carefully then to the back of the bar and lifted the phone from its cradle, dropping a dime into the machine.

She dialed the number and pressed the receiver close to her ear.

The phone clicked on the other end. She could hear the sounds of people talking in the background and then an unfamiliar female voice came on the line. "Hello?"

"Hi, hello...is Joan...is Joan there?" Vera felt a rush of nerves and jealousy and fear wrap itself about her.

"Joan? Yes, one second, dear." And there were muffled voices on the other end of the line and then the click of another phone.

"You can hang up, Claud." Joan's voice came on the line.

Another line clicked and Vera smiled in spite of herself. Relieved. To hear Joan's voice live on the other end of the phone in this dingy watering hole.

"Vera, is that you?" Joan asked.

"Yes." Vera nodded.

"Is everything all right?"

"No." Vera hummed, feeling tears well in her eyes. "Who was that?"

"Who? Oh, that was my friend Claudia. I stay at their house in the city from time to time."

"*Their* house?" Vera did not want to talk about herself.

"Yes, Claudia and Matilde. They were teachers with me years ago." She explained calmly.

"A couple?" Vera ventured.

"Yes, darling." Joan was smiling, she could tell. Vera missed her smile terribly. "Where are you?"

"A bar." Vera said.

"What are you doing at a bar? It's Thanksgiving. What happened?" Her concern was evident.

"I didn't want to be home anymore."

"Did something happen?"

Vera shook her head, lighting another cigarette. "It's terrible with my parents here. And I can't stand...I can't stand Roger."

"Did he do something?"

Vera blew smoke. "Nothing he hasn't done before."

"Vera, are you all right?" Joan's voice was sober.

"Joan," Vera wanted to tell her everything.

She noticed a man sitting nearby, watching her. It made her uncomfortable.

Everything could not be discussed here.

"What are they like?" Vera needed to know. She wanted to see it all in her mind so realistically that she could feel that she was there with Joan.

"Who?"

"Your friends."

"Oh, well Claudia is a remarkable chef. She likes reading and going to museums, very introverted and Matilde is the exact opposite. She's always entertaining someone, always very social and active. She loves going to the theatre. I don't know." Joan tried to respond.

"And the weather...the weather has been nice?"

"It's warmer in the city than there, but it might snow tonight." Joan relayed.

"When will you come back?"

"I'd planned to Saturday evening."

"And Lulu?"

"I keep her well-fed while I'm away." Joan assured. "Vera, you don't sound well."

"I'm a bit tipsy." Vera offered.

"Darling," Joan sighed. "I'm terribly worried."

"Please, don't be worried." Vera hadn't meant to upset her. "Please. Everyone is so goddamn worried about me. They think that it's because of the...but I...oh, I can't stand it. I need to see you."

"Vera." Joan's sharp inhale stopped her.

"When?" Vera pleaded.

"It's rather complicated, isn't it?" Joan was upset. "I feel the same, but we're not like other people. They won't understand it, so we have to be calm and careful. Do you understand, Vera? I want it just as badly, darling, but we simply can't...we can't."

Vera was nodding, listening to Joan speak. It all made sense to her, but it felt so awfully unfair.

"I'd give anything to be there just now." Joan whispered.

Vera's whole being calmed, the soothing words pouring over her like a balm. Joan would be there if she could. She knew it.

"Vera, you need to go home. Do you understand? I know it's horrible right now, but your parents won't be there forever. They'll be worried about you. And cut back on the liquor, darling. You might think it's helping you, but it will only make things worse. Trust me." Joan spoke as a caring mother might.

Vera fought back the tears in her eyes, not wanting to cry in front of the few men surrounding her. Not wanting to give them that satisfaction.

"Okay." Her voice was tight.

"I...I care about you so. You must know that." Joan's voice came again. "Please, take care of yourself. I'll see you Sunday morning."

Vera closed her eyes. She didn't want to hang up.

The phone was clicking for her to put another dime in, but her purse was across the room.

"Joan, I…"

"I know. Go on home." Joan coaxed.

Vera did not want to go home. The phone disconnected. She hung it up, placed a dollar on the counter, pulled on her coat, and made her way out of the bar feeling better.

Joan wanted her to go home, so she went.

Roger wouldn't look at her when she walked in.

Her father gave her a disapproving gaze.

Her mother was still cleaning in the kitchen.

"The children are in bed." Her mother told her.

She took off her coat, rolled up her sleeves and helped.

Chapter Thirty-Three

The forest was dark and damp.

There was light from the moon, shining silver on the trees around her.

She could feel the dirt in her toes, could smell the damp forest surrounding her.

A wind started up, blowing the tree branches above her. A great whooshing noise, but the under forest remained calm.

Something stirred off in the distance.

She watched without fear as the outline of someone emerged from deep within the woods.

It moved with great purpose, closer and closer toward the well highlighted by the moon.

A woman.

Beautiful, strong, with eyes that saw everything.

She came to a halt in the clearing.

Their eyes met and she seemed to hold Vera there with her gaze, not allowing her to look away.

And then, with a sudden, imperceptible motion, the woman disappeared down the well.

Vera shot straight up in bed, sweat breaking out on her brow, feverishly warm, so that she kicked the sheets off.

Roger groaned beside her. "What the hell?"

She apologized, sitting up on the edge of the bed. She reached for her cigarettes.

"Damn it, Vera." He was in no mood to deal with her.

"I said I was sorry." She reiterated as she lit the cigarette.

"Don't you start with me." Roger was awake then.

She stumbled from the bed, afraid of that tone.

"My God, you're impossible, Vera." He growled.

"It was only a bad dream." Vera whimpered, exhausted.

Her parents had left for Boston the day before.

She and Roger had quarreled all evening after that, Roger admonishing her for having left the family in a lurch on Thanksgiving.

"I thought it would be different here. I thought you'd get over your little disappearing acts."

So he'd brought her here to keep her from running away into the maze of the city on a whim? He'd wanted to trap her in his home, keep her under lock and key?

It disgusted her.

"Oh, grow up." He hissed and pulled the covers over his head.

She took her cigarettes and left for the living room couch.

The living room was cold.

She pulled a blanket over herself and sat smoking until she felt she could sleep again.

She awoke to Roger nudging her.

He was adjusting his tie. "Church." He simply said.

Lightness overcame her at the word.

Church.

A place of reverent worship.

The irony of it amused her.

Her neck hurt when she stood up.

She made coffee and breakfast for Roger, took a shower and dressed, then woke the children to feed and clothe them. There was an excitement in her actions, a wonderful stirring in the pit of her stomach as they drove to town and parked before the religious building.

They walked inside and she scanned the room. Searching.

"Oh, Vera. We were so sorry to hear about what happened." Several women blocked her vision as they offered their condolences. Word had traveled fast. The town so small. It made her stomach knot that they should know.

She smiled for them, thanked them for their kindness.

Roger slipped away to speak with Phil. Vera was relieved that Judy seemed occupied by another family for when Vera turned she went white at the sight of Joan speaking to an older couple.

Her eyes met Vera's for a brief moment and she smiled at her.

Vera felt weak in the knees, wishing she could race to the other woman, to wrap her arms about her and disappear in her embrace. It made her feel so giddy, this thought.

Instead, she continued speaking with the women before her until she turned and found that Joan was standing beside her.

"Would you excuse us?" Joan smiled as she cordially asked the other women. Her hand came to rest gently at the small of Vera's back.

The women smiled and nodded.

Joan guided Vera toward a corner of the sanctuary unoccupied by others.

Vera missed the weight of her hand on her back the instant it was gone.

"Are you all right?" Joan had turned to look at her.

Vera nodded. "Yes."

"I was worried sick about you, you know." Joan spoke softly with a half-smile on her lips for any onlooker's sake.

Vera stared at her lips and then focused on her eyes. "I'm sorry to have worried you."

Joan shook her head. "It was all right?"

Vera nodded, not wanting to think about the strain of her parent's stay and the arguments that had ensued.

Instead, an idea came to her, fully formed and perfect.

"Joan, come to the city with me."

"What are you talking about?" Joan laughed, caught off guard.

"I'll say I'm going Christmas shopping in the city for the weekend with a friend."

Joan tried to mask the surprised look that crossed her features. "That won't seem strange?"

Vera waved her off. "I'll take the children to stay with his parents. He'll probably be happy to be rid of us all for a while."

Joan's brow creased with concern at the off-handed statement.

"Oh, it's nothing." Vera said as the organist started playing the opening hymn. "Please, tell me you'll think about it."

Joan glanced away from her, as if their connection was too tight, too obvious. She waved to someone who had come in.

Her hand found Vera's for a brief moment. "Okay, I'll think about it." Her eyes were on Vera's, deep and reassuring, and then they parted. Drifting horribly, terribly away from each other.

They took their seats. Joan three rows ahead.

The service commenced and Vera was hopelessly lost to thoughts of tangling her fingers in Joan's hair as she ran her fingers through Henry's soft locks.

For that hour of worship, nothing else mattered except Joan's presence in that room so near to her.

Chapter Thirty-Four

"I'm going to the city." It was a statement and not a question.

Roger was relieving himself in the toilet as she stood at the mirror rubbing cream into her face.

"What for?" He shook himself off and tucked himself back into his boxers.

"Christmas shopping for the children. There isn't a decent shop for miles and they both need new clothes."

"There are plenty of shops downtown." He went to the sink to wash his hands and reach for his toothbrush.

"It will just be a weekend." She ignored him. "You could use a new shirt or two. You liked that store on forty-first."

"What will I do with the children?"

"I'll take them to your parents on the way. You won't have to worry about a thing."

He looked at her as he brushed his teeth. After spitting in the sink he said, "it sounds like you have it all figured out."

"I don't see why I can't have a weekend away."

"All by yourself? In the city? It wouldn't be safe."

"I've asked a friend to go along."

"Judy?"

"No," she brushed her hair. "Joan. You know Joan from church?"

There was a lack of recognition on his face.

"I introduced you the other day. From the ladies auxiliary meeting."

He seemed to remember then. He laughed. "Isn't she old enough to be friends with your mother?"

She masked the hurt on her face by rummaging through her drawer for dental floss. "We'll take the train into the city so you can have the car, if you need."

"You really have planned it out, haven't you?"

"It's not fair. You get to go to the city every day and I haven't been back since we moved." She had tried not to resort to petulance, but he seemed to match her at every turn, making it all seem impossible.

"When would you go?"

"The seventeenth."

She was relieved to see he was warming to the idea.

They moved into the bedroom and settled into bed.

She did not smoke, as she wanted to, and instead, lay beside him.

He put out his bedside lamp.

She did the same.

He shifted.

She let her hand wander between his legs and found that he was receptive to her touch.

She pleasured him to release.

He got up to go to the bathroom. She lit a cigarette and smoked until he returned to the bed. "Perhaps some time away would be good for you."

She put out the cigarette and curled on her side. Warm, happy.

She floated through the days. She was careful with Roger, with the children.

She did not smoke at the table.

She drank one tumbler of whiskey in the evenings.

Roger was amused by this change. He seemed happier with her, more forgiving.

And on Thursdays she throbbed for Joan through the ladies auxiliary meetings until they could be alone, then she would pleasure the older woman, teasing her own healing parts into a frenzy. Joan would pleasure her in other, more careful ways.

The children had finished classes for the term on the fifteenth. They were elated to be free of school and have an adventure to go on before Christmas.

The seventeenth of December arrived with a chill crisp in the air and a light blanket of snow on the ground.

Roger drove them to the train station, getting out to help with their overnight bags.

Joan was standing on the platform and waved, the children rushing to greet her with hugs. Vera longed to embrace the woman as freely as her children had, but she walked with Roger slowly, calmly.

Roger held out his hand for Joan. "So nice to see you again, Ms. DeBoer. I trust you will keep my wife out of trouble."

Joan shook his hand firmly. Vera watched the curve of her smile and noticed the slight discomfort in the upward motion. Roger made her uneasy. "I'll do my very best, Mr. Wilson."

The train arrived promptly on schedule. Roger helped them get their bags settled and then hugged the children and pulled Vera to him to kiss her.

Vera could feel Joan watching them from beneath her lashes.

Roger helped their suitcases onto the train then stood dutifully on the platform to see them off.

Vera kept her eyes on him, watching his figure recede into the background as the train picked up speed. The tightness in her chest slowly unwound the further and further away they got from him.

Vera sat across from Joan.

Henry had pushed his way beside Joan and Emma snuggled against Vera.

Joan talked animatedly with Henry, but her eyes sought out Vera's.

Vera smiled, wishing she could suspend this moment into infinity.

Emma was looking at her, a smile unlike any Vera had seen before lighting up her beautiful features. Then she buried herself into Vera's side, giggling at something Joan had said. Happy, content.

When the train reached the third station down the line, Vera saw Roger's mother and father standing on the platform. She and Joan helped get the children's luggage off the train, handing it over to Roger's father. She introduced Joan to Roger's parents and thanked them again for watching the children.

The children hugged Joan and then hugged Vera tightly. She kissed each of them as the train was about to leave the station.

A lightness overcame Vera as the train doors closed and she found herself finally alone with Joan.

They sat next to one another then.

Vera watched out the window at her children as the train departed. They waved at her, and she waved back until she could no longer see them.

Her worries faded into the background because Joan's leg was pressed against her own as they sat beside one another. Vera strained not to touch her, not to pull her against her and kiss her now that they were free.

They were free, but very much not alone.

A man was sitting two seats up from them, his eyes upon Vera.

She did not like the way he looked at her.

She looked at Joan, and Joan smiled at her, her own look of relief evident.

Vera lit a cigarette and watched the world go by until the train pulled into Grand Central Station.

Chapter Thirty-Five

oan had made arrangements for them to stay in the Village. It was a little hotel, but she assured Vera no one would bother them there, that they were friendly and she had known many people who had stayed before.

It was a generous sized room with two double beds that Vera stared at with indignation.

The hotel room door clicked shut behind them.

Joan put her bag down behind Vera and Vera was instantly in her arms, pawing at her, kissing her with intensity. "My God, I can't stand it." Vera pushed at Joan's coat, undoing her tidy travel jacket, fingers careful with the buttons at the front of her pressed white shirt.

It was a mess of clothing, of skirts and heels and pantyhose and undergarments and slips and bras.

"Is it all right?" Joan panted through kisses, afraid to hurt Vera.

"Yes," Vera guided Joan's hand between her legs. "Perfectly all right now." She assured her, having kept track of the days meticulously.

The bed was wrinkled with their lovemaking.

Fevered and hurried until the realization came over them that they hadn't anywhere else to be.

They laid together naked, hands stroking, caressing, holding.

The day had faded into darkness.

"We should get something to eat." Joan whispered as she pressed her lips to Vera's temple.

Vera held tighter to her. "No."

"Darling, we have the rest of the night to go on like this. But we should get out, get some fresh air."

Vera huffed, sitting up slightly to light a cigarette. "I can't stand to be apart from you." She let her hand trail down Joan's slender neck, fingers tracing the outline of her areola. Her nipple stood at attention.

"Jesus, Vera." And Joan leaned down to kiss her lips.

They made love again then showered together, sidetracked when Vera pressed her lips against Joan's shoulder and caressed her until she came beneath the stream of water.

They dressed to ward off the terrible chill of the night, and Joan led them to a little hole in the wall café down the road. Vera was thankful for the dim lighting and the relative privacy of the cramped space. So that their bodies could press together, hands finding the other's beneath the table top.

Vera could hardly eat but Joan insisted she do, so she at least finished the bowl of chili placed before her.

She noticed Joan did not eat meat.

"The product of growing up on a farm, I suppose." Joan explained.

Vera marveled at this revelation.

"I never had a stomach for killing animals."

"It must be awful to see." Vera agreed.

They walked, huddled close to one another, down the

street. Joan stopped in a store to buy a bottle of wine and a pack of cigarettes. She smoked Winstons.

It was a relief to return to the warm hotel room. They shed their clothing down to their slips and made love, Joan descending between Vera's legs, stroking her with her tongue and the sensation undid Vera.

They lay smoking together after.

"I should call the children." Vera sighed after looking at the clock. It was nearing eight.

"Go ahead. I'll pour us some wine." Joan kissed her and trailed out of the bed to find cups.

Vera picked up the phone and dialed Roger's parent's number.

Eileen picked up and handed the phone over to Emma.

"Are you having a good time, baby?" Vera asked, as Joan handed her a coffee cup filled with wine.

"Yes, Mommy! There are kids next door who invited us to go skating tomorrow."

Joan sat on the edge of the bed, her hand caressing Vera's naked thigh. Vera was lost in Joan's dark eyes. "Skating, well that will certainly be fun. You promise me you'll be careful?"

"Oh, I will be, Mommy!" Emma assured her. "I miss you."

"I miss you, too." Vera picked ash from her tongue. Joan leaned down and kissed her quietly. Vera let her fingers thread through Joan's hair, fingernails scratching gently against her scalp.

"Are you having fun?" Emma shyly asked her.

"Oh, yes. I am."

"Can I go to the city with you one day?" Emma asked excitedly.

"Of course. Of course, we'll go one day." And she smiled at the thought of stealing Emma away and taking her to the city and showing her what life could be like without her father, perhaps without men in general.

She told Emma she loved her, eyes firmly twined with Joan's, then asked to speak with Henry. The boy was not as patient on the phone, so it was only a matter of seconds before she could hang up and instantly she reached for Joan, pulling her close. Having missed their closeness in the few minutes the call had demanded.

"Perhaps you should call Roger." Joan insisted as she nuzzled at Vera's neck.

"I don't want to call Roger." Vera said going stiff.

Joan pulled back, looking down at Vera. "I know you don't, but it will look better that way. Don't you think?"

Vera scowled, body alive again and wanting.

She picked up the phone and dialed her own number.

It rang several times before Roger finally picked up.

"Vera?"

"Roger, we...we made it. Everything's just fine."

"Good then. Have a good evening."

"You as well."

And they hung up with one another.

Vera wiggled up to light another cigarette.

Joan sat back. "I take it that it's not an amicable relationship."

Vera snorted, smoke racing from her nostrils. "Amicable? It hasn't been amicable for years." She wrecked her hair with her hand.

"He doesn't..."

Vera shook her head. "He's never laid a finger on me. Well, never on purpose anyway. He just talks to me like he can't stand that I exist, that I get in his way, that I'm a burden. I wish he would...you know, leave me. Just walk out, but he won't do that." Vera groaned. "Oh, I don't want to talk about Roger."

"All right, we don't have to say any more about Roger." Joan conceded. "I'm perfectly content to never mention the name again."

And Vera studied her. Seeing the strain in her eyes. The pain of it. "Oh...I'm terribly sorry. I...it's very insensitive."

"What?" Joan rubbed at the back of her neck.

"Well it's awfully unfair to you, isn't it?" Vera puffed at her cigarette.

Joan shrugged. "I knew what I was getting into from the beginning. I had no delusions about it."

"I'm sorry...I wish...oh, I wish I could just leave him." Vera cursed.

"So that what? We could be together?" Her eyes had gone sad.

Vera put her cigarette in the ashtray by the bed and crawled towards Joan. "Oh, couldn't we be?" Vera wrapped Joan up in her arms, holding her close to her.

Joan laughed dryly. "I'd lose my job and you'd lose the children and the house and the life...no, I couldn't do that to you."

Vera held her tighter. "Oh let's stop. Please, let's stop. I don't want to quarrel. Not when we have this time. Please."

Joan's rigid body went slack in her arms and soon their lips sought out the other's again.

It was deeper, deeper than any time before. As if it suddenly meant more.

Vera's body was pleasantly sated.

Joan put out the light and they lay wrapped up in each other. So close, impossibly close. Simply breathing, simply existing together. Their first night to sleep side-by-side with nowhere else to be, no other responsibilities for the foreseeable future. It was only the two of them and the darkness of the hotel room.

She inhaled the scent of Joan, a mix of perfume and something that was innately *her*.

Vera was intoxicated by Joan, could not possibly get

enough of the woman. Yet in the peaceful, quiet stillness of the night, she was lulled into a deep, wondrous sleep, delighted when she awoke to the rising sun their bodies were still entwined.

Chapter Thirty-Six

Vera was fascinated by everything Joan did.

Minute things. How her hair fell below her shoulders, but how she pinned it carefully atop her head, how she applied her make-up, powdered her cheeks, lined her lips, applied her lipstick, pressed delectable perfume to all of her pulse points, how she brushed her teeth, how she pulled pantyhose up her legs, how she lit her cigarettes, how she placed things into her coat pockets.

Little things that could only be noticed when up close and personal with someone.

Little ordinary things Roger might do and yet they were transformed, transcended because it was Joan doing them.

"What are you looking at?" Joan asked as she held onto the wall in order to sink her foot into her shoe.

Vera smiled, wrapping her arms freely about Joan. "You." She pressed their freshly done lips together.

"You'll mess up our lipstick." Joan chided playfully, looking into the hall mirror, tapping a finger at the edge of her lips.

What did Vera care about spoiled lipstick?

Joan reached for Vera, inspecting her lips before lightly kissing her again.

"Well, shall we?" Joan held out her arm and Vera took it.

They had decided to take care of the gift buying all in one whirlwind trip to midtown.

Vera had planned it meticulously so that it wouldn't take any time at all.

A new dress for Emma, a toy for Henry, some slacks, a shirt, some clothes for Roger, a new diary for Emma, little knickknacks for everyone else.

Vera was finished within two hours and circled back to find Joan staring at a display case.

She startled when Vera pressed her hand to her hip.

"Don't...don't do that." She cautioned.

Vera stepped a respectable distance away and peered down at what held Joan's captive attention.

"What are you looking at?" Vera delighted in the scent of Joan near to her again. The way she had pushed her away made Vera mad with the want to drag Joan off somewhere safe, private so that she could have her again. It had been far too long since their roll in bed that morning. And there was so little time left together...

"It's nothing." Joan's cheeks were rosy.

It was a case of lipsticks.

"I think you'd look very fetching in this shade." Joan pointed to one with a rosy pink hue.

Vera's cheeks warmed. "It's lovely."

A beauty counter girl appeared before them. "Can I help you?"

"Yes, she'd like to see that one, please." Joan pointed and when the girl turned from them to find the lipstick, Joan winked at Vera.

The counter girl brought back the lipstick. "Would you like to try it, Ma'am?"

Vera allowed the girl to swipe away her lipstick and then carefully apply the new color. "It really complements your eyes." The girl said once she was finished.

Joan was looking at her over the girl's shoulder with an appraising twinkle in her eyes. "Doesn't it? We'll take it."

And Joan batted Vera's hand away and paid for the lipstick.

"Are we done here?" Joan asked as they walked with their shoulders pressed together through the department store, crowded with other holiday shoppers.

"Yes." The items would be delivered to their hotel.

They had the afternoon free to themselves.

"I'm famished, come on." Joan hailed a cab and took them to a bistro near the Village.

They ordered sandwiches and Cokes, Vera rushing them so they could go right back to the hotel. She wanted to feel Joan's skin again, she wanted to wreck her and not leave her side for the rest of the evening in the quiet privacy of the hotel room.

After they ate, they walked arm in arm down the sidewalk, protected from the chill of the cold winter wind pressed together as they were.

It was as they were about to turn down the road to the hotel that they heard a voice call out. "Joan?"

Joan startled, straightening away from Vera.

"Matilde?"

Matilde looked from Joan to Vera. "Well, I didn't know you would be in town."

"It was a last-minute trip."

Matilde's smile was knowing.

"This is Vera. Vera Wilson." Joan stepped to the side so Matilde could extend her hand to Vera. "Vera, this is Matilde Brunson."

Matilde's smile did not reach her eyes. "The infamous Vera in the flesh."

"Matilde." Joan's voice came out flustered and cross.

Matilde's eyes shifted from studying Vera to Joan again. "Well you simply must come out tonight. Claudia will insist that she see you."

"I don't think we can make it this evening." Joan tried for Vera.

"I insist. The whole gang will be there at eight."

"Matilde..."

"They'll be thrilled to meet her." Matilde was appraising Vera again.

She felt hot under her collar.

"We'll see if we can make it." Joan promised.

They kissed on the cheeks as if they were in Europe, then Matilde bid them farewell and went on down the street.

"She doesn't like me." Vera said when they got inside the hotel room.

"Don't be ridiculous, darling." Joan stepped out of her shoes as she unbuttoned her coat.

"Why?" Vera remained standing near the door. A petulant, insistent child.

She hated herself for feeling this way.

Joan tried to laugh. "Oh, Vera." She came to her and helped her out of her coat. "They're just protective of me. They don't want to see me get hurt."

"I wouldn't hurt you." Vera insisted, angry.

Joan took a deep breath and sunk onto the edge of the bed. "No. No, I know you never would on purpose. I didn't mean to say it that way."

"Then what?" Vera did not budge from her place near the door even though she ached to put her arms about Joan, to press her back against the freshly made bed.

Joan looked up at her. There was something Vera had

never seen before in her expression. She looked so tired, so terribly, terribly tired.

"Oh," Vera sighed, kicking off her shoes and falling toward Joan, placing her knees on either side of her and wrapping her up in her arms. "I never want to hurt you." She said between kisses.

They lost themselves in one another.

The hours ticked away far too fast. As if time sped up.

It was nearly a quarter to eight when Vera caught sight of the clock.

Joan squinted to see the time. "We don't have to go."

Vera sat up on her elbows. "What sort of a place is it?"

"A queer one." Joan laughed.

"I went to one once." Vera said, sitting up to light a cigarette.

"Really?" Joan watched her puff at the cigarette and then took it from her.

"Yes, with Roger when we were first married. He had a friend who thought it would be entertaining." Vera rolled her eyes as she laid back in the bed. "They laughed about it, but I didn't see the humor in it. I think it might have been the first time I came close to it. There was a girl...I'll never forget her face. The way she looked at me..." Vera delighted in the memory.

Joan handed back the cigarette. "Shall I be jealous?"

"Don't be silly." Vera leaned over and kissed her. "We should go."

Joan groaned, but they found themselves bundled up and walking the few blocks to the basement bar.

It was smokey and dark and Vera confused a woman for a man and another woman jumped before her, keeping her from following Joan any further. "Well look at you. Aren't you a delicious dish."

"Leave her alone, Kit." Joan elbowed her way in, rescuing

Vera and pulling her toward the back of the bar where they found Matilde seated amongst an assortment of women.

"You made it!" Matilde exclaimed, leaping up to pull Joan into a tight kiss on the lips. "Everyone, you'll never believe it, but our Joanie here has brought her gal pal out into the world. This is Vera."

A masculine woman seated next to Matilde looked Vera up and down from beneath thick cigar smoke, gaze dubious.

Joan helped Vera into a seat and promised she'd be right back with drinks.

The masculine woman continued to stare at her. "I'm Claud. I believe we spoke on the phone." She finally said.

Vera hung her head. "Yes." She fumbled with her cigarette case, pulling one out anxiously to place between her lips.

Claud reached over with a lighter. "We heard so much about you. Your children go to Joan's school?"

"Yes." Vera nodded, exhaling a cloud of smoke, feeling strange speaking of her children in a place such as this.

"Our Joan seems very taken with you."

"I am very fond of her, as well." Vera blew a cloud of smoke to the ceiling.

"You'd better watch yourself then. You wouldn't want to get her in trouble."

"I would never..." She felt a hand on her arm, steadying her. Joan placed a drink in front of her and sat down beside her, placing her arm firmly about Vera as a man might.

"Let's leave her alone, shall we?" Joan said civilly.

An attractive brunette seated beside her introduced herself as Molly. She leaned into Vera conspiratorially. "So tell us, how many women have you slept with?"

Vera preened at the question. "Two." She said, as if it might prove something about herself.

Molly seemed pleased by this. "How would you like to make it three?"

The group tittered with laughter and Vera turned, cheeks flushed to look at Joan. "Are they always so lewd?"

Joan pressed her lips against her ear, "yes. I apologize. We can have this drink and then be on our way."

But Vera liked the way Joan's arm felt about her in public. She liked when the others had stopped paying attention to them, how Joan kissed her right there in the bar. And after another drink, Vera wanted to dance. The music was slow and she held Joan pressed tightly against her as they swayed together. And no one looked at them as if they were strange. No one seemed to pay them any mind at all. They were just like the others.

It was nearly eleven by the time Joan excused them. The group was drunk enough to wish them well.

They stumbled back to the hotel and made love until the early morning and then clung to one another.

Chapter Thirty-Seven

She let her finger trail down the hollow between Joan's breasts.

Joan stirred beside her, half-dozing, half-awake in the early morning hours.

She held Vera tighter.

Vera couldn't sleep even if she had wanted to.

The thought of returning to her life made her stomach knot. She felt as if she might be ill each time she stared at the clock and saw more time had slipped away from them.

A countdown to the end of bliss.

Joan pressed her lips to Vera's fevered brow.

Tears clouded Vera's vision. She pressed her face against Joan's chest.

"It won't do any good crying about it." Joan's sleepy voice spoke as her fingers threaded through Vera's hair.

"Oh," Vera hadn't realized how awake the other woman was. She rolled over to look at Joan in the streetlight that filtered through the blinds. Her own wild blonde hair fell loosely atop Joan's chest. "You don't regret it, do you?

Joan pulled her close, seeking out Vera's lips. "No."

Vera smiled as Joan wiped at her cheeks.

"I want to know." Vera whispered.

Joan hummed and pressed her lips to Vera's forehead. "Know what?"

Vera peered down at Joan who looked back at her in the darkness with her large, dark eyes. "I want to know everything about you. I want to know what you were like as a child and if you were happy and what happened to your...well, Kitty told me something about what happened. But I wanted to hear it all from you...to know..."

The older woman stared up at her with delighted amusement. "Ah." She said simply and eased up a bit to reach for her cigarettes. "What is it that Kitty told you?"

"I didn't mean to upset you." Vera scampered to sit up so that she was facing Joan in the night.

She watched as the flick of the lighter illuminated Joan's face.

"No," Joan patted her thigh, exhaling a cloud of smoke. "No, you didn't. It was all a very long time ago, but I am curious to know what Kitty Daniels knew of my childhood. Her family has always been quite influential in town. It's a shame what happened to her." She extended the cigarette to Vera.

"Yes." Vera agreed as she placed the cigarette between her lips and tried not to remember the blood soaked bathroom.

Instead she focused on the taste of Joan's Winstons and found she was beginning to like them. Very much. She smoked slowly, wondering if she'd put her foot in her mouth by having mentioned anything at all about Kitty and what she knew.

"She told me about your...family. About your mother..."

Joan took the cigarette from Vera, inhaling. "Ah." Joan let smoke escape from her reddened lips. "She told you, then, about my drunk father and my mother who vanished?"

Vera sat up straighter. "Yes. But that's not really what happened, is it?"

Joan tapped off ash and shook her head. "Well, I suppose it makes for an interesting story, doesn't it?"

"I want to know." Vera curled her arms about her legs.

Joan tapped ash from the cigarette. "It's far more complicated than that and I don't know if I'll ever know the truth of it." Vera could see her eyes in the night and could see the sadness in them. "My mother was a Native, part of the Lenape tribe who lived here in the seventeen hundreds."

"What happened to them?"

Joan's lips twisted upward in amusement. "They don't teach history like they should, do they?" She took a drag of her cigarette and sat up and Vera could imagine her at the head of her classroom. If she had been Vera's teacher, she knew she would have hung on Joan's every word. "After the American Revolution the newly birthed nation wanted to run off the natives so they could take over their land. And besides, most of the native tribes had sided with the British. They were much fairer to them, but that only made it worse when the British lost. So, most of my mother's family was run off to Oklahoma or west of the Mississippi or killed."

Vera's eyes widened, marveling at Joan's knowledge of such things. That she was of these people who had been so mistreated and yet...

"My father's family immigrated here from the Netherlands. After the Revolution they purchased the farmland. There was a tribe living off the land and my great, great grandfather thought to let them remain. He saw them as an asset because they understood the land. So, when the others had to leave, my mother's family remained. But people didn't know about them. My father's family kept them well protected." She paused to smoke, running her hand down Vera's shin. "Am I boring you?" She asked, knowing full well she had Vera's undivided attention.

Vera shook her head. "No."

Joan smiled.

"My father was a good man, despite his unfortunate demise. He and my mother played together as children, in secret of course. They fell in love with one another and no one could separate them. But when the town found out..." Joan shook her head. "They burned the homestead. Up in smoke because there were natives living on the land. The town wanted to drive them away. But my mother refused to go."

"It's ridiculous that they would run them off because your mother and father fell in love." Vera stole the cigarette and inhaled at it.

Joan smiled. "Have you heard of eugenics?"

"What?"

"The superiority of the white race. A master race. The ideal human. Everyone was very taken with the idea in those days - hell, even today. A Native person was not a white person. They were primitive, ill-educated, dangerous beings who hated American settlers. Or so they've been depicted for centuries now."

Vera shook her head. "But they're humans."

"Not in the eyes of the law." She handed the cigarette to Vera. Her hand shook. "It's ridiculous to be a teacher and not be able to tell my students the truth of the world. It's such a shame they grow up being so sheltered."

Vera's heart was pounding in her chest. Anger swirling about. As if she knew without asking, but asked anyway. "What happened?"

"My mother became pregnant with me." Joan offered a small smile. "My father was afraid of what the town might do. He begged her to go with her family until I was older, but she didn't listen. She didn't want to run."

Vera watched Joan stand up, as if she needed to move or she might break apart. She went to the dresser and poured a fresh glass of the whiskey they'd bought on the way back from the bar.

She drank it back.

Vera crawled to the head of the bed and lit a cigarette.

Joan settled the glass atop the dresser, placing her hands on either side. She leaned over, head bowed. "I was so young when they came for her."

"Who?"

Joan shook her head. "I can't be sure of it, but I always suspected it was the men in charge of the town. They didn't want a Native woman owning property if anything were to happen to my father - or so I overheard my father say." Joan shook her head. "I strongly suspect the town's police were involved." Joan lifted the glass to her lips again, drinking. She took a deep breath. "My mother put me to bed that night and the next morning she was gone. I wish...oh, I wish I'd woken up that night. I wish I could have witnessed something. But it...it's all blackness."

Vera inhaled shakily at her cigarette.

"My father was a good man, but the town never looked at him the same. The drinking started after my mother...some days he was okay. He was steady, even keeled and then other days..." Joan shook her head. "He lost the farm that way. Drinking himself silly. I tried to help, I came back, but it was too late. We could only sell off the land to pay his debts. And they offered me peanuts for it. I should have known better." Joan poured herself another drink, downing it back. Her tongue had softened from the drinks.

Pain dripped from her words.

Joan shook her head. "I always thought they should have taken me too." She laughed sarcastically as she stood straight again. "I was half my mother yet they let me be because I looked white enough. With my mother gone they could just... forget. They still let me be. But they whisper behind my back and stay away. Which is perhaps for the best." Joan sniffed.

"It sounds lonely." Vera whispered.

Joan did not respond at first.

She moved back toward the bed, taking the cigarette from Vera's fingers. She laid down and blew smoke rings to the ceiling. "I suppose that's why we were drawn to one another."

"Why?" Vera laid beside her.

"I saw the same loneliness in you." Joan whispered.

Vera realized she was crying. "Oh, Joan."

Joan put out the cigarette and rolled to wrap Vera up in her arms.

"I should be comforting you." Vera sighed.

"You did." Joan kissed her forehead. "There are very few people who know the truth of it. And I appreciate that you wanted to know."

Vera clung to Joan, holding tight as if she never, ever wanted to let go. If she could stop time she would will it to linger in this moment forever.

The clock was ticking beside her.

"I love you." Vera said into the night because it was the truest thing she had ever known.

Joan held her closer.

The night was thick with the sounds of the sleeping city and silence. Vera wondered how many others were awake together like this or if they were the only two in this predicament.

The clock ticked.

"Love." Joan hummed. "Don't you know I'm in love with you?"

Vera laughed, delighted and exhausted.

She dozed in and out of consciousness, suspended in the moment. Willing the sun to never rise on another day.

Chapter Thirty-Eight

Vera startled awake, grasping at the sheets about her naked body.

"What's the matter?"

Joan.

Joan's voice near to her, calm and soft.

A hand brushed across her damp brow, smoothing out her hair.

"It's all right." Joan's reassuring voice hummed.

She'd been there again. In the forest by the well.

A woman's eyes blazing fiery hot.

Vera looked into Joan's eyes above her.

So familiar.

"It was only a dream, darling." Joan kissed her cheek.

And then Vera clung to her, holding her tight and close and kissing her into a frenzy. After it was over, she laid back on the bed and saw that daylight had broken out.

She felt as if she might be ill again.

The train was at one-thirty.

Vera looked anxiously at the clock as she lit a cigarette. It was nearing ten.

They showered together.

They stood at the vanity putting themselves back together.

Vera's hand shook as she tried to apply mascara and she ended up sitting on the toilet lid in tears.

Joan held her close, stroked her back.

"I want..." Vera groaned.

"Shh." Joan soothed but could not make it better.

Her nearness made Vera ache.

Joan suggested they have lunch before they went to the station, but Vera couldn't touch a thing. She shook as if she had the flu, smoking cigarette after cigarette.

"Vera..." Joan reached for her beneath the table of the busy bistro.

"No," Vera whispered, clasping at her fingers, "no, I'll be all right. I'll...I'll pull myself together. I won't...I won't let Roger see...Don't worry."

"I'm not worried about...Jesus, Vera. I hate this just as much as you do." Joan sat resolutely and stirred her soup. "But it doesn't help..."

"I can't help...I can't..." Vera puffed at her cigarette, nervous.

It would be the hardest thing for her to slip back into her life as if nothing had happened. As if she hadn't felt fully herself for the past two days.

"I know, darling." Joan whispered against her, pressing their bodies closer in the booth.

It was torture on the train, sitting so near one another and yet not being able to touch freely. A businessman sat across from them, eyeing Vera closely as he read a paper. She wanted to punch him, to pull Joan close to her, to kiss her a thousand times as the train raced down the track, but instead she sat smoking, hand balled into a fist at her side.

The children were waiting for them at Roger's parent's stop.

They waved at the train. Vera collected them up, despising their existence, hating how she had to give away her seat to Henry and Emma pressed herself up against her, telling her all about what they had done and seen and learned. She listened intently without hearing.

Vera met Joan's eyes and thought she might burst into tears right then, so that she could not look at Joan again.

They arrived back in town and Vera saw Roger standing on the platform, waiting for them.

The children went to him.

Vera felt weak at the knees, as if her legs might give out at any moment. Trapped between Joan and Roger.

He looked at her and she could see something curious in his half-smile at her. As if he did not recognize her.

He pulled her to his broad chest and kissed her on the lips. "Let's get home, then." He had an urgency to his voice, a tightness she recognized.

Her stomach sank.

She turned to Joan; body no longer certain of what to do. A handshake was too informal and yet a hug seemed too intimate.

Joan stood clasping her hat box before her, a sad smile tugging her lips upward. "It was a pleasure. I'll see you very soon, Vera." She whispered her name.

Vera nodded, body rigid.

"Come on, Vera." Roger called to her.

"Go on." Joan nodded with her chin.

Vera hung her head and turned, putting an arm about Emma then reaching for Henry, following them, without looking back, to the waiting car.

Roger told the children to go unpack and play in their rooms. He took Vera into their bedroom and undid his belt, helping her out of her travel suit.

She laid on the bed, fresh and clean from that morning.

She closed her eyes and thought of Joan in her arms. The artful way Joan had with her hands, her mouth...

He wanted her twice and then he wanted her to make dinner.

She showered and changed into a housedress.

Emma was standing in the hall when she went out.

"Are you all right, Mommy?" She whispered to her.

Vera bit her lip. "Yes, come...come help me with dinner."

And as Emma shredded potatoes, Vera went to the mini bar in the living room and poured herself a shot of whiskey. She lit a Winston she'd stolen from Joan and returned to her daughter in the kitchen.

"It smells different." Emma said.

"What, baby?" She spoke around her cigarette.

"The cigarette."

"Oh," Vera felt her cheeks flush. "It is different."

"Oh."

And Vera smoked the rest of it before lighting another of her usual Chesterfields and decided perhaps Winstons were for days when no one else was around.

She drank a glass of wine and stared at Roger as he ate across the table from her.

The children spoke excitedly for the week of no school before them and Christmas.

Vera half-listened, wondering what Joan would be doing just then.

Would she make herself dinner and eat alone? Would Lulu curl up on the couch beside her, happy she had returned?

Vera could see it all playing out before her and how she longed to be atop the couch with her, spread out before the heat of a warm fire, the both of them naked...

"Vera?"

She looked up and saw Roger's angry eyes upon her.

"What?"

"You're a million miles away."

"I'm sorry." She lit another cigarette.

"The chicken is burnt." He said again.

"Eat around the burnt bits." She said and he stared at her incredulously.

She was there but she wasn't there at all.

The house was closing in around her, consuming her.

The weekend felt like a far away dream, something that hadn't happened at all. A fantasy that took her away from this awful reality.

Roger put down his fork and stood up, going into the living room.

The children looked at her, frightened.

"It's all right." Vera reassured them. "Finish your dinners and then you can go play until bedtime."

They did not look reassured but slowly went back to eating.

She poured herself another glass of wine and sat at the table until they both left her.

She smoked a cigarette leisurely then went about cleaning up the kitchen. Washing the dishes, putting them in the dishwasher, cleaning down the counters, the table, the floor, fighting off the images of Joan touching her, inside of her...

Roger was watching television and pointedly ignored her when she walked up the stairs to the bedroom.

She changed into her pajamas, washed her face, brushed her teeth.

She slid between the sheets of the bed and covered her face as the tears came.

She stifled the sobs when she heard Roger come into the room. She listened as he changed and then went into the bathroom.

She feigned sleep, tightly biting her hand to keep herself

from betraying her tears when he finally slid into the bed beside her.

He did not come close to her, simply put out his light and laid down in the quiet darkness.

She laid, body tightly wound, until she heard his breaths even out.

She slid out of bed and went to the living room for a drink.

Standing at the back-porch door, tears slipping messily down her cheeks, she stared out at the snow-covered woods. Tempted to run, to flee the house.

Joan would be just through the woods. Asleep? Or still awake as Vera was?

She would call her, but Roger would hear.

So, she drank another glass of whiskey, not knowing what to do or what to feel.

The alcohol numbed the pain, lulling her into a drunken sleep.

Chapter Thirty-Nine

oger's parents came for Christmas.

Vera drank steadily.

Not enough to belay her inebriation, but enough to keep the thoughts away.

Her fingers itched to lift the receiver from the phone and call, but it was too risky with a full house.

Joan would be away for Christmas anyway, she had told her. Away in the city with her friends in a world that felt as far away from Vera as the idea of heaven and hell.

Joan, herself, could not exist if Vera were to keep a level head.

To play the role of wife and mother and dutiful housewife. To get into bed beside her husband at night and allow him to touch her.

Joan could not exist.

And on Christmas Eve Roger surprised her by telling her they were to go to a ski lodge in Vermont for a week before the school year began again. He had made all the arrangements.

So Joan couldn't exist if Vera were to go with her family, away from the town for a week.

If she awoke to a feverish dream of naked breasts and dark, kind eyes, she would simply remove herself to the living room for a smoke and a drink to quench the ache, to make it all go a bit hazy in her mind.

Christmas flew by in a haze of brightly colored foil wrapping paper and a tinseled, rainbow lit Christmas tree, baking and cleaning. Vera resented Eileen's presence with her in the kitchen. She never had a moment to herself, except to pour a splash of hidden whiskey into her drink, to light another cigarette.

It was a relief that they would only stay on to attend church the following morning and then return to their home.

Church.

Vera dreaded it.

She dressed the children up in their Christmas best, then put herself together in a simple black suit with red blouse. She took care as she applied the lipstick Joan had bought for her, smoothing it carefully over her lips.

She smoked irritably in the backseat of the car, Henry atop her lap as they drove to the service.

She hadn't a clue if Joan would be in attendance or not. If she had made it back after her own Christmas festivities in the city – would she have gone to the bar with her friends and found someone to share a bed with? The thought aroused and perturbed Vera.

She looked in vain for the woman. The sanctuary was crowded with additional family members that morning.

So she would have stayed in the city then, Vera determined as they stood for the first hymn and she felt a great depression overcome her.

Until they sat and she saw the dark head of hair carefully pinned up beneath a Christmas hat. And she felt as if she couldn't breathe. The wind went out of her, her knees weak.

She couldn't sit there between Roger and Emma a second longer.

She carefully excused herself to the restroom, climbing out from the crowded pew, ignoring the way Roger's mother looked after her. Not caring if Joan looked in her direction or not.

She went to the restroom in the lobby of the church and clumsily closed herself away in a stall and lit a cigarette.

Her heart skipped a beat when the restroom door opened and closed. She followed a pair of black heels as they walked toward the stall.

"Vera." The voice whispered.

"I can't see you." Vera whimpered.

"Vera, come now." Joan sighed. "Are you all right?"

"Of course I'm not...of course, I'm not all right. How could I possibly be all right?" Vera smoked with an unsteady hand.

"Damn it." Joan muttered under her breath. "Vera, can you just come out here so we can talk?"

"No." Vera said petulantly. "I can't...I can't..."

"It's hard for me too, you know?" Joan whispered through the door. "I used to enjoy going home to an empty house every night. I used to enjoy my life and now...Jesus."

Vera felt tears in her eyes and knew she couldn't cry because she couldn't explain a wrecked face. "I want to be with you so badly it hurts. It hurts me."

She could hear Joan's body press against the door of the stall. In defeat.

"I can't see you because it hurts too much." Vera whispered.

Joan remained silent. "Perhaps..." Joan's voice faltered and then it came clearly as she moved away from the door. "Perhaps it's better this way." And she washed her hands and left the restroom.

Vera folded over, the pain too acute to handle.

The cigarette burned down, nearly burning her finger before she tossed it away in the toilet.

She washed her hands, cleaned up her face, and then made her way back into the sanctuary.

Roger was looking at her curiously when she returned to her seat. She apologized again.

And when they got home and saw his parents off, she poured herself a shot of whiskey to make it through the next hour. Then another after that to make it through the next hour.

She ended up in bed with a headache until Roger called for her to make dinner.

That night in bed Roger lay on his back staring up at the ceiling. "What the hell's the matter with you?"

She recoiled. Everything and nothing was wrong.

Would she see Joan again?

"Is it the baby? We can...we can try again. The doctor said it would be okay."

She felt ill at the words, but nodded. "I don't...I don't think I'm ready. To try again. Not yet." She said, thankful he had formed this story to explain her behavior.

"But soon." It was a statement.

"Okay Roger." She nodded and allowed him to come into her arms. She found him ready and wanting.

The baby could explain a multitude of sins, she realized as she sat nursing a glass of watered whiskey that night, smoking away in the living room.

They left for the ski resort on Tuesday.

It snowed in the afternoon so the drive gave Vera an awful headache.

Roger took the children to the dining hall for dinner, leaving her in the dark.

She stared at the phone in the room and imagined calling Joan. She wanted to hear her voice, to make her head stop swimming for just a minute. But instead, she closed her eyes and felt the awful pulse of her head until she slid into uncon-sciousness.

Roger, an avid skier since youth, had decided to spend the days skiing, and had put the children into a day camp to learn how to ski, leaving Vera very much to herself.

She was relieved.

She did not have to make breakfast in the morning. They ate in the dining hall with the other families and then they went off to their activities.

Vera retreated to the bar.

She hadn't had a drink since they'd left the previous day. Her hand shook when she climbed onto a barstool and placed her cigarettes atop the bar.

She noticed a scattering of other wives, left to themselves for the day, but did not wish to speak to any of them.

So that she stayed far away from their groups.

She ordered a bourbon on the rocks and sipped it slowly.

She placed a cigarette between her lips, but before she could light it, she noticed the flicker of a lighter to her left, being extended toward her.

"Can I light that for you?"

She turned to take in an older man who had come to sit beside her.

His hair was dark, not yet gray, but his eyes creased kindly.

She allowed him to light her cigarette.

She did not want to talk to him, but he stayed beside her.

He got out a pack of Winstons and lit one for himself, ordering a whiskey.

"Not much of a skier?" He asked after a while.

She shook her head. "Afraid not." She downed the last of her drink.

"Another for the lady." The man said to the bartender. "My wife skis. I'm not much for the slopes, myself." He explained.

She despised him and yet liked the way in which he took control of things.

"I'm Walter."

"Vera."

"Vera, what an interesting name. Russian?"

"A distant grandmother, yes."

The conversation felt too personal. She wasn't even sure she liked him.

But the too loud tittering of the other wives at a nearby table made her relax at the idea of having a male companion for the day.

The alcohol relaxed her.

Walter was good humored. He made her laugh. Or perhaps the third drink made her laugh.

She had relaxed around him. "Can I have one of your cigarettes?" She asked, leaning in conspiratorially, closely.

He looked at her with puzzled amusement and placed one of his cigarettes between her lips before lighting it for her.

It tasted of Joan.

She noticed the clock after a while and realized the children's classes would soon be over for the day.

"I should...I need to get the children..." She said and fumbled for her wallet to pay, but Walter stopped her.

"On me. As long as you promise to come back tomorrow."

She disliked the way her stomach knotted at the request, but she nodded. For where else would she be?

"Thanks. For the drinks and the smoke." She said before slipping away to retrieve the children, feeling light headed and delightfully dizzy.

Chapter Forty

It was dark when Roger nudged her.

Her head pounded mercilessly.

Her eyes came open to the unfamiliar surroundings and it took her a moment to remember where they were.

A fresh layer of snow had descended from the sky the previous evening, the four of them had sat watching it fall. Roger had wanted to be up early to have a head start on the refreshed slopes.

But she hadn't imagined it would be quite so early.

The children were still asleep in the bed beside them. Henry had pushed off the sheets and Emma's back was turned to them.

Vera wanted to turn over and sleep off the dismal pain that was splintering in her forehead, but Roger had quietly climbed on top of her, pushing her legs apart.

"Roger." She whispered harshly, but he was already caressing her, his body taut above her.

He pulled the blanket over them and pushed her underwear to the side before entering her.

The bed rhythmically creaked along with his motions, and she closed her eyes, hoping the children would not wake.

Roger's breath came heavier with each thrust.

She bit her lip to keep herself from making any noise.

The bed creaked a bit louder.

She could feel his release coming.

"Mommy?" Henry's tired voice called out.

"Damn it." Roger cursed and rolled away from Vera. "Shit." And he stumbled from the bed and went into the bathroom and slammed the door behind himself.

Vera pulled herself back together, climbing from the bed. "What is it, baby?"

"I had a bad dream." Henry was looking up at her through tired eyes.

Emma had rolled over and was wide awake, staring worriedly up at her mother.

"Is daddy okay?" She asked tentatively.

"Everyone's okay." Vera reached out and soothed her hair away from her sweaty brow. "Henry, it was only a dream." And he nodded, climbing into her arms as if for protection from whatever horrors he'd just witnessed.

She reached for her cigarettes and sat in the children's bed smoking, coaxing them back to sleep.

She watched as Roger emerged from the bathroom, his face cross but his features relaxed. He went about putting on his ski outfit. He did not look at Vera or the children.

"I'll be back for dinner." He said then left the room.

Vera sat smoking with Henry half atop her and Emma curled into her side and watched the sun rise.

Their class began at ten.

She took them to the dining room for breakfast and ordered herself a bloody Mary to help with the pain in her head.

She wandered about the hotel lobby after dropping them

off. She stopped in the gift shop and looked at the items. A delicate scarf in a tantalizing red caught her attention.

Her fingers trailed over the material, imagining the way it would accentuate the darkness of Joan's eyes.

"It's not quite your color." A smiling sale's girl startled Vera.

"Oh," Vera released the material from her grasp.

"Someone so pale and beautiful as yourself would look good in this blue." She pointed to a periwinkle-colored scarf. "It would complement your eyes."

Vera felt her cheeks burning, uncertain whether the young clerk meant what she said or was only doing her job. "It's not... it's not for me."

The girl's eyes shimmered curiously.

Vera left the shop. She looked at her watch and found it was only half past ten.

She walked past the bar.

He was already perched atop a stool, gingerly drinking his whiskey.

She went inside and took the seat next to him.

He turned and smiled at her. "I wondered when you might show up."

She put a cigarette between her lips, and he lit it for her, ordering her a whiskey when the bartender appeared. "I'm already one ahead of you so you have to catch-up."

She drank, headache already fading away.

She could feel the other women looking at her, curious that she would rather sit at the bar with a man and not join them at their tables for idle gossip and mindless chatter.

But their interest in her waned with each passing hour.

Walter offered her a Winston sometime after noon.

She inhaled and the aborted sensations from the morning returned to her body. She thought of the women's bar and of Joan's body pressed against hers as they had danced. She thought of their hotel room in the city and how freely they had taken one another.

"It's none of my business..."

"No, it's probably not." Vera said sharply.

"But it would seem that you're pining for something. Someone, perhaps."

She turned to look at him.

What did he know?

"You're right," she blew smoke out between her lips in a thin line. "It is none of your business."

Walter laughed, because everything had become funny. Her dour demeanor delighted him. "You don't have to talk about it."

"There's nothing to talk about." She tapped off the ash and marveled at the lipstick stain around the end of the cigarette.

Walter regarded her around the smoke of his cigarette. She hated the way his lips curled upward in amusement. "It doesn't suit you."

"What?" She asked.

"Married life."

She leaned forward, itching at the back of her calf. "Why is that?" Unaffected by the observation because she'd always known the truth of it.

"You're too smart for it."

"Have I said something smart?"

He laughed again, coughing a bit until he smoked to soothe his throat. He drank back his whiskey and ordered another for the both of them. "You're not interested in it. That's all right. I've known plenty of women who hate the idea of it. You're not like these housewives here. They're content just sitting around playing bridge and waiting for their husband to pay them some attention, but not you."

"Stop it." She breathed smoke, his words causing her stomach to knot.

"I bet you'd like it if he'd leave you alone."

"What the hell do you know?" She spat and realized her anger only confirmed his words.

He drank his refreshed whiskey. "You're not really interested in me, either. But you'd go upstairs with me."

"Would I?" She swirled the amber liquid about in her glass before drinking it back.

"I suppose we could find out. I'm in room 612." He slid cash onto the bar for the both of them and then made an exit.

Vera put out her cigarette and ordered another drink.

She looked about her, the room slipping sideways when she turned her head. Her brain was sharp. She still had her wits about her. She was not drunk and yet the room danced.

She stared out of the window, out to the slopes and watched as the far away little people moved like ants down the hill.

The bartender sat the whiskey glass before her.

She lit another cigarette and sat smoking it while slowly savoring the drink. Leisurely.

There was no rush.

The glass was emptied, the cigarette crushed out in a cleaned ashtray.

She paid the bartender for the drink, tipping him far too much.

She slid off the barstool and thought to perhaps walk about aimlessly, but she stumbled and caught herself on a nearby chair.

She wanted to lie down.

Taking a deep breath, she steadied herself and moved through the lobby to the elevators.

Their room was on the fourth floor.

She pressed six and stood back, far away from the door.

Several people – a couple, a young woman, a young man – crowded on with her. The couple pressed four.

She watched as the numbers moved upward. One, two, someone got off at three, and then the doors slid open to the fourth floor.

But she did not move. The elevator emptied out and traveled to six.

The doors dinged open, and she stared down the hallway.

612 was to the right, there toward the end of the hall.

She walked unsteadily to the door and lifted her hand to knock.

She heard footsteps on the other side and then the door opened.

Walter was smiling down at her. He held the door wide for her and she walked inside.

"I suppose I was right, then." He said smugly.

"I just want to lie down." Vera whispered, slipping out of her heels, laying her bag atop the dresser. She looked about her and saw the little feminine touches spread out around the room. A bottle of perfume, lipstick, a hairbrush – a few strands of honeyed brown hair clung to it – the things of a woman. She wondered what she looked like, the woman he was married to. Who left her husband alone at a ski resort while she went out skiing for the day.

She could tell Walter was wealthy.

His wife would be young and attractive. He seemed a man who could have anything he wanted.

Vera sat on the edge of the bed.

"What does she look like?" She asked curiously.

"Who?" Walter put out his cigarette and sat down beside her.

"Your wife."

"Oh, you...you really want to know, don't you?" He pulled out his wallet from his back pocket and opened it to show her a beautiful woman. Light brown hair, clear calm eyes, a bit older than Vera had anticipated.

"First or second marriage?" Vera got out a cigarette and Walter lit it for her.

"Second." He laughed.

"She's beautiful."

"So was my first wife." He mused.

"What happened?" Vera laid back atop the bed, blowing smoke to the ceiling.

"She caught me cheating with my second wife."

Vera nodded her head. "Well, I won't be your third wife."

"I wouldn't expect it." He laid beside her, head propped atop his hand, staring down at her. "You're frigid."

"I'm not." She protested angrily.

"You don't like sex."

"You don't know me." She snapped. "You don't know one goddamn thing about me."

"But I knew you'd come."

"It doesn't mean I'll..." she sighed.

He took the cigarette from her and placed it between his lips before putting it in the ashtray beside the bed.

His lips were crushing and she fought him for a moment before she allowed him to kiss her. His body was larger than Roger's. And she closed her eyes and surrendered herself to him.

It wasn't until she caught sight of the clock that she went rigid. "I have to go...I have to get the children..." and she raced to wash herself in his bathroom and then put herself back together again.

"Tomorrow then?" He asked from the bed.

"No, I don't think so."

But the next day after drinking alone in the bar, she ended up at room 612 again.

Chapter Forty-One

Walter left Friday.

Vera watched the children ski Saturday and drank, a strange, lost feeling coming over her that depressed her all of Saturday evening.

She was grateful when Sunday came, and they drove home.

But returning home made her feel all the worse.

She felt as if she couldn't breathe until Roger went to work Monday morning.

She returned to her suburban life unwillingly, submitting angrily to her housewifely duties.

The children were still out of school and ran around the house like wild, restless animals. Henry had spilled his milk everywhere at breakfast and she'd yelled at him until he ran off crying.

After a cigarette and a sip of bourbon, she'd gone to comfort him.

She let him watch television and made chocolate chip cookies because it was too cold to make the children go out and play. Another winter storm was blowing in.

Emma had disappeared off to her room.

After pulling the cookies from the oven, Vera called out that they were hot and ready. But only Henry came running.

She pulled off her apron and went up the stairs, curious as to what was keeping her daughter so occupied in her room.

The door was shut. Vera pressed at it, and it came open.

Her eyes went wide at the sight before her.

Her daughter, her eight-year-old daughter, leaning against her bed, smoke curling from between her lips, a lit cigarette between her fingers.

Vera shoved the door open, and Emma looked up at her with wide, horrified eyes.

"What the hell do you think you're doing?" Vera's voice trembled ever as she watched the girl scramble to her feet, shaking.

"Mommy!" Emma cried, coughing on the smoke.

"What is this?" And she snatched the cigarette away from the girl.

"I just...I didn't mean..."

"How many have you had? Hmm? Is this the first time?" Vera demanded, shame and anger coursing through her, standing the hairs at the back of her neck on end.

"Yes...yes...I've never..." Emma cried.

"Come...come here." Vera grabbed the girl by the wrist and led her through the house and sat her down at the kitchen table.

Emma was crying, big wet tears streaming down her cheeks. "I'm sorry, Mommy, I'm sorry."

But her words fell on deaf ears.

"Mommy, what's wrong with Emma?" Henry was circling her, and she shooed him away.

She went to the refrigerator and got out a pack of her cigarettes and she returned to the kitchen table. "This is what my mother should've done when she first caught me." Vera stacked the pack and opened it. "You're going to smoke every single last one of these."

"Mommy, no...I don't want to."

"Too bad." And she held a cigarette out to her daughter and waited for her to place it between her trembling lips before she lit it. "That's right, go on and smoke it if you so desperately want to be like me." Vera tossed the lighter down and placed the burning cigarette she'd confiscated from her daughter between her own lips.

She sat and watched as the girl sat before her and smoked, coughing and sputtering all the while.

Emma only made it to the second cigarette before she darted from the table and raced to the bathroom below the stairs. Vera listened as she vomited.

She came out looking pale and ashen. "Mommy, I'll never do it again."

But Vera made her smoke another and then another. And by the sixth one Emma had vomited again and Vera sent her to her room.

Henry was looking at her with wide, frightened eyes.

She snatched up the bourbon and went up the stairs to her own room, slamming the door shut behind her. She laid on the bed smoking and sipping at the liquor. Tears pooled in her eyes, and she cried into her pillow.

She had failed them. Both of them.

She was not meant to be a mother.

Roger called to say he had too much work to catch up on and wouldn't be home that night.

Vera responded absently.

"Is everything all right?" He asked.

"Yes." Vera said and hung up.

She felt a horrible pain twist up inside of herself.

Henry looked up at her from his place on the couch and then looked back at the television.

She walked up the stairs and made her way down the hallway.

She could hear her daughter's sobs, loud and tortured through her bedroom door.

She turned the knob and went in.

Emma sat up and backed away from her in fear.

Vera climbed into the bed beside her daughter and wrapped her up in her arms and held her pressed close to her and allowed her to cry into her dress front. "I'm sorry. I'm so sorry." She whispered, pressing her lips against the girl's soft blonde hair.

They laid together until night fell.

Vera got up and made dinner for the children, eating bits and pieces of it herself.

Emma kept her eyes downcast at the table as she ate.

Henry looked uncomfortable. She let him go back to the television and Emma off to her room while she cleaned up after their dinner.

She took a long bath, smoking while she laid in warm bubbles.

She bathed Henry and then made a bath for Emma. She read Henry a story and put him to sleep and then went to Emma's room.

The girl was shy with her but cuddled into her side.

Something had changed between them.

Emma seemed older to her now. She was no longer a child.

They fell asleep together, but Vera awoke sometime later.

She quietly moved from the bed and went to the living room to light a cigarette and pour herself another drink, catching sight of the clock.

It was only ten.

It felt like midnight.

She wanted to call Joan.

She stared at the phone receiver for a long time before she made herself go up the stairs to her bedroom.

She laid on the bed and thought of Joan. Of Joan naked.

She thought of Walter. Of how rough he had been with her, how very opposite Joan he was and yet she had wanted that. She had wanted to be awakened out of her fevered dreams.

She thought furiously of running away with Joan. Of disappearing in the city, never to be found again by anyone.

She thought perhaps neither Henry nor Emma would even miss her. For how awful she was to both of them.

The thought aroused her.

Of simply leaving, of beginning again.

Of taking Joan however she wanted, whenever she wanted. To rent a little apartment in the Village and walk around naked so they could make love whenever they wished.

She put out her cigarette and buried her hand beneath her pajamas.

She cried out Joan's name when she brought herself over the edge then turned over and pressed her face into the pillow and sobbed.

She willed sleep to come, but it eluded her.

She got out of bed and wrapped a robe about herself and went down to the kitchen and lit a cigarette and picked the phone up from the receiver and dialed the number she knew by heart.

"Vera?" The voice on the other end startled her.

"Oh, Joan." And she started crying. "I can't...I can't go on like this. I miss you...I miss you terribly."

Chapter Forty-Two

The excuse was incoherent even to herself, but Judy didn't seem to mind taking the children the following day. Vera thanked her profusely, promising to be back before it got too late.

The sky had opened up and the snow came down silently onto the freshly cleared streets. She dreamed of getting stranded, of not being able to return home.

She drove carefully, cigarette clasped between her teeth as she concentrated on the road, thankful she didn't have to travel very far.

She turned into the drive and skidded her way to a stop before the house.

Her boots sank in the snow, wetting her ankles.

The door opened and Joan appeared wrapped up in an oversized sweater and slacks, Lulu at her side, too cold to race to Vera so she simply meowed her greeting.

Joan clasped Vera's face between her hands and their lips met the instant Vera stepped onto the porch. "Get inside, it's freezing out here." Joan pulled her in, shutting the door to the cold winter day.

A fire was blazing in the fireplace, a cup of coffee sat atop the coffee table, a discarded blanket, a book split open and face down beside it.

It was unbearably warm until Joan began undoing Vera's coat and removing it from her shoulders. Then she leaned down to help her out of her boots. "Your stockings are soaked." Joan laughed and pulled Vera to the couch. They wrestled her out of the offending garment and Joan hung them near the fireplace to dry.

"Joan," Vera whimpered.

Joan came to her, wrapping her up in her arms, pressing kisses to her neck.

"I'm no good. I'm no good, I've never been good." Vera cried, inaudibly at first until the words were coming loud and clear.

Joan clasped her wrists, forcing her to look at her. "Don't say that about yourself."

'But it's the truth." And she felt big wet tears slipping down her cheeks.

"It isn't." Joan reached for a box of tissues and wiped at Vera's cheeks.

"I can't stand it, Joan, I can't...I can't take it." Vera's voice broke as the tears continued to flow. "I never wanted this. I never wanted...I hate..."

Joan sat wordlessly.

Vera reached for her purse, for her cigarettes. She lit one with a shaky hand, Joan pulling out her ashtray. Vera blew a stream of smoke toward the ceiling. "I do these...these impulsive things. I lash out, I go cold, I retreat, I can't...I can't relate to anyone except you. You're the only one...you're the only one I can talk to. Really talk to. And we hardly even get to do that!" Vera gestured wildly with her cigarette. "I've never fully felt myself until I was here. With you. And now that I've...I've felt it, touched it...I can't make it go away. It's always there, always pestering me. And I'm miserable."

Joan touched her cheek, wiping at a tear with her thumb.

Vera's lip trembled at the touch.

"Oh, Joan. I'm an awful person."

"Why?" Joan smoothed out one of Vera's errant curls.

"I slept with a man. In Vermont. I don't know why. He reminded me so much of you and I...I slept with him. And I didn't even like it, I just wanted it to be you." The tears slid from her eyes. "I thought maybe I could make you go away, I thought he could just...make it better somehow, but it didn't. It didn't make it go away."

Joan looked at her, a shade of hurt or pain crossing her features.

"Please don't...don't be upset." Vera whispered, putting the cigarette between her lips to inhale, stomach knotting that she'd said it, that she'd said anything to Joan, but Joan deserved the full truth of things. Joan mattered.

"Upset...well, I..." And Joan turned from her to fetch her own cigarettes from the side table. "I'm not your husband." Joan said, lighting the end of the cigarette with a match.

Vera felt fresh tears cloud her vision. "No, but you...you..."

Joan shrugged. "It was something you needed to get out of your system, I suppose." And she sat back on the couch.

Vera wiped at her eyes, smoking furiously. "No, it was...my God, I don't even understand it. I don't even understand myself half the time."

"Why are you telling me about it?" Joan stood up, staring down into the fireplace at the dancing flames.

"Because I love you." Vera whispered.

Joan did not turn to her. "Jesus, Vera."

Vera bit her lip, fresh tears welling in her eyes. "Joan, I..."

"Don't say it." Joan turned on her. "Don't say that."

"Why not?" Vera shot back, indignant.

"Because I can't...because then it would..." Joan's fingers curled into her hair.

"It would what?" Vera demanded.

Joan sank onto the chair opposite the fireplace, away from the couch and Vera. She sank her head into her hands.

Vera had never seen her like this.

Joan was always poised, always the steady rock she could cling to. Joan did not falter, but now she looked as if she were about to cry and it shattered Vera.

She put out her cigarette and went to sit before Joan, to wrap her arms about her legs, to press her lips against Joan's temples. "Joan?"

Joan did not look up at her.

"I'm sorry, Joan. I'm so sorry." Vera whimpered. "Please."

"Oh, Vera." Joan sat up, looking down at Vera as she smoked. "It hurts me. It hurts me terribly to love you this much."

Vera's eyes widened at the statement and then she was crying again.

"And there's nothing I can do about it but take it for what it is." Joan did not reach for Vera.

"But this isn't...my God, this isn't just some fling. This matters, Joan. This matters to me." Vera sat up on her knees so that she could look Joan dead in the eyes. "You matter to me."

Joan flicked ash absently. "So what do you want to do about it?"

"I want to run...I want to run away with you."

Joan shook her head. "Vera..."

"I'm serious."

Joan was laughing again. "Oh, Vera. Oh, my sweet, darling." And she tossed her cigarette into the flames of the fire and leaned forward to pull Vera to her, to kiss her lips.

She took her upstairs and they took their time. Slipping

beneath Joan's bedsheets for warmth until their bodies warmed and they pushed them away.

They took wantonly, leisurely. Kissing away tears, distracting with touches and caresses.

They laid smoking in the bed, cuddled together for warmth afterwards. Lulu curled herself at Vera's side, purring contentedly, Vera's hand buried in her soft fur.

"I wish it could always be like this." She exhaled a cloud of smoke.

"So do I." Joan conceded, taking the cigarette from Vera.

Vera turned to look at her. "Did you ever...did you ever want to...with a man?"

Joan coughed on smoke. "Well, no...I don't suppose I ever did."

"So you've never..."

"It might surprise you, but no. I've never." Joan's lip quirked upwards at the admission.

"Not even when you were engaged..."

"What? Oh. You mean to Peter Kendrick. The man I told you I almost married?" Joan turned to face Vera, their legs still entwined together beneath the warm sheets.

"Yes." Vera took the cigarette from Joan.

"Well, he was gay."

"He was...gay?"

Joan laughed. "Yes, very gay. And he knew I was very gay so he thought that if we married it would solve all our problems. But along with his marriage proposal were a million other little stipulations of how he wanted his wife to behave in public. And I didn't want to give up my job or my autonomy for him, so...we parted ways. He moved back to the city years ago. I hardly hear from him."

"Would you?" Vera peered at her curiously.

"What?"

"Move back to the city?"

Joan laid back onto the bed, looking up at the ceiling. "Sometimes I think about it."

Vera put out the cigarette and curled atop Joan's side. "I want to move there with you."

"Do you?" Joan put her arm about Vera, kissing her forehead.

"I want to get a little apartment in the Village – maybe only two little rooms. Less cleaning that way." Vera smiled against Joan's breast, teasing the other with her fingers.

"What about your children?" Joan asked soberly.

Vera rolled away from Joan, covering her face with her hands. "I don't want to think about my children."

"Nor do I, but they're..."

"They'd probably be just fine without me. I only cause them more pain than happiness. All they ever do is see the worst of me." Vera sat up and pulled the sheets about her, reaching for another cigarette. "It might be better if I left them."

"Don't say such a thing. Children need their mother."

"Not a mother like me." Vera exhaled a cloud of smoke. "Well, damn it. What else can we do?"

Joan stroked her thigh. "Go on like this?"

"It's not enough." Vera pulled her body away. She saw the clock and wanted to cry again that it was nearing four in the afternoon.

"Give me some time." Joan's voice whispered.

Vera turned to look at her. "You'll consider it?"

Joan sat up, a worried look creasing her brow. "It would have to be handled very carefully."

A smile found its way to Vera's lips. She bowed over Joan, pressing their lips together until their bodies were rolling about the bed again, this time more urgent and passionate than before.

Chapter Forty-Three

Roger was looking at her over his dinner.

She ate a steamed carrot then picked up the glass of wine she'd poured for herself.

His gaze made her uneasy.

The children asked to be excused and she allowed them to go but wished they would stay to distract from whatever it was that Roger had on his mind.

"Where were you yesterday?" He asked, voice low.

She drank the wine and furrowed her brow. "Did you call?"

"I saw Phil on the train. Said the children had been with Judy."

"I was running errands."

"He said they stayed all day."

Vera cut a carrot in half and shoved it to the opposite side of the plate. "I told you. I was running errands."

"The whole day?" He asked incredulously.

Vera nodded. "The car got stuck in the snow. Someone passing by had to help me out."

Roger eyed her. She could tell he wanted to believe her.

Damn Phil. Damn the children. There was only one day left of Christmas break that Vera could escape to Joan's. One more chance and she wouldn't have Judy to rely on or perhaps any of the other mothers and so any plan to go to Joan was shot to hell.

She wanted to cry, but she couldn't let him see that he was getting to her.

"You're drinking too much." He finally said.

She sat the wine glass onto the table a bit too roughly.

"That bottle of whiskey is nearly gone, and I only bought it the week before last. Goddamn it, that was expensive, Vera." He hit his fists slowly, angrily against the table.

It jostled her and she felt a headache coming on.

She'd gotten sloppy about adding a bit of water to keep the levels in the bottles up. And besides, the watered-down whiskey hadn't packed the same punch.

"If it's about the baby..."

"God, Roger." Vera lit a cigarette.

"Then what the hell is wrong with you?" The anger was back in his voice.

She couldn't look at him.

They avoided one another the rest of the night.

Roger didn't even try anything with her, and it sent a wave of panic racing through her.

What did he think he knew?

After she took him to the train the following morning, she returned home and called Joan.

"I can't...oh...I can't make it today. I can't leave the children. Judy told her husband I was out all day and now Roger is suspicious."

Joan was quiet on the other end.

"What?" Vera demanded. "You can't be cross with me."

"No, darling. I'm not cross...I'm worried."

"Roger won't do anything. He's only trying to figure me out. He hasn't a clue...it's all right." Vera tried to soothe over the situation, but she could tell that Joan was afraid.

"You don't know men, Vera."

"How would he know?" Vera's voice felt small.

"We went away together..."

"He didn't suspect..."

"We have to be careful, Vera." Joan's voice had hardened.

"Careful...all we ever are is careful." Vera hissed, putting out a cigarette so she could light another.

"Vera, I am a teacher in this provincial little town. Those parents are already suspicious of me. You told me yourself that they warned you off me. So, I'm on shaky ground as it is, darling. Don't you see?" Joan's voice was pleading.

Vera pressed her eyes closed, fighting off the tears.

Joan was right. Joan was terribly right.

She was being selfish.

With her wants, with her unquenchable desires.

"You're right...you're right...I'm so sorry." Vera whispered out through tears and saw Emma staring at her from the foot of the staircase, all sleepy-eyed and concerned. Oh, how she was awful to everyone.

Awful to Joan, awful to her children, awful to Roger.

"Don't cry, Vera. Don't cry when I can't properly comfort you." Joan was saying on the other end of the line.

"Well, what am I supposed to do?" Vera turned her back on her daughter and covered the receiver with her hand, as if the girl might not hear anything. She'd already seen enough. "I'm just awful."

"You're not awful, darling. We're just in an impossible situation." Joan assured.

"It doesn't seem so impossible for you." Vera said and then regretted it.

"And why is that?" Joan's voice had an edge to it.

"You're free to do what you want. You have options. I don't understand why you stay here. I couldn't stand it." Vera blurted out, temper flaring again.

"You're right. You don't understand." Joan's voice was flat.

Vera whimpered and sank to the kitchen floor ungracefully. Tired of the goddamn phone between them. If she could just be there, if she could simply reach out for Joan, see the expression in her eyes, then she would know, would understand.

But she was stuck.

Stuck in this house with these children in this life she despised.

"Mommy, are you all right?" Emma's timid voice came from the kitchen doorway.

"It sounds like you should go." Joan said in her ear.

"No, I..."

"In a week the auxiliary meetings will begin again." Joan reminded her.

And then the phone line went dead.

Vera felt tears slipping down her cheeks as she let the phone fall, swinging back and forth on its cord, the dial tone beeping incessantly.

Emma slipped her arms about Vera's neck and hugged her tightly. "It's okay, Mommy. I love you."

Vera wrapped her arms about her daughter and held her close as the tears came hot and heavy.

Sunday came and she stared at the back of Joan's neck and thought of caressing it. They barely spoke two words to one another, as if afraid even looking at the other might arouse some suspicion within Roger.

Vera felt stifled by it.

On Monday morning, after she'd taken the children to school, she purchased her own bottle of whiskey and spent the day drinking little sips of it and then hid it amongst her things in the dresser drawer.

The whiskey was gone by Wednesday.

She was drunk at dinner that night but tried to hold herself as if she were not.

While cleaning up, a plate slipped from her soapy hands and shattered all over the floor.

Roger appeared in the doorway. "Goddamn it, Vera."

"It's only a plate, Roger." She shot back, on edge, a bit dizzy.

He caught her arm and looked into her face. "You're drunk."

"Take your hands off me." She shook her arm free.

He left. He took the car keys and left.

Henry came to her crying, Emma appearing at the bottom of the steps in tears.

She shooed Henry away from the broken pieces, told the both of them to leave her alone, and then sat down on the kitchen floor to light a cigarette with a shaky hand. Roger had bruised her arm.

Roger came back late that evening. Well past midnight, and she thought she could smell someone else's perfume on him.

She laid quietly in the bed, feigning sleep when he crawled in beside her.

He did not try anything with her, and she felt relief and fear.

She was nervous the following evening. Smoked cigarette after cigarette to try and calm her nerves, as she drove to the church.

She hadn't spoken to Joan since their last phone conversation.

She had hurt her, she knew.

She was afraid to face her and yet she needed to see her.

And there she was. As beautiful as ever arranging cookies on a plate when Vera walked in a few minutes late.

Joan looked at her with those wide, beautiful eyes. She smiled at Vera and Vera wished they were alone and not before the other women.

The meeting was insufferable. Vera was absent, nodding when she thought a response was needed, but otherwise wholly occupied by furtively watching Joan.

Vera stole to the kitchen the minute the meeting was done, wishing to make quick work of cleaning up.

The women lingered far too long, one speaking for what seemed like hours to Joan.

Vera had nearly cleaned up the entire kitchen space when Joan finally appeared with the last of the teacups.

Joan placed the teacups in the sink and Vera wiped her hands on a towel.

"They're gone." Joan said simply.

Vera bowed her head, fighting back frustrated tears. "I'm so sorry, Joan. The other day..."

Joan took her into her arms and held her close. "Shh. You weren't wrong, darling." Joan conceded. "I'm sorry I was short with you. I guess I'm just a coward."

Vera looked up at Joan and their lips met. "You're not a coward."

"I'm afraid I am." Joan pulled away and held out her hand for Vera to take. They traveled through the church, to their hideaway in the library and Joan undressed Vera. "I don't know if I could leave this place."

"Why not?" Vera asked as she helped get Joan's shirt off, fear gripping her at the idea that Joan might never leave. Fear that her whole dream of running away might never come to fruition.

"I don't know...I suppose I feel stuck here. My mother...my father...they're gone but they were here." Joan's voice was quiet.

And Vera suddenly understood. "Oh, Joan." And she took her into her arms and laid her down and loved her.

273

Chapter Forty-Four

On Thursdays she stayed sober.

For the most part.

If the other days she drank a little too much, then it was only to get through, to help her face her husband and her children and her duties.

On Thursdays she had Joan.

Vera talked dreamily of leaving and Joan listened.

But Joan did not commit to it wholeheartedly.

It irritated Vera.

In the rumination of their conversations, over a glass of whiskey, Vera would find Joan had not agreed to anything.

One Thursday she drank a bit too much before the ladies auxiliary meeting.

Joan tasted it on her lips when they kissed.

"Jesus, Vera." Joan had said.

"What?" Vera let her hand trail over Joan's backside.

"You're quite soused, aren't you?"

Vera laughed at it. "No, just a drink or two. Harmless."

"Vera, darling, the drinking to make things better isn't helpful." Joan warned.

"Then how are we supposed to make things better? You won't even go away with me." Vera pouted.

Joan pulled away from her and went to finish up the dishes.

Vera was hurt.

She lit a cigarette in irritation.

"Vera, it's not so simple. Your children..."

"My God! What about them? I've told you I'm not a decent mother to them."

"They love you, Vera. They *need* you." Joan did not look at Vera, instead continuing to wash the dishes.

"They don't need me." Vera said as she felt the tears coming.

"You would miss them." Joan said simply, placing the last dried cup back into the cabinet.

Vera shook her head. "No." She thought of Emma wrapped up in her arms and the sweet smell of Henry.

But there was also the sweetness of Joan, the smell of her skin, of her sex, of her comfort, the beauty of her on the inside and out.

It was all mixed up in her mind.

She wished there was something to drink in the godforsaken church.

"You love them." Joan said as she turned to look at Vera.

Vera covered her face. "It...it shouldn't have to be a goddamn choice. I'd take them if I could, but Roger..."

Joan's lips turned upward in a sad smile.

Vera puffed at her cigarette. "He hasn't the slightest clue what to do with them, but he'd certainly keep them away from me."

Joan went to Vera, wrapping her up in her arms, kissing her neck. "So, you see, it's not so simple."

Vera put out her cigarette in a nearby saucer and let Joan take her to the library.

She hated that Roger looked at her when she came home that night. That he followed her with his eyes as she went up the stairs to kiss Henry and Emma goodnight and then disappear into their bedroom. She wanted to wash herself but as she undressed Roger came into the bathroom.

"You're home late."

Vera hadn't noticed the time. "No later than normal."

"You'd better tell me..." his face was red.

"Tell you what?" She stopped mid-undressing, knowing that her ruined underwear might give her away if he were to see.

"It's someone else, isn't it?"

She felt a loud thump in her chest, her throat tightening in fear.

"You've been fooling around with someone. Ken?"

"What?" She almost laughed at the suggestion. "My God, I wouldn't go near him. He disgusts me."

"Then who? Which one of these husbands are you sneaking off with?"

Vera fought back the smile that threatened to show. "Darling, I'm not fooling around with any other man. There's not one of them in this town that remotely interests me."

He looked at her a bit incredulously.

"Roger," she stepped toward him.

He didn't move away from her.

She could handle this.

He let her touch him, let her kiss him.

She wished she could have bathed. She wished his face wasn't so stubbly and rough against her cheeks. But she kissed him as if she meant it.

He pulled her into the bedroom and put her beneath him. She let him dominate her, and he marveled that she could be so wanting for him.

It soothed him, it made him happy, and she whispered

false confessions of love and devotion to him and fell asleep in his arms, the way he had liked to hold her at the beginning of their marriage.

Her insides churned in his embrace.

She waited for his breaths to even out and then slipped from beneath his strong arm.

She went to the bathroom and showered, washed out her mouth, then wrapped herself in a robe and padded down the stairs for a cigarette and a drink to calm herself.

How long could she put him off?

After another splash of bourbon, she felt an ache running along her spine. A pain that went deep in her bones.

She groaned.

Would she be trapped in this home for the rest of her life?

The pain intensified and she sank down on the couch.

She crawled back to bed that night, knowing she would have to prove herself a devoted wife. She didn't want him to find her on the couch in the morning.

He kissed her with a renewed fondness when she dropped him off at the train station the following morning.

She masked the banging in her head, the awful pain that pinched her brow.

She went home and was sick before she got the children ready for school.

She stole a nip of whiskey and then took the children to the school and ached for Joan.

She drove aimlessly after she dropped the children off. She stopped at the store to buy cigarettes and a fifth of whiskey.

She drove and drove and ended up in the city. She drove from the tip of Manhattan down through the winding traffic of the city. She had no idea where she was going, but she ended up near Fourteenth Street.

She parked the car on the street and wandered the streets of the winding Village, smoking cigarette after cigarette and stealing nips of the whiskey when no one might notice.

She found the bar they had gone to.

It was open early on Friday afternoon.

She felt self-conscious, as if she did not belong in the light of day. She was a married woman alone who scarcely looked like a normal patron.

But the lure of a drink amongst women who could openly love women enticed her enough to enter.

A mannish looking woman stopped her. "What do you think you're doing in here?"

"I...I just came for a drink." Vera stuttered.

The woman looked her over head to toe. "You know what kind'a place this is?"

"Yes." Vera lowered her eyes.

The woman softened only a little and nodded for Vera to go on.

Her nerves were frayed when she took a seat near the back corner of the bar.

An attractive young woman in trousers was behind the bar. She looked Vera over as she settled her purse atop the countertop and smiled sweetly at her. "What'll you have, sweetheart?"

"Whiskey." Vera said, cheeks flushing at the way the woman looked at her.

"You've got it." And she flipped a cup over with a flourish and made a spectacle of pouring the liquid into the glass. "Been here before?"

Vera sipped the liquid and delighted in how it made her whole body warm. "Yes."

The girl looked surprised. "Haven't seen you before."

"It was only once." Vera shrugged.

"And you came back for more."

Vera nodded.

"Special occasion?" The girl inquired, insistent on talking to Vera for there were hardly any other patrons about them. A few women were scattered about, but no one of interest to either Vera or the bartender.

Vera swirled the liquid about in her glass and wished Joan could be there with her, at her side.

If they could only live here openly.

She let the dream overcome her. That Joan might be coming from a teaching job in the city and would meet her at the bar and kiss her on the lips and they might have a drink out and then stumble back to their little room on the second floor of a brownstone...

She sipped the drink again, washing it all away.

"It's my birthday."

Chapter Forty-Five

It was the beginning of March, the first stirrings of spring in the air.

Vera had spent the day between a bottle of whiskey and cleaning the house.

She was drunk enough to ask Judy if she would mind picking the children up from school, feigning a headache. Judy told her to take aspirin and go right to bed and not to worry.

Vera's hand shook when she hung up the phone. She had to light a cigarette to calm her nerves.

She would have to sober up before Roger came home.

He had not been home the previous two nights, but had not called that day. So she expected him as ever on the six thirty train.

She hid the empty whiskey bottle beneath the sink along with one from two days before. She would have to do something about it, but that would be later.

Just then the room was spinning and she did want to lie down.

She made herself some coffee and took it to the living

room, where she laid atop the couch and ended up snoozing until she heard the front door open and the children race in.

She sat up and her head splintered and her back ached.

Judy appeared with the children at the top of the stairs. "You look awful."

"Oh." Vera tried to smooth back her hair.

"Let me get you a glass of water."

Emma was eyeing her curiously but Judy gently shooed the children off to their rooms. She disappeared into the kitchen and returned with a glass of water and an ice pack. "Just lay down." Judy told her in soothing tones.

Vera fought back tears, allowing the woman to care for her.

"Is everything all right?" Judy asked.

And Vera blinked, wishing in that moment she could tell her everything. That she was slowly drowning herself, that she was in love with a woman, that she wanted to get out...

But Judy couldn't possibly understand any of it.

So she nodded lightly. "I'm fine."

Judy patted her arm. "Just rest. You'll be better in the morning."

She got up to go.

"Judy..." Vera called weakly.

Judy turned back to her, a little smile forced across her lips.

"Th...thank you."

Judy nodded and left.

Vera pressed the cold pack to her head and groaned.

She had to force herself to make dinner for the children and prepare food for Roger's return. The coffee seemed to help sober her, but her body still ached.

She watched the children eat with a cigarette between her fingers.

She went upstairs to put herself together and then she drove to the station.

Roger was waiting for her.

He leaned over to kiss her. She gave him her cheek.

"You don't look well." He said after studying her.

"Headache." She said.

His brow creased at the excuse, as if he no longer believed her. He shoved her out of the driver's seat and drove them home.

She sat at the table with him, watching him eat and picking at her own food.

She watched his fist tighten around his fork.

She swallowed a piece of asparagus, waiting.

"You're drinking too much." He finally said.

Her jaw clenched. "No."

"I can smell it on you, Vera. The headache...I mean, come on."

She put out her cigarette and reached for another. "I have a nip here and there. It's not like you're not putting away a drink or two at a business lunch."

"It's not the same and you know it." Roger's jaw had tightened. "You've been drinking all day. What's your goddamn problem?"

She rubbed her forehead. "I haven't."

He slammed his fists against the table. "Stop lying to me, Vera."

"I won't be talked to this way." She spat as she stood from the table, angrily putting out her cigarette.

"And I won't allow this, Vera. Do you hear?" He had risen too.

"You can't punish me like I'm a child, Roger." She shot back as she carried her plate to the sink and shoved it atop the other dirty dishes.

"You certainly act like one." He was behind her then. "What is it, Vera? I thought maybe you needed a change of scenery, that the city was too much for you."

"I feel stuck here, Roger. Can't you understand? At least in the city there were places to go, people to see…"

"Too many places for you to hide."

"I was never hiding." She rolled her eyes, head splintering.

"You're my wife, Vera. You can't just go off and disappear on a whim. And you can't sit around getting drunk all day. You have two children to take care of."

"The children! All I ever do is think of the children!" She smashed a plate on the floor.

His eyes went wide and then he was furious. "What the hell are you doing? Are you mad?"

"No, but I'm mad to stay here and take this from you." She brushed past him in his confusion and went for her boots, for her coat.

He was upon her and grabbed her, holding her tightly.

"Let me go!" She cried, flailing in his arms.

He held tighter. She dug her nails into his arm and he hissed in pain but his grasp only tightened.

The children were on the stairs in tears, watching.

"Go back to your rooms." Roger growled.

Vera hit him in the groin and he dropped his grasp. She managed to get away fast enough to race through the kitchen and toward the patio door. He reached her in that moment and she turned, scratching her fingers across his face. He howled in pain.

It gave her enough time to get out the door, pulling on her coat as she ran through the chilly night, racing as fast as she could through the woods.

"Vera! Vera, goddamn it, come back here!" Roger was following her.

She could hear his footsteps behind her.

A twig tripped her and she went tumbling to the ground, looking wildly about for a place to hide.

She rolled until she was wedged between a fallen tree and

a ditch. She tried to remain completely still, listening as Roger called out for her, listening as his voice got dangerously close and then slowly, slowly further away.

"Vera?! Damn. Damn it." She heard him cursing. "You're going to regret this!" He finally announced.

She did not move.

Not a single muscle.

She was hardly aware if she was breathing or not.

The minutes passed by. The moon was a sliver in the sky. She watched it make its slow trek across the sky.

Roger had been in the military.

He could easily outsmart her.

Or could he?

There was only the sound of the earth around her. A little wind in the empty branches above her. The call of a nighttime animal.

She let her head come slowly up to survey the area.

There was no trace of movement, of anyone nearby.

Her eyes had adjusted to the dark. Her mind was crisp and clear.

She rolled herself over, feeling pain in her foot and knee. She began to crawl slowly, quietly away from where she had been, all the while looking out for Roger at every turn.

Would he be sitting silently, waiting for her to make a move?

What would he do when he caught her?

Her heart pounded in her chest as she crawled as quietly as possible through the brush of the forest. And when the fear and panic welled inside of her, and she thought he couldn't possibly be near to her then, she stood up and started to run.

She raced through the dimly lit forest as fast as she could.

Until she felt her foot catch at something and she went tumbling forward again. "Shit." She cursed, feeling that her legs were banged up, her hands bruised and bloody.

She turned to see what she had fallen over and recognized the well.

It sat there, covered over by cement and fallen branches.

The sight of it frightened her and she scurried up and away, moving faster through the forest. Running with all her strength until she saw the lights in the windows of the little house in the woods.

And she raced onto the porch and pounded on the front door, tears pouring from her eyes.

The door opened.

"My God, Vera!" Joan gasped and made quick work of helping Vera inside.

Chapter Forty-Six

"You're bleeding." Joan began to undress her. First her boots, then her coat, her torn dress, her bloodied stockings. "What happened?"

Vera felt a migraine coming on.

As the high of it all began to wear off she found her body was in immense pain. She could hardly keep herself up.

"Can you make it upstairs? I'll draw you a bath." Joan was holding her about the waist and carefully guided her up to the second floor and sat her down on the toilet while she carefully went about preparing the bath.

Vera hunched forward over her knees, shaking and crying.

"Did he hurt you?" Joan asked as she worked.

Vera shook her head. "No."

"Does he know where you went?" Joan asked softly.

"No."

"Come on, let's get you in the tub." And Joan carefully helped her into the hot water that burned where she'd cut and scratched herself along the way.

Joan washed away the dirt and dried blood. She cleaned

her up, whispering sweet things to Vera, pressing her lips against her shoulder, her back.

"What happened out in those woods?" Joan asked.

"I tripped." Vera said simply, surveying her bruised and banged up knees and legs.

Joan did not believe her as she continued to scrub at her skin. Vera saw there were tears in her eyes and it made her want to cry again.

Vera shivered and Joan helped her up. She wrapped her up in a towel then half-carried her to her bedroom where she laid her atop the bed. Joan sat before Vera, lighting her a cigarette before bandaging her wounds. Then she helped her into a pair of her pajamas and tucked her in. "You'll stay here tonight." Joan insisted.

"Joan." Vera grasped at her.

Joan wiped at the tears in her eyes. "It's all right."

"It isn't." Vera covered her eyes with her hands. "It was my fault. It was all my fault." Vera whispered through her own tears.

"What was?" Joan sat at the edge of the bed.

"He was upset with me. He was upset that I...I drank."

Joan nodded. "You've been doing a lot of that lately."

"Don't you...don't you start with me, too." Vera couldn't bear it if she had to hear it from Joan.

Joan stroked her forehead. "I'm worried."

Vera closed her eyes tight and hard. "It's the only goddamn way to escape, to make it all go away." A tear slid from her closed eyes. "I have to leave, Joan. I have to get away from here." She opened her eyes, pleading with Joan. "I love you, Joan. I love you and I want to be with you. Not like this. Not hidden away with only stolen moments between us as if it's some horrible crime."

"Oh, darling," Joan pressed her lips against her cheek. "But it is a crime no matter where we go. We'll always be hiding away from something."

"I'd rather be hiding with you than apart from you." Vera insisted.

Another tear slid down Joan's cheek.

Vera pulled herself up in the bed and reached for Joan's hand. "You're scared."

Joan laughed humorously. "Perhaps."

"I've upset your life terribly, haven't I?" Vera held her hand tightly.

Joan wiped at her eyes. "I'm older than you, Vera. Just up and leaving and running away isn't so easy for me."

"But is hiding out here in this godawful town any easier than being with me? Surrounded by your friends in a city that could look the other way?" Vera tried.

Joan nodded. "No. It's not easier." Joan took a deep, shaky breath. "Oh, Vera. How would we do it? Hmm? Do you have any money to your name?"

"Yes. I have a personal account in the city from when I was working. Roger doesn't know about it."

"And I have savings and this house. There wouldn't be a teaching position for me until the fall, perhaps, but we could find little things to do in the city. There's always substitute teaching. Claudia or Matilde could put in a good word for me and I would just hope that they don't contact the school here for a reference." Joan was reasoning it all out. "We could stay with them for a bit until we find a place."

Vera's eyes were getting wider and wider. "So you'll go?"

Joan looked uneasy but shook her head up and down. "Yes."

Vera wrapped Joan up in her arms. "When can we go?"

"I...I need a day to put my affairs in order. Friday?" Joan reasoned.

"I'll have to get some things from the house..." Vera was smiling.

Joan laid down beside her as if she were exhausted by the thought of it all. "How will you explain it to Roger? You can't tell him..."

"I'll ask for a divorce."

Joan looked at her with wide, surprised eyes. "On what grounds?"

"We don't get along. We haven't for years." Vera turned to face Joan, stroking her cheek. "I won't mention you. He was suspicious, but he thought it was a man. I assured him it certainly was not another man."

Joan was looking into her eyes. "But you like men?"

Vera twirled a bit of Joan's hair about in her fingers. "It's nothing like being with you. I want to be with you, Joan. You."

Joan let Vera kiss her, but the same worry from before was furrowing her brow.

"What is it?" Vera stroked Joan's hair, delighting in their closeness, in this stolen night with her. Roger, the children, the house, the chores, so far from her...

"I'm...well, I'm much older than you, Vera." Joan said. "It will be different in the city. There are many women in the village, all very beautiful and you'll be free..."

Vera grasped Joan's face in her hands. "Don't talk like that."

"You slept with that man..."

"I wanted it to be you, Joan. I wanted him to be you the whole time." Vera cried. "I want to devote myself to you, don't you understand? I'm myself with you. I'm who I was supposed to be with you. Don't you think I saw it when we were there? Those bars full of women...all hot and ready for one another. But none of them compare. I only want you, Joan." Vera insisted. "You. I love you. I love you for your age and everything else that is you. You're the only good thing I've come across and I wouldn't want to lose that for anything."

Joan's furrowed brow showed she didn't believe it.

"I wish you wouldn't worry about such things. I'm yours. I'm all yours." Vera had rolled on top of Joan, burying her face in her neck and kissing it.

"I want to believe you. " Joan wrapped her arms about Vera, holding her close. "I want to."

"Believe me." Vera insisted as their lips met, hungry for one another. "I'll happily spend the rest of my life proving it to you."

Joan whimpered and let Vera touch her between her legs.

They made love and then laid in the silence of the night.

Vera startled awake the next morning.

The sky was overcast.

Joan was not in the bed beside her.

Lulu was curled up atop Vera's feet.

Joan appeared in the doorway half dressed with a cup of coffee in hand. Vera could tell she was surprised to find her awake. "Good morning." Joan smiled slowly.

"Morning." Vera stretched and Joan came to her, pressing a kiss to her lips and offering her the coffee.

"I'll go to school. I think it's best if I continue as usual until Friday." She explained.

Vera reached for her pack of Winstons and lit one. "Roger will be at work. I'll go get my things."

"Be careful." Joan caressed her cheek.

"He won't hurt me."

Joan looked doubtful. "Just be careful."

"I will be." Vera reassured her, pulling her close to kiss her.

Joan made breakfast and they ate together.

How domestic it all was.

How wonderful it would be if this could be their life together.

Vera wished they could simply stay in this home together. That she could go and collect her children and leave Roger behind on the other side of the forest and live a life with Joan and the children in this beautiful home.

But it couldn't be so easy, could it?

She saw Joan off, kissing her goodbye. They smiled at one another.

She put on Joan's clothes, some trousers and a sweater and put her coat over herself before slipping into her boots.

She walked back through the woods with a cigarette between her fingers, body aching.

The home loomed before her. Ugly and modern. She would not miss it.

The backdoor was unlocked.

She slid inside and found the table had not been cleaned from the night before and cereal bowls sat half-eaten atop its surface. The smashed plate had remained on the ground, only it had been shoved away from the sink and the fridge. The fragments crunched beneath her boots.

It looked like a disaster.

Roger had done nothing to clean it up.

She put the dirty dishes in the sink and swept the remnants of the plate up before tossing them away. The final housekeeping she would do in the home, she thought, then moved to go upstairs to pack.

But she froze when she felt two eyes upon her.

"What the hell are you doing here?"

Chapter Forty-Seven

"It's my home, isn't it?" Roger sat dressed in a fresh suit.

"Where are the children?" Vera asked.

"I had Judy take them to school. Said you weren't feeling well." He replied. "It seems you've been sick a lot lately according to her."

She crossed her arms over her chest, not dignifying him with a response.

"So, where were you then?"

"A friend's." Vera said simply.

He laughed. "Come on, Vera. I'm not an idiot. You were with someone last night."

"Yes, a friend." Vera said again. She longed for a drink.

Roger shook his head.

"Roger," Vera pressed herself against the wall, as far away as possible from him. "I want a divorce."

Roger looked at her with a strange smile, and then he was laughing. He was laughing at her. He sobered and looked at her with a silly half-smile. "You don't honestly think I'll just let you run off with your little lover."

Vera felt her cheeks flush at the implication. "Oh, Jesus,

Roger. As if you aren't sleeping around on me all the time. You think I don't notice it when you don't come home at night? You think I'm an idiot, don't you? That you could move me out here to the middle of nowhere so you could go on fucking whoever it is you're fucking in the city...because I know Roger. I knew all along. When we were at Lake George she was there. When we were at the ski resort, she was there. I'm not stupid. I just don't understand why you won't let me go so you can take up with her. Or is she not interested in the children? You just keep me around to raise the kids, is that right?"

"Now you listen to me." Roger was on his feet, but his voice remained calm, restrained. "You haven't any idea what you're talking about."

Vera felt her head begin to throb, she groped for her cigarettes atop the kitchen table.

"What the hell are you wearing?" Roger was eyeing her legs.

She looked down after she lit a cigarette to Joan's trousers that encased her legs.

"You know I didn't want to believe it."

"Believe what?" She turned on him.

"You haven't any idea what they say about you, do you?"

Vera hadn't a clue what those gossipy housewives had cooked up about her now.

"The little whispers here and there. I didn't want to believe it. I thought it was all a lie, but it all rather makes sense, doesn't it?"

"What are you talking about?" She held her ground near the kitchen.

"I was an idiot to ignore it in the beginning." Roger wasn't even listening to her. "But I guess I couldn't fathom it being true."

"What isn't true, Roger?" Vera demanded.

"You're sick, Vera. Just admit it to me."

"What the hell are you talking about?" Vera cried.

"You wonder why I'd go outside our marriage bed, well you should see your lack of response, the apathetic way you let me fuck you. It used to be good, Vera. It used to be passionate. And now you just lay there and take it. How do you think that makes me feel?" He kicked the edge of the coffee table.

She jumped. "And how do you think it makes me feel to be an object you put your dick in?"

Roger set his jaw. "You're my wife, dammit."

"Roger, tell me right now what the hell you think you know." She shot back, no longer worried about pacifying him.

"It's not real, Vera. Whatever it is you're doing or feeling isn't real. You're not one of those women."

"What women, Roger?"

"She's corrupted you, hasn't she?"

Vera's blood ran cold. "She?"

"Just tell me, Vera. Be reasonable with me and we can make it all go away. I know it's not you. It's not like you."

"What's not like me?" How did he suddenly know so much about her?

"I shouldn't have let you go. That weekend. Before Christmas." He ran his hands through his hair. "She did something to you."

Vera wanted to laugh at him, but she was afraid. Afraid at his abnormally cool manner. "She had nothing to do with it."

He looked at her strangely.

"Oh, God, Roger. I'm bored out of my mind in this town. I've fucked some people, too. There, now we're even. Now you know. But I want out of this marriage. I can't stand it a minute longer."

"You can't just walk away, Vera. What about the children?"

"I'll go and get them from school and take them with me."

"You wouldn't dare."

"Then let me go." Vera pleaded.

"You're not a....a queer, Vera. You're married to me."

"You don't know the first thing about me, Roger. I could have really been something if I hadn't met you."

"This again. Always this. You think you'd be some big shot in your father's company, probably running the show at this point, but wake up, Vera! You're a woman. It's not your world, it's not your place. You belong here. With me. I saved you from your own demise."

"Oh, right. You just waltzed in and slept with me, ignored me for a few months until you found out I was pregnant and then decided to grow up and marry me to protect my honor"

"I loved you."

"You liked sleeping with me and for a time I liked it too and that's all it should have been." She cried, folding onto the ground with her cigarettes and an ashtray. "You should just admit you can't stand me anymore than I can stand you."

"That's certainly nice, Vera." Roger shot back. "I do love you, damn it. And you love me, too. If you liked it once then you can like it again. It's not something you forget."

"It's not as simple as that." Vera covered her face with her hands. "Please, would you just let me go? You can have anything. You can have everything, I don't care."

Roger was laughing again. "What, so you can run off to that dyke?"

She winced at the word. "Don't...don't you call her that."

"It's not real, Vera."

"It's more real than this." Vera puffed out a cloud of smoke.

"You're just confused, Vera. Don't do this to me." Roger insisted, trying to come closer to her.

But she put out her cigarette and stood, moving away from him.

He reached for her, his arms strong and big about her. She

could see the wound she had inflicted upon his cheek the night before. The scratches that went down his face.

He held her close to him.

"Please, Roger. Let me go. I'm no use to you or the children. They'd be better off without me and maybe you would be too. Don't drag this on." She pleaded.

"You love me, Vera."

She looked into his eyes, felt tears welling in her own. "I don't, Roger. I don't love you."

He pressed his lips to hers, rough and heavy. She felt as if she couldn't breathe, but he kept kissing her and she kept fighting him off. "Stop it, Roger! Raping me won't make it any better." She shoved at him. "Let me go!"

And she hit him between the legs and he released her to sit down on the steps.

She raced upward, away from him, up to the bedroom. She locked the door so it might keep him away while she went about throwing items into a suitcase. She packed only what was essential then carefully unlocked the door and peered out, afraid to see Roger standing on the other side waiting for her.

But he was sitting in the living room, drinking a bourbon.

He did not look up at her when she lugged the suitcase down the stairs.

"You're not going to do this." He said resolutely.

"Please, tell the children I love them. I'll send a mailing address as soon as I know where I'll be. I'd like to hear about the children."

He just laughed at her, not giving her the satisfaction of looking at her as she spoke.

She took her cigarettes and placed them in her purse, then lifted the telephone to call a cab. She wouldn't let him follow her. She'd throw him off. He hadn't a clue where she was staying just then and she didn't want him to know.

She smoked anxiously.

He sat drinking, lost in thought.

When the cab pulled up, she wondered if he would stop her, but he let her get out the front door.

She felt a tension release in her shoulders when the cabbie helped her load her bag into the trunk and he asked her where to. She gave him the address of the home that sat across the road and down from Joan's.

He stared at her curiously, but drove her out of the town and down the windy country road. She told him to leave her by the mailbox and paid him nicely for his services.

She watched him drive away then carried her bag and purse across the street to Joan's house. Joan had left a key beneath a rock. She used it to unlock the door and went inside.

Once the door was closed and locked she felt the first wave of relief wash over her.

Lulu wound herself happily about her legs and she bent down to scoop the cat up into her arms. "It'll be all right, won't it?" She whispered into the cat's fur and left her bag and purse by the door, and carrying the cat to the couch and curling up atop it. She drifted off into delusional sleep.

Chapter Forty-Eight

Joan woke her with a gentle kiss to the cheek. Vera awoke happy and elated, wrapping her arms about her neck, inhaling her scent, until the memory of the day began to seep back into her consciousness.

"You're all right?" Joan asked, lighting them both a cigarette and passing one off to Vera as she sat next to her on the couch.

Vera took the cigarette gratefully. "He was home." Her hand shook.

Joan's dark eyes widened.

"He was strangely calm." Vera pulled her legs up beneath her to sit cross-legged.

"What did you tell him?" A worried look crossed Joan's brow.

Vera smoked long and deep. "I told him I wanted a divorce."

Joan smoked.

"I told him I knew he was cheating on me and then he threw it back in my face. Apparently there has been talk about me...and you." Vera looked at Joan anxiously.

Joan nodded. "How *much* does he know?"

Vera bit her lip. "Not all of it." She leaned forward to tap off ash. "He thinks it all started when we went to the city together. He thinks you corrupted me."

Joan let out a hoarse, mirthless laugh at that.

Vera wasn't sure if she was upset, angry, or concerned. Her lack of words frightened Vera, made her feel uneasy. "What is it?" Vera demanded.

Joan looked at her uneasily. "It's unnerving. He just let you walk out?"

"Yes." Vera nodded. "I told him I wanted a divorce, that I was leaving. He kept insisting I wouldn't, that we could fix it. But I can't, Joan. I can't take it anymore."

Joan stroked her arm gently. "Did he hurt you?"

Vera shook her head then. "No. He tried...but I wouldn't let him."

Joan shook her head. "I suppose there's no choice then. You can file the paperwork when we're in the city."

Vera nodded.

Joan's face had not softened. She smoked inelegantly, as if deep in thought.

"Are you upset with me?" Vera asked quietly.

Joan shook her head. "No. No, darling. It was all going to fall down around me at some point." She smiled at her sadly.

Vera put out her cigarette and crawled atop her lap and cupped her cheeks and kissed her. "Something like this shouldn't be so difficult." Vera said as they held one another close atop the couch.

"Maybe one day it won't be." Joan hummed absently.

Vera made dinner while Joan packed her bags. She decided they should leave early in the morning so as not to delay any longer.

They ate together at the kitchen table, Vera staring around at the welcoming kitchen, inhaling the aroma of their meal, the logs burning in the fireplace, the very scent of Joan that clung to everything about her.

She was home. In this house with Joan.

They did the dishes together, and Joan drew a bath for them and they luxuriated in the tub, washing one another, touching, sharing a cigarette. They dried off and Joan rubbed Vera with an expensive oil that made her skin feel soft and smell of flower petals.

They went to bed naked and made love and then lay anxiously beside one another, hands clasped together.

Neither slept.

It was Joan who arose at five thirty. Her usual time, she explained.

They kissed one another and Joan wrapped herself in her robe to make coffee.

Vera remembered those moments so clearly.

And then Joan walked down the stairs and Vera lit a cigarette, smoking leisurely as she stretched, watching the oncoming daylight slowly, slowly creep into the room.

She listened to Joan's footsteps on the stairs.

They would be on the road to a new life soon. It would not be this home, but anywhere would be a home with Joan.

Vera smiled at the thought of it. A place in the Village all to themselves.

"Vera?"

Panic laced the name.

Vera's heart began pounding in her chest.

She stood from the bed feeling suddenly lightheaded.

She left the cigarette burning in the ashtray.

Something was terribly wrong.

Vera pulled on one of Joan's nightgowns that she found in a drawer.

She walked to the top of the stairs and could see Joan standing frozen in the center of her living room.

Vera walked down the stairs.

She came to stand beside Joan, peering through the front window.

Roger.

She felt a terrible shock go through her at the vision of him standing in Joan's front lawn.

"What the hell is he doing here?" Vera cursed under her breath.

Joan wrapped her arms tightly about herself.

Vera stepped toward the door.

"Be careful." Joan hissed.

"I'll just talk to him." Vera assured, opening the door, but leaving the screened door closed between her and Roger. "What are you doing here?" She called out.

Roger did not come any closer. He smiled at her. "I wanted to catch you before you made the wrong decision."

"Couldn't you just leave me alone?" Vera was shaking. She could feel Joan standing just behind her.

"I'm afraid I can't because you're my wife." Roger laughed easily. "Why don't you come on out here and I'll take you home?"

"I'm not going home with you, Roger." Vera stated firmly.

"Ah, come on, Vera. You don't want to get mixed up in this type of life. You'll come to resent it just like you seem to resent me right now. But we can work on it, honey. Why don't you come on out here?"

"You're disgusting." She hissed. "How many times do I have to tell you I'm leaving you, Roger?"

Roger was just laughing at her. "Come on. Get your bag, sweetheart. We're going home."

Vera felt Joan touch her arm, pulling her back. "Vera, I don't think he's alone." She whispered.

Fear rushed through her veins.

"What the hell are you here trying to accomplish, Roger?"

Vera called out, eyes searching for anyone else that could possibly be nearby.

"Honey, if you really care about your little friend in there you'll come on out of her house and home with me. It's as easy as that. No harm no foul."

"And what if I don't come home with you?" Vera hated that her voice broke on the question.

Roger looked amused by this. "Well, honey, there are laws against that sort of thing. I'm afraid your friend would get herself into a great deal of trouble."

Vera turned wide, frightened eyes to Joan.

Joan was crying quietly.

Vera clasped Joan's hand. "I love you." She whispered so that only Joan might hear. "I love you, I'll take care of this. I won't let them hurt you."

"Vera!" Joan cried out, but Vera had already turned and pushed open the screen door intent on telling Roger off, on telling him he couldn't touch her and she wasn't going to go home with him.

But the instant she stepped outside two pairs of arms went about her.

She froze in fear and then her instincts kicked in. She began to fight, to push and kick and scratch and bite.

"Let me go!" She cried out, kicking and screaming and fighting them off, but they held her tighter. They pushed her arms against her body, Joan's nightgown all in disarray on her body. "What the hell is this, Roger?!" She screamed, catching sight of him standing there looking as serene as ever.

The two men, two police officers, she realized, restrained her arms and pushed her into the backseat of her own car. She fought at them, trying to push them so she could run, run back to Joan who now stood on her front porch with a myriad of emotions playing out on her face as tears slipped from her eyes.

Roger got into the driver's seat and started up the engine.

"What the hell are you doing?" Vera screamed.

The men on either side of her did not look at her as the car went quickly in reverse down the driveway.

Vera railed against her restraints, watching as Joan raced barefoot from her porch toward the car as if she could stop it. But the motor outpaced her.

She disappeared in a bend in the driveway.

The car turned away from the town.

They were not going home.

She pushed her foot into the back of the front seat, trying to get Roger's attention, but he did not even glance back in her direction in the rearview mirror. He drove on as if she weren't crying and screaming in the backseat.

Her gown had come up about her body, exposing a breast and a thigh in the struggle.

She shoved at the back of the seat again. "Roger, damn it. What is going on?" She demanded, wrists hurting where they had handcuffed her.

Roger did not acknowledge her again.

The car came to a halt at a stop sign and she twisted, as if she could push her way out of the car, but the police officer to her right simply shoved her back into place, not so nicely.

"Don't touch me." She spat at him.

He glared at her.

"Roger," she pushed at the seat again. "What the hell is going on?"

"Such a loud bitch." The officer to her left said.

"What did you say?" She turned to him. "Don't you call me a bitch. What right do you have to restrain me? I haven't done anything wrong. You have to let me go, Roger. What are you doing?" She shoved her body against the seat again and then felt a rough slap across her cheek.

It knocked her backward.

She tasted blood in her mouth.

She was dazed.

"Would you cover her tit, for Christ's sake?" She heard Roger ask.

The officer on the left reached over and let his hand touch her as he made quite a show of covering her up.

"Too bad she's cracked up." The officer on the right said under his breath.

Vera pulled her legs tightly together. "I'm not crazy." She muttered.

The officer on the left laughed at her words.

"I'm not crazy, Roger!" She pushed on the seat again and the officer raised his hand to hit her so she sat back to avoid another blow, heart racing.

She sat quietly, legs pressed together, arms uncomfortably restrained behind her, for what seemed like hours.

She watched the sun rise in the sky.

And then she knew where they were going. Perhaps even before Roger turned off the winding road and they crossed beneath an arch and up a winding, tree-lined drive.

She knew what was about to happen, and she felt fear and panic overtake her.

She screamed so loudly that Roger hit the brakes and sent her reeling forward. Her face hit against the front seat and she felt tears rolling down her cheeks mixed with something warm. "I'm not crazy, Roger. I'm not crazy. I'm not crazy." She kept saying over and over again.

"Get her out. They're expecting her." Roger got out and the officers made quick work of dragging her kicking and screaming from the car.

Two men in white and several uniformed nurses were waiting on the stairs, watching the scene with indifference.

"You can't do this to me, Roger!" Vera screamed, fighting

against the officers, only to be handed off to the waiting personnel, handcuffs replaced with tighter restraints.

"Don't you worry, little darling." A man in white said calmly. "We'll get you sedated and settled in in no time." And she felt the prick of a needle in her arm and a strange warm sensation overcame her. She collapsed into their waiting arms.

Chapter Forty-Nine

"Mrs. Wilson?"

Someone was tapping a pen on a piece of paper before her.

She stared blankly.

Her back hurt where they'd shoved a needle into her spine.

She'd been washed and scrubbed roughly clean.

They had put her in a less revealing but dreadfully unfitted dress and scratchy undergarments.

"Have you had impure thoughts about someone of the same sex?" The doctor was asking her.

He was young.

He looked at her with both fear and power in his eyes.

The sedative had yet to wear off. Everything echoed about in her brain. Everything looked as if it was moving in slow motion.

The doctor's eyelashes fluttered open and then closed. His lip had curled up at the end, waiting for her response.

She laughed. Because it was a strange question.

What was impure about thoughts of another woman?

What *was* impure was the way the doctor was looking at her.

"Why are you laughing, Mrs. Wilson?"

She hated the name because it was Roger's name.

Vera had once been Vera Nilsson.

"Can I have a cigarette?" She asked because they had promised her at the beginning of the interview.

The cravings had only grown stronger with each new idiotic question they asked her.

"You haven't answered the question." The doctor insisted.

"Impure thoughts?" She pretended to think and picked at a thread on her awful prison dress.

"Mrs. Wilson, we're here to help you. But you have to be willing to help yourself, too." He insisted.

"I'm sure I could help myself a lot more if I had a cigarette." She attempted, eyeing the pack in the doctor's pocket.

If he wanted to be her friend he could offer her a cigarette.

He folded his hands neatly over her paperwork. "We'll wait then."

She folded her arms over her chest, wishing she could bolt for the door and race out. But she hadn't a clue where she was in the building and the door had been firmly locked after her. So she was stuck. In this room with the doctor and a nurse.

"Well," she finally said. "Why is it that my husband says I'm here?"

The doctor looked at her curiously. "He has informed us of your drinking habits, your depressions, and your deviance."

"Deviance." She repeated the word. "Did he also tell you about his own affairs? Or did he leave that part out?"

The doctor's face did not move.

"Mrs. Wilson..."

"My God! Don't call me that." She covered her ears. She couldn't take it another second.

The nurse came towards her with a needle and she shied away.

"Please...please don't."

The doctor held up a hand to stop the nurse. "All right then, Vera. Can you tell us about your immoral behavior?"

Vera looked from the nurse's cold eyes to the young doctor's curious gaze. "What is this immoral behavior? What is it that I've done?"

It was only the slight reddening of the doctor's cheeks that showed any hint of his discomfort. "Impure thoughts of other women? Let's see, deviant acts with another woman."

Vera laughed. What had been impure or deviant about what she had done with Vera? "I might say what I had to do with my husband was far more deviant and disgusting than anything else I've ever done. The way he forced me against my will..."

"That's enough." The doctor was looking at her sternly.

Vera swallowed.

The doctor wrote something on a piece of paper.

Vera continued to stare at his pocket that held the cigarettes. Perhaps if she were to leap toward him she could get it. But then there was the nurse and her needle.

The doctor finally looked up. "I think that will be all for now."

"Can I have a cigarette?" Vera asked eagerly.

"Nurse, will you please escort Mrs. Wilson to the C ward. I believe she will need a bit more care than we first suspected."

"What does that mean?" Vera felt a wave of anxiety course through her.

"It's nothing bad, Vera." The doctor looked at her again as he pulled out his pack of cigarettes.. "I'm prescribing you to an open ward where you'll be given a slightly more vigorous course of treatment." He paused to place a cigarette between his lips and light it. His face eased into a smile as he exhaled a cloud of smoke. " If you succeed then you'll move up to the A ward. Trust me, you'll want to move up."

"Goddamn it. Give me a cigarette." But the nurse was hauling her up to her feet and dragging her out the door.

"Don't you give me any trouble." She roughly grabbed Vera's arm and led her through the hall.

Vera's hands were shaking, her resolve weak. If she didn't want the sedative then she had no choice but to obey.

There were distant screams that frightened Vera. They passed through several sets of locked doors that had to be unlocked and then locked again. A prison.

There was a glimpse of a gymnasium, a dining hall, a television room. People scattered the surfaces. Faces weary, tired, far away, devoid of humanity.

She startled when a man looked right at her yet there was nothing in his eyes.

Dead.

They walked through a facility where she heard a woman's shrill cry reverberating off cinder block walls. And when she peered inside she saw a giant silver tank with a tiny little head that popped out of the center of it. The head was crying.

The nurse yanked Vera away and they were off again down a hall.

She was escorted through another door, into a room with rows of beds.

The nurse led her to the row beneath the windows and she was given the third bed from the wall. "There are toiletries in here, but we're not allowed to give you anything sharp so we will cut your nails and your hair once a week. If you become a risk to yourself or others we will not hesitate to isolate you in the isolation room. Dinner will be in an hour. You can come with me to the recreation room. You're not allowed to be in here except to sleep." The nurse pulled her again toward another door.

Vera stumbled as the woman yanked her. "When can I have a cigarette?"

The nurse laughed at her. "You get three a day. That's the rule. And you can't have a lighter so a nurse will have to light it for you."

"Three?" Vera felt her throat constrict, her palms sweating at the awfulness of it.

She was shoved into a room full of zombies. Sedate humans. Expressionless, gone.

Vera was frightened by the vacant stares of the other women.

The nurse pulled her through the room to a station where nurses sat smoking.

She stared enviously as their pretty pink lips wrapped about the sticks and then expelled clouds of smoke.

"This is Vera Wilson. She'll be on the Monday, Wednesday, Friday schedule for now. And I do think she'd like a cigarette." The rough nurse relayed to the young girls behind the counter.

A younger, dark haired nurse smiled at her. "You'd like a cigarette, would you?"

Vera disliked her immediately. The condescending tone was more than she could bear.

"I'll light it for you." The young nurse, Betty, her name tag said, placed one between her lips and lit it, inhaling the first drag before dangling it out to Vera.

Vera was furious. She hit Betty's hand away, the burning cigarette dropping onto a pile of paperwork.

The nurses scrambled then, the rough nurse at her side pressing the needle into Vera's arm while the others jumped to keep a fire from starting.

Vera went weak and had to be helped to a chair.

The rough nurse leaned down into her face. "And that's one way to lose your smoking privileges for the week."

Vera stared coldly at the nurse until she turned and walked away from her.

She looked up to find Betty staring furiously at her.

Vera hated them. Hated them all.

She was too tired just then to throw a fit, but by God she would.

The nurses had forgotten her. She sat watching as Betty put a fresh cigarette between her lips and inhaled. They were all laughing again.

Vera forgotten.

"Looks like you could use this." A wide-awake voice spoke near her.

Chapter Fifty

era turned to find an older woman sitting by the window.

Her body was exhausted with age, but her eyes...her eyes were sharp.

She was extending a half-smoked cigarette in Vera's direction.

"Well, take it dear before it burns out and then we'll both have wasted it."

Vera peered back at the nurses, but they had lost interest in her.

She took the cigarette gratefully and inhaled deeply.

The smoke filled her lungs and for a second her body calmed; her mind was still.

The older woman watched her smoke. "You're quite beautiful." She finally said.

Vera's eyes went to her again.

"I'm not a queer, but we don't get many like you around here." She amended as if it needed to be stated. "I'm Pat. Short for Patricia." She held out her weathered hand.

Vera studied her more closely and found that beneath the

institutional veneer, she was quite a handsome woman. "Vera." She said after exhaling a cloud of smoke, taking the offered hand in her own.

"What a pretty name. A little old for you, but it suits you." Pat said, then covered her mouth as she coughed.

Vera held the cigarette between her thumb and pointer finger as she pulled the last remnants of smoke from it. It was undignified, but she could scarcely care if she were dignified or not in a place like this.

"You'll get used to it." Pat noticed her unease.

Vera grimaced at that. "I can't imagine."

"What're you in for?" Pat inquired. "I, myself, was brought here by my loving son after my husband had the audacity to die without a cent to his name."

Vera frowned. "Is that so?" She hadn't a clue if the woman before her was crazy or if she were actually telling the truth. She seemed quite normal, but they were in an asylum.

"No, I'm not mad. Quite clear in the head, in fact." Pat said quietly. "It's enough to make me feel mad though, being around all these doped up lunatics."

"Why on earth would your son bring you here?" Vera looked at her pointedly.

"To get me out of the way. Why are you here? You seem like a well-adjusted young woman."

Vera sucked the smoke out of the end of the cigarette and crushed it out in a nearby ashtray. "My husband put me here."

Pat nodded. "Over there," and she pointed across the room to a group of younger women who sat about a table, "are women just like you. Their husbands just bring them here to get them out of the way."

Vera looked at them with wide eyes. They spoke to one another haltingly. They did not smile. They stared off into space or read quietly. They were no longer people.

Vera shivered.

"You don't have to become like them. But you can't let these people break you. And believe me, they will try everything to make you go insane." Pat cautioned.

Vera felt as if she might cry, a mixture of fear and frustration sent a jolt of anger through her. She rubbed her forehead. This couldn't be real.

She was meant to be in the city with Joan.

Joan.

Joan seemed like a distant memory and yet it had only been hours...no a day...she was no longer sure of the time.

She tried her hardest to recall her, to pull her back and all she could see was a blank face.

No, she couldn't have forgotten her so easily.

"Vera." Pat was gently nudging her. "They're calling us for dinner."

Dinner was an awful mush of unidentifiable items they passed off as food.

Vera was not hungry and pushed the plate away from her.

Pat leaned into her. "You'll have to get used to it, or else they'll stick a tube down your throat."

Vera's eyes went wide. "But it's terrible."

"This isn't the Ritz, baby." Pat laughed.

"I noticed." Vera responded.

"Just be a good girl and humor that nurse over there who keeps looking at you."

Vera looked up to see Nurse Betty eyeing her closely.

She picked up a spoonful of whatever the white stuff was supposed to be on her plate and put it in her mouth.

She wanted to puke it up, but it went down just fine.

Nurse Betty looked away from her.

"That's a good girl." Pat applauded her.

"It's disgusting." Vera said in return. "Jesus, I want a drink and a smoke."

"Wouldn't that be nice?" Pat laughed.

From dinner they were lined up for nightly toilet time that had to be supervised.

Vera had never had to wait so long for the bathroom before. She stood in the line with a growing migraine, hopping from foot to foot.

When she finally got to the front of the line, it was Nurse Betty who grabbed her and pulled down her underwear and shoved her down on the toilet. It was all so very rough, so very unnecessary. "What the hell are you doing?" Vera cursed.

Betty ignored her. "Would you hurry up?"

Vera turned her head away, flushed, and annoyed. She relieved herself and was shoved into another line.

"What is this for?" She asked when she saw Pat again standing in the line next to her's.

"Nightly pills. Trust me, you'll want them."

The line gave way to a counter where a nurse was handing out cups with pills.

"Swallow it down, honey." The nurse said when Vera simply looked down at the two pills resting at the bottom of the cup.

"What is it?" She asked.

"Just take the pills." The nurse was irritated by her reluctance.

Vera wanted to throw them in her face, but she caught sight of Nurse Betty eyeing her. She knew there were needles in her pockets and her arm was already sore from being poked more than once that day.

She threw the pills down her throat and swallowed as best she could without water, then she was roughly led to the room with beds to collect her toiletries and then there was another line to brush her teeth.

It was all so very tedious.

Her head was pounding by the time she was allowed to

return to her bed. She searched the room in an attempt to find Pat. The only friendly face in the whole place.

She finally located her across the room and their eyes met right before the nurse called "lights out" and the room went dark.

Vera felt terribly alone.

The bed was horribly uncomfortable and there wasn't any way to get comfortable.

She stared drowsily at the ceiling and began to realize one of the pills had been a sleeping pill.

She watched, hypnotized, as the shadows of trees moved across the ceiling in the gentle breeze of night.

The movement seemed to lull her into sleep, pulling her down, down into darkness.

There were no dreams, nothing to grasp onto, only emptiness.

Until her eyes shot open.

She coughed, reaching out in the dark night for her cigarettes, but she quickly realized the room about her was unfamiliar.

And then she saw the rows and rows of beds and a sinking feeling overcame her and she began to cry out in terror of the world she found herself in.

She screamed and screamed until a door burst open and three people in white came rushing in. A needle was shoved into her arm and she was forcibly removed from the room kicking and screaming until the sedative kicked in. She fell limp in an attendant's arms.

They took her to a dark room and placed her on a cot and closed the door.

She lay shaking with fear, eyes wide open.

She did not see the sun rise that day nor set.

She peed on herself.

They did not bring her food.

Her head splintered in pain, and she vomited despite having scarcely eaten the day before.

The time dragged on painfully slowly.

She called out, searching for anyone, until she started sobbing and screaming because it frightened her. This dark room with no light and no sound.

A nurse came in and gave her another shot and she fell back, numb, onto the bed. She tried again when the fear overcame her and again they sedated her.

She hadn't a clue how long they kept her there.

She became complacent, no longer able to scream.

They dragged her out of the room and two attendants striped her bare and showered her down and put her in fresh clothes.

Nurse Betty appeared before her. "You try it again and we'll send you to the D ward."

Vera was taken back to the recreation room, and she found it was daylight.

It took a while for her eyes to adjust to the light.

Her stomach growled and she stared wistfully at the patients with cigarettes.

Pat found her, helped her into a chair in a dark corner, and lit a cigarette from the butt of another woman's and gave it to Vera.

Vera took it thankfully.

"Are you all right?" Pat asked quietly.

Vera shook her head, her eyes wide.

She felt wild. Feral. A scared animal.

"Vera, I'm going to tell you something so you'd better listen to me. You're a smart young woman, so be smart. Be in control of your emotions or else they'll have control over you. Do you understand?" Pat was whispering.

Vera looked at her, looked into her calm, reassuring eyes.

"You're not insane, Vera." Pat spoke firmly.

Chapter Fifty-One

Vera sat near a window, arms wrapped tightly about her knees, staring blankly out at the trees that lay just beyond the dirty windowpane.

She rocked lightly back and forth. Soothing.

The sky was overcast.

She could hear a bird calling out and watched as it took flight, sweeping gracefully out of sight.

There was a commotion behind her.

"Everyone, line up!" A nurse was calling out.

Vera felt panic well up inside of her.

She whimpered, on the verge of crying until a soft hand came to rest on her shoulder.

"Come on." Pat's gentle voice whispered to her.

She unfolded herself and got up, slipping into the line behind Pat.

"Where are we going now?" It was only midafternoon. It was not yet time for dinner.

Pat did not answer right away. It was only once they were headed down the hallway and no attendants were about. "It will only hurt a little bit." Was all she said.

Vera began to shake as they were led into the gymnasium. A woman near her was crying silently.

"What do you mean?" Vera hissed.

Pat clasped her hand surreptitiously, eyeing her for a brief moment. "Just don't scream when you see it. I don't want to see you end up in isolation again." And then she released Vera's hand and Vera saw at the center of the gym partitions laid out in a square.

A woman at the front of the line was shaking and fearful as a nurse grabbed her and pulled her into the partition. There was the sound of straps, the woman's fearful sobbing and then the sound was muffled by something.

Vera wrapped her arms about herself, body shaking.

She stared at the partition, listening to a clicking noise and then a light flashed and the woman screamed through her muzzle.

It was all done in an instant and Vera thought she might faint.

She felt an arm go about her. Pat was holding her up.

"What are they doing in there?" Vera whispered.

"Electroshock therapy." Pat responded.

"I can't...I can't..." Vera's body was desperate to flee suddenly, but her legs were leaden.

Pat held her firm, strong for her age. "I told you not to make a scene. It'll only hurt a bit. You can handle it."

Vera was shaking roughly as she looked at Pat. Into those calm, serene eyes.

"Promise me." Pat pleaded.

And Vera nodded her shaky head, clinging to Pat.

The first woman came staggering out from behind the partition, crying and shaking and looking as if she might tumble over at any moment. An attendant grabbed her roughly and escorted her out of the gymnasium.

"Don't watch." Pat pushed her head to look in the other

direction, to look anywhere but at the parade of women into the center of the gym.

It felt like hours and yet no time at all before Pat was gently prying Vera from her. "I'll see you on the other side. Be brave."

Vera wanted to cry, wanted to scream, but Pat sent her a warning glance.

Instead she wrapped her arms about her still quivering body and steeled her gaze at the opposite end of the room.

The screams echoed about in her head.

Before she was ready, she was dragged behind the curtains and told to remove her shoes.

And as she did, she looked up to find Pat strapped to a table, a rubber strip wedged between her lips, her eyes closed. She looked so serene, so calm as they placed two metal plates on either of her temples.

A machine flashed and a man in a doctor's coat nodded at a nurse to press the button.

A current raced through the lines and Pat's body began to convulse terribly, as if she were having a seizure.

She only cried out a little, but as soon as the procedure was over her face became serene yet again.

Vera was pulled up from the chair she had been sitting on and was taken to the bed. She wanted to drag her heels into the ground, to not allow them to touch her, but she caught sight of Pat offering her a calming smile.

And she went with the attendants to the bed and allowed them to strap her to its surface.

They pressed the same rubber guard into her mouth.

She closed her eyes.

She thought of anything but what was about to happen.

She saw sunlight streaming through a window, the orange fur of a cat, a cup of coffee and a cigarette.

And Joan at her desk, head bowed, grading papers.

Joan looked up and Vera realized she could make out every detail in startling clarity. Every curve and wrinkle and line. Those eyes, so dark and lovely.

She felt the coldness of the metal plates at her temple, but Joan was kneeling before her, telling her "don't be afraid. They can't hurt you." And she clasped Vera's hands in her own and kissed her fingers. "I love you, darling."

The shock went through her body, the pain so acute in her temples, zapping her mind into blackness.

Nothingness.

The pain stopped.

They pried the rubber guard from between her clenched teeth.

She felt her body being released, rough arms lifting her up and shoving her out.

She was unsteady on her feet, she could hardly see anything. She was left staggering about until a nurse grabbed her arm and pulled her out of the gymnasium. The motion was too swift.

She had to stop, she had to lean over to vomit.

The nurse cursed at her.

She hadn't a clue what happened after that, only that she found herself sitting in the recreation room. A stain on the front of her dress.

Pat was sitting near to her.

Pat, her angel.

Her eyes looked so similar to someone she knew. But she couldn't remember who.

"I got you a cigarette." Pat said, holding it out to her already lit.

Vera took the cigarette from her and smiled hazily at her. "You're so kind to me, Joan."

"Who is Joan, dear?" Pat asked calmly.

Vera startled.

Joan.

Who was Joan?

Vera felt tears in her eyes at the name but she didn't know why.

She curled into herself and smoked the cigarette.

"Don't worry...it will come back." Pat reassured her.

She went back to her reading but eyed Vera from time to time.

They were taken like cattle to dinner and then to the bathrooms and then to pills.

Vera looked down into her cup and found there were three pills now instead of two. Two blue and one white.

The nurse eyed her with contempt. "Please take the pills, Mrs. Wilson."

Vera tipped the cup back but tried not to swallow.

The nurse told her to open her mouth and she pushed the pills beneath her tongue and opened briefly.

It was enough.

They were taken to the bathroom to brush their teeth and she spat the pills down the drain when no one was looking.

She went to her bed and changed into her slip; the soiled dress, she realized, would remain soiled for a while, but she did not wish to sleep in it.

She felt dirty but also realized they would not be allowed to bathe regularly.

She got into the bed and looked across the room to seek out Pat.

Had she really called her Joan?

Pat was looking at her.

They smiled at one another and then the lights went out around them.

Vera sank back onto the intolerable bed.

She stared at the ceiling and watched the trees dance in the shadows.

There were the distant cries and screams that filtered in from down the hallway.

Bone chilling, unsettling.

She pressed her hands against her ears and tried to think of anything but of where she currently was.

Joan.

Joan came back to her.

Joan was sitting on the bed beside her, stroking her cheek.

As long as she could remain sharp and aware, Joan would be with her.

Joan leaned down and pressed their lips together. Vera put her arms about Joan and held her close to her.

She fell asleep clutching her pillow to her chest.

Chapter Fifty-Two

When she awoke to the early light of day and looked about, her heart began to pound rapidly. She opened her mouth to scream, but quickly clasped a hand over her lips to stop the sound from emitting forth.

It was simply a nightmare.

A never-ending nightmare she couldn't wake from.

She laid back against the bed and tried to calm her racing heart.

It was all blurring together in her mind. The asylum, Joan's bedroom, Joan's face.

Darkness.

They were awakened by seven, taken to the bathroom and then forced to breakfast.

Vera's head hurt and she longed for a cigarette to make the pain go away.

She did not see Pat until they were led to the recreation room.

Pat let her have the rest of her cigarette and Vera pulled the smoke into her lungs as if it were oxygen.

The headache began to loosen its grip. Her shoulders relaxed down from her ears.

She studied Pat more closely as she went back to reading the book in her hands.

Why on earth was she in a place like this?

"How long have you been here?" Vera asked, tapping ash off the cigarette before inhaling deeply.

Pat looked up from her book, thinking. "Well, what year is it?"

"Nineteen fifty-five." Vera said.

Pat laughed at this. "My, how time flies. Let's see...it was right after the war. Nineteen forty-six. I suppose nine years now."

Vera's eyes widened. "My God."

Pat shrugged.

"But you're completely sane. Can't they see it?" Vera demanded.

"How can anyone be considered sane if they end up in a place like this? Even if my case had nothing to do with my psychological soundness." Pat's eyes saddened.

Vera huffed out a cloud of smoke and realized she was near the end of the cigarette. "It's not right." She flicked ash, not caring where it scattered.

Pat offered her a sympathetic smile.

Vera smoked the last of the cigarette and put it out in a nearby ashtray. She pulled her knees up to her chest and stared out the window.

Where would Joan be?

Sadness welled inside of her.

She felt miserable not knowing what had happened.

Was Joan all right? Had they left her alone or was she as sunk as Vera?

Would she have gone on to the city without her? She certainly hoped she had.

She wished she could pick up the phone and call but she had gathered it would not be possible.

"Pat," Vera looked at the older woman.

"Mmm?" She asked looking up from her book again.

"Is it possible to get letters out?"

Pat's expression did not give her hope.

"They won't let you correspond for some time. They're monitoring you for the first few weeks to see how you adjust and they think that the outside world would be a bad influence. But even if they give you the privilege I would be careful. What you write is read and only a portion of your message will get to its intended recipient."

Vera felt panic rising within her.

To not be able to correspond with Joan. To not be able to tell her where she was and what was happening to her and in return to not know what was happening to Joan.

It was enough to drive her mad.

She hoped Joan was unscathed, that Vera hadn't soiled her reputation too horribly.

Oh, Joan should hate her.

She pressed her forehead against her knees and let the tears fall.

"She means a great deal to you, doesn't she?" Pat's voice was quiet.

Vera looked up, startled, wiping at her cheeks. "What?"

"Joan."

Vera fought off the flood of tears that threatened to fall at the mention of the name aloud.

"There are others just like you." Pat assured. "The doctors think they can fix it." She laughed a little at that. "What a laugh that is. Hey, don't worry, I've been here long enough to know some things. Nothing can shock me."

Vera's lip was trembling.

She lowered her chin to her knees and let the tears fall down her cheeks.

"You can tell me about her." Pat spoke softly.

Vera shook her head, burying her face again to softly weep. "Thank you. Thank you, Pat. I...I can't. Not right now."

And Pat understood.

She went back to reading and Vera curled into herself, allowing herself to cry, to think back, to remember everything. And for a while the memories made her feel better.

"Mrs. Wilson?" A nurse's curt voice broke into her reverie.

She startled, looking up to find the rough nurse waiting for her.

"Get up."

Pat looked at Vera anxiously, but could not intervene.

Vera wanted to scream, to demand to know where it was she was being taken, but she caught sight of Pat shooting her a warning look.

She bit her tongue instead and allowed the nurse to take her by the arm and drag her down the hall.

She was taken to an office and found the young doctor from the first day seated behind the desk.

"Mrs. Wilson." He gestured toward the chair across from his desk.

The nurse shoved her down onto the seat and then left. However, she knew the nurse would not be far away. Waiting with a needle. Just in case.

"It seems you've had a rough first few days with us." He was looking at a folder of notes. Notes about her? Had the nurses been watching her every movement?

What did the notes say?

"It says here you had a very disruptive outburst in the middle of the night and had to be sedated."

Vera did not know why he was recounting this to her.

She did not speak.

He looked at her over his glasses.

"Have there been other outbursts?" He asked.

She looked down at her lap, at the vomit stain still present on the front of her dress.

She hadn't a clue why he was asking her. It would all be there in the notes before him.

"Mrs. Wilson."

She thought of Pat.

"No." She said tightly.

The doctor gave her a strange smile.

He reached into his coat pocket and pulled out his pack of cigarettes.

She watched the motion of his hands as he tapped out a cigarette and placed it between his teeth. He struck a match and held it against the end until the paper caught. He inhaled.

Vera bit her lip, foot tapping lightly against the floor.

The doctor's eyes returned to the papers before him as he puffed at the cigarette.

Vera sat with her hands tucked beneath her legs. A schoolgirl in the principal's office.

Only it was more than that. Much more than a slap on the wrists and a note to mother and father.

"I see you had your first shock therapy treatment yesterday." He said as he eyed her papers. "We find it has a high success rate for women like you."

"Women like me?" Vera's foot stopped tapping.

The doctor gave her a smile she did not like.

A cloud of smoke escaped from his lips.

"Yes, women with unnatural sexual tendencies."

"Unnatural." Vera repeated the word.

It had never been unnatural. Any of it.

The doctor sat back and puffed at his cigarette. "We find it generally stems from an unhappy childhood. Something that happens when the father is a tyrant, and the mother is too kind."

"I see." Vera nodded but did not see.

"Or sometimes it simply just happens. The wires in the brain get a little crossed and you mistake the affections intended for the opposite sex for someone of the same sex. In either case, the electroshock treatment can be very beneficial. It can reset the brain and help you return to normal." He sounded like a car salesman.

"Normal." Vera found herself repeating the word.

"Mrs. Wilson, are you listening to me?" The doctor was irritated.

"Mmm." She nodded, watching the cigarette burning between his fingers.

"You *do* want to be normal, don't you?" He urged her.

She looked blankly at his face. "Do I?"

He stared at her before he laughed. The laughter did not reach his eyes. "Every woman wants to be normal, Mrs. Wilson. They want to belong, they want to fit in, they want to be like everyone else."

Vera tilted her head to the side. "Is that so?"

He crushed out his cigarette and sat back, folding his hands over his chest. "You haven't a clue how sick you are, do you? What you've done goes against nature. But I can tell you're not like those women. You're only confused."

"Like what women?" Vera needled, wondering just how far she could push this.

"Vile, unhappy, unattractive women who think they want to be sexually involved with another woman. You haven't got it in you to be that kind of a woman. You're very beautiful, Mrs. Wilson. You must know that. You belong at home with your husband and children."

"If I'm not mistaken my husband put me in this institution far away from my home with him and my children."

"He did it for your own good." The doctor responded. "He said you very nearly ran off with another woman. That sounds quite sick to me. To leave a loving husband, your children... why, he did the honorable thing."

Vera stifled a laugh.

"You were confused." He said again.

"I wasn't confused." Vera responded coldly.

He looked at her intensely.

"I loved her more than I could ever love a man and that's the truth of it." Vera spat.

He did not speak for some time.

Then he leaned forward and offered her a cigarette.

She stared at it, not certain why he was handing it to her now.

She felt as if she were making a pact with the devil. She did not want his cigarette. She did not want to take anything from this man.

But the need won out. She took the cigarette and put it between her lips.

The doctor moved from behind the desk, coming to stand before her with a match.

He lit her cigarette.

She inhaled deeply, her mind easing as the smoke filled her lungs.

"She touched you a little. She showed you some care, some concern, perhaps?" He said as he crossed his arms and leaned back against his desk.

Vera puffed at the cigarette but could not meet his gaze.

"She lured you in, tricked you into loving her because she was sick herself. It just rubbed off on you a little." His voice was so quiet.

Vera tapped ash against the ashtray on his desk.

What was he doing?

"She just infected you a little, didn't she?" He urged.

Vera sat back in her seat. "If I was infected it was by Roger."

"It's far worse than I suspected." The doctor lamented.

"Far worse? Worse to be used as a body for a man night after night than to actually love someone?" Vera looked up at him.

The doctor laughed at her. "Love. You think it's love. It's perversion."

"There was nothing perverted about it." Vera said coolly.

The doctor slammed his fist on the desk. "I think you need to cool down."

Vera startled in her seat. "I need to cool down?"

"Nurse!" The doctor yelled and she heard the door open behind her.

"My God, I haven't done a thing!" Vera cried.

"Take her to the baths." The doctor instructed.

The nurse reached for the cigarette, but Vera clasped it and in the process succeeded in burning her palm. She cursed and the damn thing dropped uselessly to the floor. The nurse pressed a needle into Vera then supported her half-sedate body down the hall.

Vera drowsily saw where they were headed.

The room with the water tanks.

Little heads poking out from beneath covers.

She didn't want to be inside a bath.

She tried to scream, but her body was too limp, too relaxed.

A male attendant undressed her, and with the help of the nurse she was eased into the freezing cold depths of a bathtub, strapped in and then enclosed inside.

The water shocked her senses, putting her into overdrive.

The medicine working through her veins and the intense cold overwhelming her.

She shivered, whimpered.

Her eyes and teeth clenched shut.

She hallucinated the warmth of a claw foot bath tub, Joan's naked body wrapped in her arms.

Chapter Fifty-Three

She sat with a cigarette pinched between her fingers, staring idly out the window.

The trees outside were revealing the green of their leaves.

Spring was unfolding. Summer would be upon them soon.

She hadn't a clue the day.

Someone was coughing.

She turned to look at Pat, watching as her body heaved with the cough.

It had only grown worse over the course of the week.

Vera moved to sit beside her, to pat her on the back gently. "You need to see a doctor."

Pat laughed at that. She coughed again before she could say, "not one of these."

Vera rolled her eyes and smoked deeply, watching as Pat began coughing again. Vera looked up, looked for a nurse, wondering if they were paying attention at all, but the young girls were all laughing and having a gay time all huddled around their station.

Vera looked back to Pat and noticed the blood on the cloth that she held in her hands.

Pat moved it out of sight.

But Vera had seen it.

"Jesus." Vera cursed under her breath. She stood, ignoring the hand that reached out to pull her back.

She moved toward the nurses.

Nurse Betty eyed her as she approached, disdain in her gaze.

"That woman over there is ill. She needs to see a doctor." Vera said simply, gesturing with her cigarette.

The nurses looked blankly off in Pat's direction. "She looks just fine to me." A nurse shrugged.

"She just coughed up blood." Vera insisted.

Nurse Betty laughed at her. "She can come ask for help if she needs it." And then she turned her back and took up a conversation with another nurse and soon they were both laughing again.

"She needs help now." Vera spoke clearly and loudly, jaw clenched tight.

Betty turned cold, unkind eyes toward her. "I would suggest letting it go, unless you'd like some time alone again in the isolation room."

"Vera," she felt a hand on her arm. Pat was pulling her away.

"The nerve." Vera cursed under her breath as Pat weakly led her back to their spot by the window.

Vera watched as Pat tried to stifle a cough, but it only made it worse.

"You're ill and you need care."

Pat shook her head. "It will pass. Don't you worry about me."

"But I am worried about you." Vera cried, raking her fingers through her hair, tears pooling in her eyes. She puffed at the last of her cigarette and stubbed it out in a nearby ashtray, longing for another but knowing she would have to wait until after lunch if she were to make it through the day on the three lousy cigarettes they were given.

Pat was coughing again, the force of it shaking her whole body. She gasped for air.

Vera could not lose Pat.

"Damn. Damn them all." Vera balled her hands into fists.

She was on her feet in a matter of seconds, walking again to the nurses. "You listen to me, that woman over there needs medical attention. She has been coughing for the last five days and it's only gotten worse. She can hardly breathe. You need to get her to a doctor." Vera said very levelly, very civilly.

"Mrs. Needham is a frail, older woman who has delusional fits of hysteria. There ain't nothing wrong with her." A larger nurse who sat at the desk exclaimed coldly.

Vera felt her pulse quickening, frustration mounting by the second. "Now you listen to me, Pat isn't hysterical at all. She's ill. She has pneumonia or bronchitis or something awful. She needs to see a doctor. A real doctor."

They were surrounding her.

There was a needle in her arm and the tingling, sluggish feeling she'd become used to overcame her.

She could hazily see Pat standing near the window.

She wanted to run for her, to grab her hand and pull her out of this place and get her to a doctor, but she didn't have feeling in her limbs.

She was taken to the isolation room and thrown inside.

She landed against the wall and curled into herself, wrapping her arms around her knees in a fetal position.

The sedation wore at her, made her drowsy and tired.

She slipped into sleep.

She woke up craving a cigarette and realized where she

was and nearly screamed until she cognitively remembered it wasn't wise to scream.

She picked herself up from the floor and went to the cot in the corner of the windowless room.

She sat in the corner and put her arms about her legs, pulling them close to her chest.

She closed her eyes tight and tried to remember the way the sun looked through the windows of a house in the forest. The way the fireplace looked, dancing with flames. A leather couch. A woman with dark eyes and a gentle smile.

Joan.

Joan sitting on the couch, Vera watching her.

Vera laid on her side.

Joan caressed her cheek, pressed her lips to Vera's willing lips.

They had all the time in the world.

Joan touched Vera between her legs.

Vera sighed.

Joan moved deliciously against her.

Vera panted, gasping at each motion until the perfect place was found and she could not contain the cries that escaped from deep inside her throat.

She laid, breathless, grasping at Joan.

But it was only empty air and a dark room she opened her eyes to.

A tear slid from the side of her eye.

And then another.

For a brief moment she wished the continuous shock treatments could make her forget. That they might erase her memory completely.

Because Joan was still so vibrant, so alive to her.

And Vera was dead.

She laid soundlessly in the darkness of the isolation room.

She did not know for how long she was there.

It felt an eternity.

She tried to keep her mind as blank and free from thought as possible. She recounted pointless details of her life. She did not think about that woman and those children or anything that would make it feel impossible to go on existing.

She thought of Pat.

She hoped they had helped her, that her pleas had not been in vain.

The days and nights ran together. She slept when she was tired. She got up and paced to keep her body moving and then when that tired her, she laid on the cot and thought about frivolous, mindless things.

The door unlocking sent a shock through her whole system.

Light filtered into the room, and she blinked, blinded by it.

She was pulled to her feet and forced out into daylight.

She was weak and stumbled, but the nurse held tight to her.

She was taken to the showers and forced under a strong torrent of water. They scrubbed roughly at her skin, and she felt tender all over when it was finished.

They put her in a new gown and returned her, without food, to the recreation room.

She looked wildly about but knew, almost immediately, Pat was not there.

"Where is she?" Vera whispered to a passing nurse.

The nurse hardly looked at her. "What is that Mrs. Wilson?"

"Where the hell is Pat?" Vera's voice shook. She hadn't spoken for days.

"Pat? Oh, Mrs. Needham. She's no longer here."

Vera blinked, incredulous. "No longer here? What does that mean?"

The nurse was losing her patience. "Mrs. Wilson, that's all

you need to know. She's not here anymore. It's as plain and simple as that."

Vera set her jaw as the nurse walked away.

She looked again over the now familiar group of women. Some returned vacant gazes in her direction.

She whimpered and then blackness pulled her under, and she fell to the ground.

Chapter Fifty-Four

L istless.

The sun was shining outside the window.

The sky was a brilliant blue, the trees fluorescent green.

It was too bright.

She put her feet up on the window ledge.

She brought the cigarette to her lips.

"Join us for a round of bridge." A woman's voice said.

Vera exhaled a stream of smoke.

She did not move.

"Leave her alone, Agnes." Someone else said.

They were taken to lunch.

She lifted a spoonful of food up, and then let it fall back to the plate.

They were moved back to the recreation room.

Vera waited as long as she could and then asked for a light to her cigarette.

She took up her spot at the window.

She smoked, staring at the change in the sun's position, how it shadowed the trees in a different way.

A bird flew past the window.

She watched it apathetically as it landed on a tree branch and then took off again in flight.

The sun followed its daily trajectory across the sky and the world dimmed in increments.

They were taken to dinner.

She moved food from one side of the plate to the other, picking at some green beans and eating a buttered roll.

They were taken to the bathroom. They were taken for pills. She took the pills, swallowing them. They were taken to brush their teeth. She brushed obediently. They were taken to bed. She climbed onto the scratchy surface.

But before she laid down, she glanced across the room.

She thought...

But it was another woman she did not recognize.

She laid down and the lights went out.

Darkness consumed her.

Someone shook her awake.

They were taken to the bathroom.

They were taken to breakfast.

She drank the weak coffee.

They were taken to the recreation room, and she sat at the window and lit a cigarette.

They were taken to the gymnasium. She waited to be strapped to the table and reveled in the pain.

She did not scream. She did not vomit.

They were taken back to the recreation room.

She sat lethargically staring out the window, a second cigarette between her fingers.

Lunch. Recreation. Dinner. Bathroom. Pills. Bed.

The days bled together.

Until one afternoon.

They were allowed outside.

The fresh air hit her sharply, accosting her senses.

It smelled of grass, of earth, of leaves, and flowers.

She inhaled and stumbled on the uneven ground.

She felt sun on her skin. She closed her eyes and relished the sensation.

The large, brick buildings were surrounded by a dense forest.

She peered out through the trees.

She thought if she could simply run fast enough, far enough...

But there were people watching.

She looked around her and saw male attendants walking about. Monitoring.

There was a path into the woods.

She moved quietly toward the path.

No one called out to her.

She walked into the forest, following the path. She saw several people ahead of her, so she knew it was not restricted to her.

She continued on, head down, looking at the underbrush of the forest, the strong trunks of trees.

The path ended at the edge of a gently flowing stream. A small waterfall gurgled.

She sat down at the edge of the water.

Leaning forward, she let her fingers skim the surface of the cool, clear surface. She watched as the gentle current worked against her hand, causing ripples to splay out behind her fingers. She marveled at the sensation, transfixed.

A bird cawed overhead.

She looked up through the branches to the sky above.

She felt eyes upon her. Someone watching.

The sensation startled her.

She turned to find the interloper, but she was all alone in the woods.

No one was there.

"Mrs. Wilson!" Someone was calling to her. "Mrs. Wilson, it's time to go inside."

She wanted to run, to dart further into the woods, but she heard rapid footsteps coming up behind her. If she did not move quickly then there would be a needle.

She stood up and went willingly with the attendant.

They were taken to dinner. They were taken to the bathroom. They were given pills.

That evening she hid them under her tongue. She spat them down the sink as she brushed her teeth.

She got into bed, and she laid wide awake. Staring groggily up at the ceiling.

There were screams coming from down the hall.

They no longer made her flinch.

She drifted off into a fitful sleep unhindered by medication.

The dreams came.

The well.

The well stood before her.

A woman stood staring at her.

She was no longer afraid.

The woman had kind eyes.

The woman had a face she recognized.

She awoke, startled.

She knew.

Vera's mind raced.

A new vitality returned to her.

She laid back in the horrible bed but could not fall back to sleep.

She wanted the dreams to return, but sleep did not come again that night.

The following day Vera anxiously awaited a chance to go outside, but it was another two days before they were given the privilege.

When they were finally taken outside, she made her way quickly - but not so quickly that anyone might take notice of her - to the path.

To the stream.

She sat at the edge, and she looked out past the water, out into the forest.

But she saw nothing.

She stood and walked through the forest, keeping the sanitarium to her right.

An attendant was watching her.

She walked past several other women who ignored her.

She kept her eyes on the ground. The men in uniform in sight.

And then it appeared. There before her.

Hidden beneath some brush, forgotten.

A well.

Chapter Fifty-Five

"We've seen tremendous improvement, Mrs. Wilson." The doctor was looking at her over his notes. "It's been nearly a month without incident."

Vera stared out the window in the corner of the room.

"Would you say your...unnatural...urges have dwindled?"

Vera remembered the ladder she had seen pressed up against the side of the building. She hadn't a clue if it would be long enough to reach the bottom.

"Mrs. Wilson?"

She looked hazily at the doctor.

"Hmm?" She stared at him in confusion. What had they been talking about?

"Your feelings about women. You would say the shock treatments have helped?"

She thought about the biweekly electroshock treatments. She thought about her brief moments of memory loss.

But the memories always came back to her.

"Yes." She said sedately.

The doctor nodded, pleased.

The other matter would be getting away without anyone noticing her absence.

The attendants were always watching. Always keeping an eye out.

She had taken to noticing doors.

She knew the doors to the rooms were not locked at night.

The nurses thought the sleeping pills would keep people sedated.

Vera had not been taking the pills.

However, she did not know what would happen once outside the dormitory room.

"Do you think about women in a sexual way?" The doctor lit a cigarette.

Always these questions.

"No." Never mind the dream she'd had the night before that had driven her to touch herself beneath the scratchy sheets. She hardly had the appetite to touch herself any more, but there was a new hope pinned on her discovery in the forest.

Something to fixate upon.

Something to keep her mind occupied.

"Not even a little urge?" The doctor smoked for her. A performance.

She shook her head.

"I see." He took some notes. "Well, if you keep this up then perhaps we can move you out of the C ward."

She eyed him then. Infuriated that it had taken submissive compliance to make him amenable.

But she gave him what she hoped would be a happy smile.

He smiled back at her. "A nurse will be right outside to escort you back to the recreation room." He dismissed her, bending down to study his case notes.

She stared at his burning cigarette. "What did they do with Pat?"

He looked up at her, confused. "I'm sorry, who?"

"Patricia Needham." She said the name crisply.

He frowned at her. "Why she died. Two weeks ago."

Vera's mind went blank.

Feeling dissolved from her body.

She nodded and stood, moving for the door, to return to the nurse who pulled her like a fugitive down the hallway.

Vera paid attention at each turn. She noticed a hallway that led to a door that seemed to go outside.

She looked for other doors.

Would they all be locked?

She was pushed back into the recreation room.

She stared around her at the women and thought she should feel something. Sadness, anger, upset, anything...but she felt nothing.

She asked for a light to a cigarette and went to sit near the windows on the right side of the room. Because from those windows she could see the edge of the woods. And just beyond that edge was the well.

She felt weak. She was swimming in the outfit they had given her to wear.

After she smoked she took to pacing the recreation room. She needed to keep up her strength, her mobility.

They were taken to dinner.

She looked at the food and found it revolting but knew she needed to eat.

The bathroom, the pills, bed.

She laid in her bed. Wide awake.

There was screaming.

She waited, stiffly still.

She watched the branches dance on the ceiling.

Hours passed.

The screaming died down and then started up again.

She stood from the bed.

No one stopped her.

She walked slowly, quietly toward the doorway.

She turned the knob and slowly inched the door, centimeter by centimeter, open.

There was a squeak.

She stopped.

Her heart was pounding fiercely in her ears.

She couldn't move, only stood. Waiting to see if anyone would come.

There was no sound in the hall.

No shuffling of feet.

She stood like that for what felt like an eternity and then began to push the door further and further open until there was enough room to slip out.

The hallway was sparsely illuminated.

She looked in both directions but did not see any of the attendants nearby.

There was a desk to the right. The night staff would be there.

She went left, pressing herself up against the wall and continually glancing ahead and behind herself.

Her pulse beat loudly in her ears.

She reached the stairwell doorway. She hadn't a clue if it would be locked or not. She was pleasantly surprised when it turned in her hand and she carefully began to ease it open.

It creaked and she paused again, looking around to see if anyone had heard, if anyone would be coming around the corner to stab her with a needle.

But the corridor remained quiet, save for the laugh of the night nurses and the screams of other patients.

She continued easing the door open and was able to squeeze through and into the stairwell.

She raced down the stairs but slowed toward the bottom. Someone could be there. Watching.

She looked both ways down the hallway.

She startled at the sight of another station where a nurse sat with her feet propped up, reading a novel.

Vera's pulse raced loudly in her ears. She pressed herself up against the wall to steady herself, to press a hand against her mouth, willing herself to calm down.

When her heart had stopped hammering away in her chest and there was no movement around her, she realized the nurse had not seen her and she was safe.

She peered back around the corner and saw the nurse still reading her book, still preoccupied.

She quietly turned the corner in the opposite direction of the nurse's station and made her way toward the hallway where the exit would be. It was just down a bit further, she was certain of it. She had memorized the layout of the place.

"What do you think you're doing?"

A hand on her arm, another about her waist.

She tried to scream, but her mouth was covered by a hand. A needle was pushed into her arm and she found herself locked away again in darkness.

Chapter Fifty-Six

She was given ice baths daily and then wrapped in cold, damp towels like a mummy and left to freeze for hours at a time.

This treatment went on for a week.

To calm her nerves, to make her numb.

They supervised her with extra care each night to ensure she took her pills.

She slept like the dead.

It was while being taken from the resting room where they mummified her, that she saw the first half-gone patient.

A man.

Staring blankly at her through a crack in a door.

He laid on the bed with unseeing eyes, a huge cut in the side of his head.

Vera felt ill at the sight of him.

"What's wrong with him?" She asked the attendant who was escorting her roughly.

She was now escorted by men, so that they could handle her if she got out of line.

The attendant pulled her away. "Lobotomy." He said simply.

What was a lobotomy?

The man took her back to the recreation room.

She was shivering in her gown, cold from the treatments. She had a cigarette lit and went to sit at the window, heavily watched now. For she was deemed a runner. She needed constant surveillance.

She stared wistfully out the window.

The well would be right there and yet she was stuck where she was. Close and yet so far away.

She smoked with a shaky hand.

They were taken to dinner, to the bathroom, to pills, to bed. The cold chilled her bones.

The next day she was taken to the doctor.

He did not look pleased with her.

"I thought you'd really turned a corner, Mrs. Wilson." He clasped his hands together atop the desk.

She bit her acid tongue.

She did not have the strength to be isolated again so soon.

"Where do you think you were going?" He asked her. "It's miles from the town. There's really no place to go. Don't you know it's better to simply remain here for the duration of your treatment?"

"Duration." Vera repeated. "And what might that be now?"

The doctor gave her a half-smile. "That depends on you, of course. I must say I was about to recommend you to the B ward, but after your little stunt the other night, I don't think we can do that."

"I figured as much." She sighed boredly.

"Mrs. Wilson, don't you want to get better?" The doctor prodded. "You have two children at home. I would imagine you'd want to get back to them. They need a mother."

She felt her blood boil at the mention of the children. He hadn't the right to use them against her.

She balled her hands into fists. "Then let me go back."

The doctor laughed, "ah, but I don't think you're well enough. Someone sane wouldn't be up and roaming about at night. They would be getting much needed sleep and relaxation."

Vera let him talk to her. Let him tell her how unwell she was, how much she needed him and this facility. That her nerves were simply shot, that she wasn't thinking clearly because she had been afflicted by a bad crush on a woman. She was still a child and she needed to become a grown up, with grown up affections.

Women loved men.

"Mrs. Wilson?" He yelled.

She startled in her seat.

"Are you paying attention to the words I am saying? You are a very sick woman, and it is my duty to save you."

She looked at him, frightened by the intensity of his words.

"If things don't begin to improve we'll have to discuss the possibility of a lobotomy."

Vera felt her palms sweat. "A...a lobotomy."

"Perhaps it might make things easier, Mrs. Wilson."

She saw the face of the half-there man who had been laying in his bed vacantly, no longer a living thing and she shook her head.

No.

She could not be like him.

"No, no please." She begged, tears welling in her eyes.

She hadn't a clue what a lobotomy meant, but she knew it would not be good.

"Then you'd better learn how to behave." The doctor threatened.

She was returned to the recreation room.
She sat stunned, unable to even ask for her third cigarette
of the day.
Paralyzed.

Chapter Fifty-Seven

She watched the storm clouds gather in the evening sky.

She was careful to hide the pills.

The nurse forcefully cupped her face in her hand and stared down her throat. She thought she would be caught, but the nurse shoved her roughly to the side and she was shuffled to the bathroom to brush her teeth.

She spit the pills down the sink and then was taken to her bed.

The lights went out.

She laid in darkness.

She waited.

Waited until she felt everyone around her drift off to sleep.

She listened to the screaming down the halls.

She listened for the movement of the nurses.

She listened to the hum of the place.

A storm had whipped up outside.

She listened as it approached, closer and closer.

Wind in the trees, whistling past the window panes.

A flash of lightning illuminated the bodies in the beds

around her. They looked like corpses and it suddenly frightened her, making it all the more unbearable.

A rumble of thunder sounded off in the distance.

The rain would come soon.

She laid, listening to the perfect symphony of noise drum up around her.

The rain began pounding against the building.

A flash of lightning disrupted the sky and thunder crashed loudly very nearby.

The storm was upon them.

She listened out to the sounds of the building.

After another clash of the elements the hum of the building died down.

She could tell the electricity had gone out.

She stood from the bed and made her way to the door.

She pressed her ear against the surface.

There was a frantic shuffle on the other side. She listened until the voices disappeared down the hall. They were moving in the opposite direction of the stairwell.

Vera opened the door carefully and made her way silently out of the room, looking from one side to the other.

No one was at the nursing station.

Someone was screaming in agony down the hall.

Vera moved soundlessly to the stairwell.

She opened the door carefully and slid down the stairs.

There was no light in the hall below.

She pressed herself against the wall and peered around into the main hall.

Lightning flashed and she could see no one was at the main desk.

She waited, peering in the opposite direction until the lightning lit up the hallway and she could see no one was in the direction she needed to travel.

She pressed herself against the wall and moved toward the hall with the exit.

She tried not to think of her previous attempt. She tried to stay aware of her surroundings so no one would catch her by surprise again. She looked back and forth carefully. She moved slowly, slowly.

The hallway came and Vera ducked down it.

The exit was there.

Lightning flashed and she caught sight of a doorway on the right. The door was slightly ajar.

There were screams echoing loudly inside the room.

A woman.

Atop a table.

Something metal pressed against her temple.

And she was screaming.

Vera put a hand over her mouth, legs weak.

But she could not stop, she could not stop.

She had to keep going. She was so close to the exit.

She darted for the outside door, hoping and praying it would not be locked and she could get out, get away.

Her hands pressed at the push bar and she realized it was unlocked.

The door fell open and she found herself in the pouring rain.

She would have to move fast.

There was no time to stop, to think.

She moved around the edge of the building, pressed up against it for dear life in case anyone were to look out, to see her.

She found the old ladder leaning against the side of the building.

It was heavier than she had thought it would be.

She hoisted it up and half-carried, half-dragged it behind her, moving as quickly as possible to the woods.

She had memorized the direction and distance from the ladder to the well.

It did not take her long to find the well even in the darkness. It felt like second nature to return to it, as if returning home. Home.

She let the ladder drop in the brush, shivering with a chill from the rain.

She pushed at the fallen branches and leaves, pulling them away from the top of the well. The pieces cut into her body, scratching her arms, her cheek, and yet she did not stop until she had unearthed the mouth of the well.

There was a wood cover stretched atop the surface. She yanked at it and it gave way.

The hole opened before her.

She turned and reached for the ladder, easing it up and then angling it down, down into the well.

She hadn't a clue how deep it would be, but the ladder fell from her hands and clattered to the bottom. She was relieved that she could feel the top rung if she reached down inside the well.

She looked up and saw power had been restored to the sanitarium.

It glowed like a beacon.

She would have to hurry.

She threw a leg over the side of the well and felt for the ladder.

She would have to be careful, careful.

The water made everything slippery and she clasped tightly to every stable surface she could find.

Once she was inside, she pulled the wood cover back over the top and then descended down, down into the cool, cold, dark well.

It was silent in the well.

Calming.

She could not hear the incessant screams of other women.

She could hardly hear the rain as it pelted the earth above.

She reached the bottom of the well, a mixture of dirt and stone.

She sat down in muddy dampness and wrapped her arms about herself and shivered.

She rested her head against the cool stone wall.

She closed her eyes and tried to steady her breathing, the rapid beating of her heart.

She was free.

She was safe.

She shivered.

She wrapped her arms about herself.

Exhaustion overtook her and she drifted off into sleep.

Chapter Fifty-Eight

Her eyes came open to darkness.

She nearly screamed until she remembered where she was.

Her neck hurt from sleeping half sitting up. The space was cramped.

She looked up, up above her and saw little spurts of sunlight filtering in through the cracks in the wooden cover.

Daylight had come.

She would be free now. If she could only wait the day out and then, then at night she could...

But a terrible feeling overwhelmed her.

She reached out in the semi-darkness.

The ladder.

It was no longer there.

Vera began to search more frantically, wondering if it was a mirage, some mistake.

But all she felt was the cold wall of the well.

Where had the ladder gone?

Her heart began pounding roughly in her chest.

She pressed against the wall but it was only solid rock. She grabbed at the stones, trying to find a hold for her fingers, for her feet so she might be able to climb, but she only succeeded in slipping and falling painfully to the ground again.

There was no escape.

Panic rose in her chest and she fell back, slid down onto the muddy dirt of the floor.

She called out weakly. "Help! Help!"

But then thought better of it and put a hand over her mouth.

No, she would not want their help.

She curled herself into a ball, breathing heavily. Afraid.

The fear overcame her then. So overwhelming that she slipped into oblivion.

Chapter Fifty-Nine

D arkness.

She was freezing.

She shook, reaching out in vain for the ladder she knew was not there.

She heard voices in the distance but was too weak to call out and too afraid to be found.

She closed her eyes.

She remembered the quiet stillness of a green street.

A broken teacup.

The well in the woods.

A path that led to a house.

A leather couch upon which she curled herself against a dark-haired woman with dark, enchanting eyes.

"Just give yourself over to it." A soft, feminine voice whispered.

Vera whimpered, not wanting to surrender and yet when she let her body lay still and her mind go blank she felt a great calmness overcome her.

A fire in the fireplace warmed her body and she was suddenly warm all over.

Life returning to her limbs.
The more she let go the more it came to her.
Bright and brilliant.

Chapter Sixty

"Vera?"

That voice.

So near to her.

"Vera! Jesus, where are you? Vera?"

Her eyes fluttered open, and she saw the sky above her. Clear and brilliantly blue. The leaves verdantly green above.

"Vera! What are you doing over there?"

She looked up and her heart leapt at the woman walking toward her.

She recognized her and yet she did not.

Her long dark hair with hints of gray hung in two braids and she wore a T-shirt that said "Niagara Falls" and men's blue jeans.

She was beautiful.

Joan.

"Joan?" Vera startled. "Joan!"

Joan was before her, a look of concern on her face as she kneeled beside her. "What happened to you? Did you fall and hit your head?" Joan was cradling her in her arms, examining her forehead.

Vera pulled at Joan, wrapping her tightly up in her arms. "You're here. You're really here."

"Of course, I'm here." Joan laughed.

"You're...it's you...you're okay! My God you're okay." Vera stuttered.

"Of course, I'm okay. What in the world happened to you?" Joan rocked her in her arms.

Vera pulled Joan close to her and pressed their lips together hungrily. "They took me away." She breathed between kisses, pawing at Joan's strange shirt, seeking out skin.

Joan held her off, looking down at her. "What are you talking about? Who took you away?"

"Roger." Vera was panting.

A frown creased Joan's forehead. "Roger was here?"

"He came to your house; he took me to that awful place..."

"My house? Honey, I don't know what you're talking about. Roger and Nat came to get the kids last weekend so we could pack, but you most certainly stayed with me."

"Nat? Who is Nat?"

"Natalie. Roger's wife. I really think we should get you to the hospital."

"I'm just fine!" Vera snapped, pulling herself up into a seated position. She noticed an unfamiliar pack of cigarettes on the ground beside her. The logo was different, the brand something she'd never heard of before. The outline of an Indian set on the dark green of a package. American Spirit.

"You're smoking again." Joan lifted the pack and examined it.

Vera frowned.

Had she ever given it up?

"Where's the lighter?" Joan asked.

Vera touched her hip and realized she was wearing nicely tailored blue shorts and a breezy deep cut, sleeveless white shirt.

The hospital gown was gone.

There was a lighter in her pocket. She gave it over to Joan and Joan sat down beside her to light a cigarette. She inhaled deeply then passed the cigarette off to Vera. "I think you've been working too hard at the firm."

"What firm?" Vera inhaled the strange tasting cigarette, but found she quite liked it.

Joan gave her a worried glance. "Your accounting firm. Jesus, and here I thought I'd be the one we needed to worry about having memory problems. Are you sure you're all right?"

"Well, I'm alive." Vera decided, after looking herself over. "How long have I been gone?" She asked curiously.

Joan pulled a device out of her pocket and tapped at the smooth glass screen. It lit up to a picture of Vera and Emma and Henry. They looked so very much like themselves and yet she had never seen them in such outfits before. "You told me you were going for a little walk about two hours ago and when you didn't come back I got worried. I figured you were sneaking away to smoke, but I didn't expect it to take this long. You must have fallen. Do you remember what happened?"

Vera shook her head. "I don't know. It all...it all seemed so real."

Joan took the cigarette from her. "What did?"

Vera glanced around and thought that there was something familiar about the woods. "I don't know. It was like I was in another life...I...it was like something out of a movie. It was so real...I...I can't imagine..."

"It sounds awful." Joan handed back the cigarette.

"It was awful." Vera inhaled deeply.

They heard the distant cry of a voice in the woods and Vera's heart sped up in fear.

But it was the cry of a young girl who came bursting through the roughage. The fiery young thing came to a halt before them, panting and excited.

"Eww, you're smoking?" The girl wrinkled up her nose.

"Oh!" Vera cried, crushing the cigarette out into the dirt beside her. "Emma!" And she lunged at the girl, crushing her in her arms. "Emma, look at you!"

Emma was rigid in her embrace but soon gave in to her mother.

"What's the matter with her?" Emma was saying.

"I think she hit her head." Joan replied.

"I'm just fine." Vera insisted.

"We've been looking for you for forever. We're hungry and Mama Joan said we could order pizza from the local place because they have vegan options." Emma was jumping from foot to foot.

Vera looked from Emma to Joan.

Mama Joan?

What in the world had happened?

"What's that over there?" Emma's eyes had fixed upon something.

Vera turned, following her pointed finger.

Under some brush was a line of neatly stacked stones.

Vera stepped closer, reaching out to move some of the brush away from the surface.

A chill went through her.

"It's an old well." Joan said at her side. "I'm glad it's covered up."

"That's so cool!" Emma exclaimed at Vera's other side, reaching out to touch the stone surface.

"Don't..." Vera clasped her hand. "Don't go near it."

"It's only an old well, Vera." Joan put an arm about her.

Vera shook her head. She was being ridiculous.

Emma was looking up at her with concern in her brilliant, young eyes.

"Is that what you tripped over?" Joan asked, still inspecting her as if she were injured.

Vera felt just fine, but there was something about the well she didn't like.

"Are you okay, Mommy?" Emma had her arms about her.

"I'm fine, baby. I just went for a walk." Vera stroked her daughter's back, begging Joan with her eyes to believe her. That everything was fine.

Joan still looked worried.

"I'm fine." She reiterated.

"Come on, let's get back to the house." Joan brushed off her jeans and reached for Emma. "Emma, go run ahead and ask your brother what he wants on the pizza."

Emma nodded and darted off through the woods.

Joan put her arm through Vera's and began guiding them back through the forest. "I think we should pay a visit to the clinic just to have you looked over. I'm worried about your head."

"There's nothing wrong with my head." Vera insisted haughtily.

"Do you even know what year it is?" Joan asked, putting her arm about Vera's waist.

"Sure," Vera shrugged.

Joan gave her a disbelieving laugh. "Do you know who the president is?"

"Of course, I do." Vera felt her cheeks go red.

"Do you know why we moved out here?" Joan was genuinely concerned.

Vera did not even know where 'here' was, but when she glanced up, she came to an abrupt halt.

The house in the woods.

It all came flooding back to her.

Her previous marriage to Roger, the births, the fights, his affair, the divorce.

Joan was a dean at a college in the city and Vera worked at an accounting firm.

She'd met Joan one night after a client meeting at a bar.

Henry had been six months old when Roger had informed her he was divorcing her.

Joan had listened sympathetically and had told her in turn about her wife who had recently left her for a man.

She and Joan had been married three years.

They had decided, amidst the pandemic, that they should move upstate to give the kids fresher air and a quieter life.

Joan was watching her closely. "You remember now, don't you?" She put an arm around Vera, and they began walking back toward the house.

"I do." Vera marveled. "Thank God we don't live in the fifties."

"What on earth are you talking about?" Joan laughed.

Henry was running like a madman through the backyard. He came racing toward Vera and Joan as they approached.

"I'll explain later." Vera murmured and then held out her arms for her son. "Look at you! You're really enjoying having a backyard, aren't you?"

He nodded enthusiastically. "Can we get a dog?"

Vera laughed, hugging him closely, inhaling the scent of him.

She relished, later that evening amongst moving boxes stacked high in the living room, the warmth of Joan near her and the happy voices of her children as they recounted the banalities of the day over pizza.

She tried to hold on to the warm feeling that surrounded her.

She was safe, happy, relieved and yet...

As they were cleaning up the kitchen later that evening, Vera noticed something sticking out from behind the refrigerator.

She bent down and clasped the edge of the thick card stock and dislodged it from its place.

Her heart beat wildly in her chest as she stared at the blank backside of a yellowed postcard.

She already knew what would be on the other side.

Acknowledgments

First, thank you, as always, to my most amazing reader Lorrie. You're always there to tell me if it works or not and to bounce ideas around with. You're the best writing partner.

Thank you to Lina for your support throughout the process.

To my amazing editor, Laura, who omitted my 'that's and extra, unnecessary letters. You're so encouraging and helpful!

And to the amazing readers I've met this past year. You're all so wonderful and I love getting to know you all. Come join in on the fun on Instagram! I always love connecting with new people.

And to C. You know what you did and you're the best.

About the Author

Anna Woiwood is a writer of mid-century Sapphic stories. Her debut novel, The Veracity of Lies, was a finalist for a 2023 Golden Crown Literary Award in historical fiction and A Tiger in Suburbia was a 2024 Golden Crown Literary Ann Bannon Popular Choice finalist. She lives in Kansas City with her small cat son, Walter. Find her on Instagram @anna.w.writes

Also by Anna Woiwood

The Veracity of Lies

The People Next Door